Your Dreams Taste Like Candy

Horror Stories From the Depths of the Internet

By P. F. McGrail

Delora Publishing

Your Dreams Taste Like Candy

Your Dreams Taste Like Candy

To Rebecca, for making my words dance in just the right way

Your Dreams Taste Like Candy

Your Dreams Taste Like Candy

CONTENTS

Your Dreams Taste Like Candy

Your Dreams Taste Like Candy

FOREWORD

A writer friend of mine once asked, "Why do you lean toward perverted stories?" She quickly added, "They rule, I'm not complaining, just curious."

I maintain that the allegation assumes a vicious half-truth; and, since I was half proud of it, I feel that it warrants an honest answer:

It's because I hope to write beautiful things.

The greatest risk of any attempt at a deep and meaningful creative endeavor is cheesiness. I feel that the best way to avoid such a calamity is by embracing the horrific fact that life's pain is sometimes meaningless.

That explanation will make more sense after reading a select few stories contained in this book.

The price of crossing to the opposite extreme is unavoidable. In my previous collection, "Fifty Shades of Purple," I shared certain stories at a known cost. Specifically, some readers pointed out that I crossed a line. I have only one response:

They're right.

This book, like the one that came before, sometimes pushes boundaries. The shifts in tone from tale to tale will be jarring. One of my favorite stories in this collection turned friends away with its title alone, and the opening line nearly got it banned from Reddit's NoSleep community. I did not know any other way to tell the tale, though, so it is contained here in its uncensored form.

I'm following the pattern that life hands us; we can only find true joy *because* it is so frail and vulnerable, rather than *despite* that fact. Simply put, the world is filled with shit, piss, blood, rape, gore, and needless death. Only after we accept that can we articulate what it means to be beautiful, because true beauty stems from the reality that there is no guarantee of its existence.

I've attempted to find wonder and happiness at the bottom of a cesspit, because I don't know where else to look.

Whether I've succeeded is entirely up to you.

To those who make it to the very last line — what I've always wanted was for someone to listen.

Thank you for giving me the courage to share my words.

-P. F. McGrail

September 2019

Your Dreams Taste Like Candy

LET ME INTRODUCE
THE DEMON INSIDE YOU

I WAS FIVE YEARS OLD WHEN THEY CAME FOR ME.

I believed – at least in the beginning – that they took me because I was different.

But Mama explained that they took us because *we* were different, and I did not understand.

Because I had learned from an early age that I was the only one who saw them.

Before we left, there was a change in the way that people looked. Tall, thin figures stood over most of them, with ugly blood dripping down wiry, burnt arms as the demons forced every action of the people below. Sinewy limbs would turn their heads downward whenever people attempted to see what was controlling them.

No one was able to see these figures besides me.

The only thing that I understood completely was that I should never speak of them.

When the uniformed man came to our house, I asked Mama about what I saw. I wanted to know why he appeared as a man at first, but when I looked closer he became red and wheezy and hot. The creature ground his teeth together, back and forth, back and forth.

I wanted to know why he was angry.

Your Dreams Taste Like Candy

Mama silenced me, pinching my shoulder so hard that her hands shined red. I could see her wings wrapped around my body, but they trembled so.

I did not see Papa spread his wings at all. He appeared very blue and cold. I could feel his shame, but I did not understand why.

I knew better than to ask.

We packed little more than our clothes before leaving the next day. I asked Mama how long we would be gone, and she told me that it would be just a short vacation. We had never taken a vacation, and she turned green as she spoke, so I knew that she was lying. I cried and told her to tell me the truth.

That's when Papa slapped me. It was the first and last time he ever did so, and I silenced myself immediately.

He stayed blue for the rest of the day. Throughout the train ride that took us farther and farther from home, no one spoke.

When it came close to nighttime, we got off of the train and walked past a large sign. I struggled to sound out the word before asking Mama what it meant.

"What is 'Manzanar'?" I asked, breaking my hours-long silence.

Mama did not look at me when she answered. "It's an American word. It means we're home."

She was glowing bright green.

I did not understand why there were so many men with guns. I had never been allowed to play with one, no matter how fun I thought they would be.

When I looked at them closely, I was afraid of what I saw. Most appeared red, with their muscular arms bulging as they ground clawed fists around their weapons. They licked long, angry tongues around sharp, jagged teeth.

One that scared me more than the rest was a man who got shorter when I looked directly at him. He turned different shades of pink as the crowd of people walked past. Every time that he looked at a woman or a little girl, the shade of pink changed.

He stared at Mama much longer than all the rest.

That was when the pink glowed brightest.

Mama had told me that the word meant "home," but that did not make any sense. We slept in a big tent with many other strangers, so I did not understand how we could be home. Whenever I asked Papa about it, his wings drooped, and he became very blue.

He never had an answer for me.

One of the guards, a man with the name "Schuld" written on his uniform, was not like the rest. Instead of glowing red or pink, he was blue just like Papa. He was the only one with wings like my parents. But they must have been dead wings, because they dragged behind him wherever he walked. I didn't understand why this made me want to cry.

I could not ask anyone to explain why I saw people as special shapes or colors. No one else saw the world in such a way, and that made people afraid.

We're no exception to the rest of the planet's animals. Scared people are the most dangerous ones.

In the beginning of our stay, the toilets did not have walls built around them. Everybody who walked in or out glowed much bluer than normal.

But almost everyone was blue in our new home.

The guard who became short when I looked at him spent a lot of time near the women's toilets. He was very pink when they were blue.

Papa rarely looked me in the eye at our new home. He would say "shikata ga nai" and say no more.

Your Dreams Taste Like Candy

But while Mama wrapped her bright wings around me whenever she was near, Papa's only dragged on the ground. He turned blue more often than anyone else.

The short, pink guard once followed as the three of us walked alone between two large tents. He quietly told Papa and me to turn away from him. We immediately did as he told us, because Papa had taught me that obedience was a virtue.

Mama started crying as soon as we could not see her. I tried to look, but Papa grabbed me and turned my head toward the tall mountain that towered over the camp.

That's when Schuld, the guard with the fallen wings, appeared before us. "Verrater, what the fuck are you doing?" he shouted to the other man.

I did not understand what happened next, because Mama and Papa never spoke of it again.

They said nothing to one another for a very long time after that.

I witnessed the brightest blue light I had ever seen while I was in bed that night. Its brilliance woke me, and I struggled to discern its source.

It was my father. He was sitting on the edge of his bed, quietly sobbing into his hands.

I had never seen him cry. It made me so uncomfortable that I snuck out and left our tent, despite knowing that this was a cardinal sin.

When I emerged into the cool and endlessly windy night, I did not know where to go, so I hid in the shadows. No sooner had I disappeared than a guard emerged from around the corner.

Schuld walked past me without noticing. His wings still dragged, but no blue shined from his body that night.

The greatest changes tend to come when we think all the changing is already done.

I don't know why Mama and I were outside alone after dark that night. I do remember her wings wrapped snugly around me. Her eyes were unusually wide as she looked rapidly back and forth, and her hand gripped me so tightly that I thought she might break my tiny bones. The light around her was gray that night – far grayer than I had ever seen it.

Your Dreams Taste Like Candy

We walked quickly, our rapid footsteps muffled in the dirt. We took a long and winding route back to our tent, which confused me.

The sudden stop confused me more. Mama hid me behind her back, enveloping my body completely within the shimmering folds of her wings.

It was all I could do to peek around and see the guard Verrater. He was smiling.

The man's hands were around Mama's wrists faster than I could comprehend. She gasped and sobbed. A part of me knew that she wanted to speak, but for some reason she could not find the words.

Part of me also knew that she wanted me to run. Far away. She wanted me to leave her behind, and never to question why.

But I remained frozen in place, as though my mind had retreated to safety and left my body to face the dark.

I saw red liquid, and I knew it came from my mother.

I didn't cry, because tears are meant to encapsulate fear and to process it. I understood then that some things are beyond comprehension or reason, and that sometimes pain exists simply of its own accord. It was how I learned to be afraid of the world, and terrified of the species that made it go round.

A golden hue blinded me. I squinted at it and saw that, for the first time, Schuld's wings were held aloft. He strode confidently toward Verrater.

There was screaming, and I was thrown to the ground.

I groped in the dark and found my mother's arm. I grasped it so hard that I expected to feel the skin erupt and spill blood beneath my grimy fingers, but I refused to relent. Her arm was limp and unmoving, and I cried and begged her to be alive as I shook her unresponsive body.

I remember hearing one more thing from Verrater. "You're going too far, Schuld! Stop!"

He said nothing more after that.

I don't know how long I held my mother. Pain distended time.

When I looked up again, I saw just one man walking out of the darkness.

He had no wings.

My heart screamed against my ribcage. I grabbed Mama's arm and pulled her, but she would not budge. I dropped the arm, dove to the ground, and covered her body with my own.

The man stepped into the moonlight.

Your Dreams Taste Like Candy

It was Schuld. Bloody stumps protruded from both shoulders. The blood covered his hands as well.

He knelt down next to Mama, clutching her neck and chest.

He looked at me sadly.

"She's alive, kid."

Mama stirred, and my world turned upside down. The feeling was too intense for me even to recognize as happiness.

Schuld lifted her up. "It would be better if nobody knew you two were around. This… is going to be bad."

He carried her from the moonlight into the shadow. I followed, my eyes fixed on the sad, broken stumps of his back.

It was the last time that I saw either Verrater or Schuld. It took me years to understand what had happened that night.

The greatest of angels are the ones willing to shed their wings.

We left Manzanar when I was eight years old. By that time, my mother's lie had become truth: we were leaving home, because there was nothing left for us anywhere in the world. Our former house had long since been inhabited by other occupants.

The three of us were together when we left, and Papa said that was the most important thing. "Shikata ga nai," he explained confidently, and said that our lives were beginning again.

Except that wasn't entirely true. Papa glowed a steady blue that followed him from Manzanar for the rest of his life. He died in 1953, just two days after his fortieth birthday.

Mama continued to manage the landscaping company he had created. By the time I graduated from college, she was the quintessential American success story.

I continued to see the animals within people for the rest of my life, though age and experience honed my understanding of what was being shown to me.

My mother never remarried, and I was never able to quench her loneliness. I grabbed her arm and begged her to come back one more time, on August 5th, 1993.

It didn't work.

Your Dreams Taste Like Candy

Part of me — a deep part, one so fundamental that I had not known of it existence — broke as I watched her aura of solitude finally disappear into the sterile sheets of her hospital bed.

I'm afraid of what I would see if I could step outside my body and look at myself. The ability does not work in mirrors, so I have spent a lifetime wondering how I really look.

I can imagine, though.

And I am glad for what I do not see.

Loneliness feeds fear, and fear feeds itself. It is a simple beast, and one that is much more easily nurtured than destroyed.

And fear is the worst one.

He's tall and thin, perpetually crouching over the people in his grasp. He uses bloody and sinewy hands to manipulate the limbs of unknowing men and women. Whenever they look up and risk seeing his face, he tilts their heads back to the ground and forces them onward.

When I encounter large groups, the quantity and power that he wields is overwhelming.

So I stay away from large groups.

I am simply unable to bear the fear that seizes me in those moments, and how quickly it can take control.

JANET'S STUPID BOOB JOB

1) Pack the diaper bag and haul it in one hand
2) Lift the car seat in the other (oof, Lily is getting heavy)
3) Set the diaper bag on the ground
4) Put Lily on the roof of the car (the ground is fucking filthy)
5) Pull out my cell phone and figure out where the damn park is
6) Finally give up and type the address on Google Maps
7) Phone dies. Piece of shit!
8) *Throw* the diaper bag in the car
9) Remember the ancient Thomas Guide in the glove box
10) Crawl over to the passenger side
11) Pull three different pacifiers out of said glove box
12) Finally find the map
13) Spend five frustrating minutes figuring out my route
14) Spend three more minutes hunting for the charging cord
15) Plug it in and turn on the car to see if it works
16) The cord doesn't fucking work. Of course
17) I didn't even want to spend the day with bubbly Janet
18) Or her perky boob job. Let's just get this trip done with
19) Pull out of the driveway and head down the street
20) Did I forget something?

SHREDDED FLESH SOUNDS LIKE HAPPINESS

BEGIN AUDIO TRANSCRIPT

Charlie Minton: *crying* You've already taken enough. My family will never heal. Please just stop.

Talia Minton: *gasping* He forces my head *gasping* underwater every time you beg, Charlie. *gasping* Please stay quiet when he's torturing us.

Charlie Minton: *crying* What am I supposed to do, Talia? Watch my wife and daughters suffer without saying anything?

Talia Minton: *screaming* YES!

Charlie Minton: *crying* He's not even talking, he's just smiling and moving the damn microphone in front of us… what the FUCK do you want?

Talia Minton: Oh my God, Charlie… he's moving his finger back and forth between me and the girls… I think he wants you to choose one of us…

Charlie Minton: *sobbing louder* NO!

LAPSE IN AUDIO TRANSCRIPT

19

Samantha Minton: Daddy... please don't make him do that again. It hurts so much.

Charlie Minton: I... I-I'm so sorry, Samantha. I'll do everything he asks from now on, okay? I promise, sweet girl.

Talia Minton: *whispering* He still wants you to pick one of us, Charlie.

Charlie Minton: I can't...

LAPSE IN AUDIO TRANSCRIPT

Charlie Minton: Okay! Okay! I'll choose! Talia, I'm sorry, but we have to protect the girls!

Talia Minton: Don't you do it, Charlie! Don't you pick me, we can have more kids! As many as you want! You can't make another mom for them!

Charlie Minton: But they're so young, Talia. *crying*

Talia Minton: Samantha's seven and Abby's five, Charlie. Do you really want them remembering this for the rest of their lives?

Charlie Minton: *crying* No, I don't...

Samantha Minton: DADDY, NO! DON'T POINT TO ME, PLEASE, I DON'T WANT TO DIE DADDY-

LAPSE IN AUDIO TRANSCRIPT

Charlie Minton: *softly* You bastard. You could have killed her quickly. You fucking bastard.

Talia Minton: *deadpan* Don't be a fucking idiot, Charlie. He's going to kill us all. He just wants to make you feel responsible before you die. There's nothing you can do to save our lives or your soul.

Charlie Minton: He's… he's shaking his head, Talia. He's… telling me that two of us are going to die, and one will survive. He's saying… I think he's saying I get to choose the survivor? He's nodding. One of us will make it out.

Talia Minton: You've fucked up enough already, Charlie – and Abby just watched her sister slowly get pulled apart like taffy. Hell, Samantha's eyeball is in her fucking lap. Neither one of you will ever recover from this. Just save me and face the end, you fucking coward.

Abby Minton: Please don't kill me, Daddy. Please don't listen to Mommy.

Charlie Minton: *weakly* I can't watch another daughter suffer like that, Talia. I'm sorry. I love you.

Talia Minton: I don't love you anymore, Charlie.

Abby Minton: Will you tell me that you love me before you die, Mommy?

Talia Minton: No.

END AUDIO TRANSCRIPT

Elm Grove Police Department

Evidence Item No. 110220181913

Incident Type: Multiple Homicide

Your Dreams Taste Like Candy

Coroner's Conclusion: The remains of Charlie, Talia, and Samantha Minton were positively identified using the DNA of close relatives. Dental records were not practical, as no intact mouth was found. A total of 1,913 discrete body parts were strewn about the remote cabin on the outskirts of Elm Grove.

One intact eyeball was determined to belong to seven-year-old Samantha Minton.

Notes: The attached audio transcript [Evidence Item No. 110220181913] was mailed to Elm Grove Police, along with instructions on how to find the cabin where the bodies were discovered.

The Minton family had been missing since July 2019.

206 bones were found in a crawl space beneath the cabin. DNA analysis revealed that these bones were the remains of five-year-old Abby Minton.

Scratches on the bones were determined to be human bite marks.

Within the chest cavity was a short note:

"He chose the smallest one, but she still fed me for three months. The flavor is always so succulent when I eat one morsel at a time and keep them alive until the very end."

M (37) & F (31) SEEKING A THIRD. MUST BE INTO LIGHT BONDAGE AND DEMONIC POSSESSION

LUBE, ANAL BEADS (ALBEIT SMALL ONES), A LEATHER WHIP, A butt plug, three different vibrators, and a rainbow collection of lingerie inhabit an unused drawer in the top shelf of my marital dressing cabinet. They were purchased a couple of years ago in a mutual fit of carnal excitement on a random Friday night. Our intention was to plan an evening "sometime soon" where we could put them all to good use.

Would I be administering the whipping to Joshua? Or would he be turning my ass a healthy shade of red?

Por qué no los dos?

After the Amazon shopping, we fucked each other, because no one "makes love" past the first year of marriage. We stopped after four minutes, because he can't stay awake after cumming. You might think that I'd be disappointed to fall asleep without an orgasm, but I hadn't expected one.

There's a distinct kind of comfort in familiarity.

But I hadn't purchased a butt plug out of a search for comfort.
The term "seven-year itch" was coined for a reason.
Joshua and I had been married for seven years, and dating for ten.
I was *itchy*.

Your Dreams Taste Like Candy

So let's take a moment to share a little advice with every man who's ever pursued a female orifice with lusty intent. Are you listening?

Sex begins three hours before the clothes come off.

If you can't wrap either one of your heads around that concept, then I have an explanation for why you need to masturbate so much.

Joshua used to take me out on epic dates. They were romantic. We would come home and fuck for hours. It was amazing.

As time wore on, however, we found a new kind of intimacy. It's the sort of connection that comes with staying in to watch a movie on a Friday night while dressed in nothing but gray sweats and a haphazard bun.

The thrill of the chase comes from knowing that starvation is always just around the corner. There's a sheer kind of terror that underlies every first date: not a single person on earth is free from the very real prospect that they might die alone.

Agreeing to marry someone means giving up on that terror. It's nice. Really.

But there's nothing that can compare with the thrill of watching a man try *so hard* for three straight hours, knowing that you have complete control of the final decision. It's wonderful to dangle it just beyond his grasp for the sake of testing his obedience.

Especially when you've known the whole time how things are going to play out.

And there's *nothing* that can compare with making the decision that he *has* succeeded, knowing that you *will* make him split you open within the hour, and keeping that decision to yourself.

The 'comfort' type of intimacy is nice. Honestly. But things get dulled when there's no *edge* to the romance.

That's why I decided to accept Malia's book.

Malia is the type of person I'm scared to be. Spiritual, Wiccan, bisexual, promiscuous, naturist, and vegan. So when she asked me "how dark do you want to go?" I was initially afraid.

Then I thought about the four minutes of sex. About how it had been the longest session in a month.

And in one truly horrifying moment, I asked myself if it would get better or worse in the years ahead.

I swallowed. Then, voice shaking, I asked, "How dark can it get?"

Malia turned ashen-faced. "Darker than you can handle, Mandy."

Your Dreams Taste Like Candy

I felt a chill cascade from my shoulders down to my toes. I thought about how long it had been since the last time Joshua evoked that sensation in me.

"Okay. I'll take that option."

"This is stupid," Joshua whined as I positioned the full-length mirror against the middle of the living room wall.

I grunted as I wedged the mirror against the wood. "You've been begging for anal sex for a decade, babe. Are you *really* going to jeopardize the agreement by bitching about my conditions?"

And just like that, I was the marionette once again. I bent over, making sure to stick my ass out just a little farther, and pushed against the mirror.

Josh reached out to caress my rear. I suppressed a grin as I slapped his hand hard enough to sting my own.

I could *feel* his blood rushing faster.

We hadn't even started, and Malia was already being proven right.

The tan pantyhose matched the black lingerie, so that was my outfit. We didn't have a need for panties, because sex *was* the foreplay in Malia's plan, and there was no time for inhibition.

I stepped gingerly onto the white sheet in the middle of the living room. As I positioned myself carefully into the center of the pentagram, my toes landed in the goat's blood that had been used to draw it. The slick, crimson fluid was still warm and fresh.

Joshua was nervous, so I pulled him by the hand until he was standing directly behind me. I had decided to dress him in nothing other than black boxer briefs, because that really got my motor running and he was currently doing everything that I commanded. He wrapped me in a full-body hug from the rear, and I could actually feel his pecs pressed up against my shoulders.

The pudge in his stomach was still evident, don't get me wrong. But I couldn't remember the last time he'd hugged me so tightly from behind.

25

Your Dreams Taste Like Candy

I reached my head back and kissed him. He kissed back like he *meant* it, like he wanted to fuck me and be fucked by me and was *terrified* that I'd say 'no.' I drank it in. He smelled of Old Spice and sweat. His chin was *really* fucking scratchy against my neck, just under my left ear, so I grabbed his hair and pulled hard enough to cause pain.

He whimpered.

I looked into his verdant green eyes. Shimmering light from 32 candles danced in his pupils as he stared back with a mixture of dominance and fear.

By this point, his erection was poking through the boxer briefs like a tent pole ready to rip through canvas. He knew that I could feel it, so he nuzzled the head of his cock between my asscheeks and pressed his pelvis tightly against me. His smothered cock lay flat against my rear, squished between both cheeks and running up against my lower back.

My pussy felt like a sauna. So I slipped him the hunting knife.

I held very, *very* still as he ran the tip of the blade gently along the part of the pantyhose that covered my pussy. The edge of my lips met a cool rush of air as he started near my clit, then slowly and delicately freed every inch until my asshole was exposed. It felt so *naked* to have my most intimate parts freed while the rest of my body remained (lightly) covered.

Then Josh threw me to the floor.

I crouched on my hands and knees, staring into the mirror as I watched my husband undress behind me. I kept my legs spread in anticipation.

Josh was rock hard (good for you, babe), proudly admiring his erection in the mirror.

Then he pounced.

First a half-inch thrust to get things wet. Then a full inch.

Nothing compares to that initial moment of complete penetration. The feeling of sudden *fullness* in what had once been empty is why the three hours of buildup is so worthwhile.

And then?

…It was nice.

Josh and I got into a rhythm that was pleasantly in sync. After about a minute, I realized that he wasn't planning on changing his pace at all. This comfortable thrusting was enjoyable in the same way that eating a Hershey's Kiss or finding a dollar on the ground is a pretty decent moment.

But it wasn't the best sex I was going to have for the rest of my life.

Your Dreams Taste Like Candy

No way in hell.

Time to execute.

I pressed my palms onto the warm, sticky blood, then looked directly up into the mirror.

A lot of women can't look at pictures of themselves without being critical. Seeing images mid-fuck just makes things worse, not better. Did my hair really hang so limply when I was in the doggy position? Ugh.

And Joshua didn't look any hotter. His "thrusting" face honestly made him seem like he was in the middle of a particularly challenging fart.

I felt my pussy begin to dry out.

I smeared the blood with my hands, stared my reflection in the eye, and spoke.

"*Fuck* me, Ba'al." I repeated it. One time, two times, three, thirty. I stared deeply into my own eyes as I chanted. To him? To Josh? To myself?

Who knew?

After the thirtieth, I looked for a difference.

I *found* a difference.

The thrusts got faster. My pussy got fuller. I felt an arm wrap around my waist like I was a delicate little waif that needed to be handled with the utmost care as she was torn apart.

The dick inside of me became longer and thicker.

I looked up into Josh's face, but it was obscured by shadow. Nineteen candles on the tables and lucky thirteen on the floor were not enough to illuminate his countenance – but I knew that his head was larger. Darker.

Different.

It wasn't Josh.

I groaned and winced as the thicker cock thrust faster. A *lot* faster. Like Olympic-level-fucking faster.

I laid my face down on the sheet. My head swirled.

Powerful arms grabbed my wrists and hoisted my chest above the ground. He pinned my hands against my sides and held my back parallel to the floor.

We fucked *hard*.

The entire lower half of my body seemed to detach from me. It was so perfectly *intense* that it transcended physical sensation and everything below my belly just floated away.

Your Dreams Taste Like Candy

My tits, however, shook with the ferocity of an earthquake. My body was being penetrated with a frequency far greater than the natural resonance of my breasts, leaving my c-cups to rattle like erupting volcanoes.

Then the claws *yes claws* holding my arms in place squeezed against the tender, meaty sides of my torso. They dug into the pasty flesh of the often-overlooked sidebody. I could feel rivulets of blood erupt as the claws tore my skin.

It hurt in the most *wonderful* way.

The pain grounded me, brought me back to earth with its bite, enabling me to feel the penetration in all its intensity. *Now* I could sense the energy as I was entered three distinct times per second, *now* I could feel every square inch of my vaginal walls being probed, *now* I could taste my own delicateness as I was simultaneously handled with the fragility of a flower and the roughness of an untamable stallion.

It was the first time I came from fucking alone. Feeling my hands pressed against my hips was just too much, and I sailed deliciously over the edge.

I don't know how long it lasted. I don't know how many orgasms consumed me.

I *do* remember feeling more and more empty. It was like the cock inside my pussy was shrinking.

Josh finally bobbled in his discombobulated shamble that signified he had finished. He withdrew a limp dick from me with an anticlimactic slide, then collapsed on the sheet. I fell into his arms.

"Whoa," he offered, "that was neat."

Then he started snoring.

I clutched his arms as my heart rate slowly returned to normal.

As I began to calm down, I noticed a burning. It was coming from my side.

I looked at the flesh alongside my torso.

God *damn*.

Three long strips of skin were torn open as though claws had ripped me apart. I checked my other side and found the same. They oozed blood and burned to the touch.

The entire room smelled like sulfur.

Your Dreams Taste Like Candy

I snuggled into Josh's familiar arms and drifted off to sleep in the pentagram on the living room floor.

It was nice. Comfortable, even.

But that just won't do anymore.

I know that it wasn't my husband who fucked me that night.

There's no way he could leave scars that deep.

I also know that I need to do this again. You can't move back to the farm once you've seen Paris.

I'll fuck a demon once more.

Though Malia was right. I don't know if I'll be able to handle this.

But I'm going to try.

See, the price of admission changes for the second ride.

Where I can find four pints of human blood?

AN HONEST CRITIQUE
OF THE HOWARD PHILLIPS RESTAURANT

EVERY PERSON HAS AT LEAST ONE DISTINCT MOMENT THAT fucks up the rest of their life in some small way. That moment can never be un-fucked, and that person will never again see the world in quite the same light.

Howard Phillips served the best seafood in Boston, Massachusetts. The calamari had a cult following, but its crab was second to none. At $19.13 for a whole, fresh, deep-fried, soft-shell crab, it was nothing short of a steal. It was decadence incarnate, with neither spritz of lemon nor dab of sauce needed to detract from its buttery cascades of flavor. Paired with a dry German Riesling, the taste lingered in a way that transcended culinary excellence and entered Zen-like satisfaction.

No one noticed the tiny droplet of spittle fall from my lips as the dish was placed before me.

And after the first crunch, I noticed no one else.

I was nearly unaware that I had consumed half the crab. My hand had been floating to my lips of its own accord, completely detached from the conscious discretion of my brain.

It took several attempts for the waiter to get my attention.

Sweat covered his bald forehead.

"Sir!" he insisted as loudly as possible without attracting even more attention from the nearby guests. "*Sir*! I need to speak with you, please!"

I swallowed. "Yes?" I was annoyed.

Your Dreams Taste Like Candy

With my attention fully given, he seemed at a loss. "Um." He swallowed. "It seems, sir, that one of our staff was upset with a recent online review that you gave concerning our calamari." He breathed deeply. "The employee – who is being dealt with! – chose to, ah, express his frustration in a most unprofessional manner."

I looked at him in confusion as my hand reached for another forkful.

"Sir, *stop eating.*"

I was shocked.

Then I followed his eyes to my plate.

I remembered that the first bite had been crunchy.

It shouldn't have been crunchy.

The deep-fried crab was supposed to have eight legs. But two of those should have been claws.

This crab had no claws.

Just eight legs.

Then it twitched.

Though deep-fried, my dinner was not dead.

Nausea attacked like a fucking hurricane. But instead of bile, I felt a solid object rise from my throat. Its hairy, bristly legs raked my uvula as it burst forth between my teeth.

Those tiny little hairs fucking *hurt.*

It caressed my tongue as it tumbled from my mouth and landed on the plate with a soft *clunk.* My stomach had dissolved the breading, revealing the true nature of the meat beneath.

The long, black leg of a spider – which had just been in my stomach – jittered on my plate.

"It seems, sir, that the man sought revenge…" he gulped. "So he acquired a tarantula and deep-fried it instead of a crab."

I puked my dry Riesling onto the plate with a *splorch.*

"I'm so sorry, sir."

The uneaten half of the tarantula was in full squirm, mindlessly pushing itself around the vomit-filled plate. The tiny, razor-sharp hairs were now poking through the breading as it flaked off and dissolved in the Riesling puke. Its four remaining legs slowly waved at me like half a hairy hand.

I wanted to faint and never re-awaken. Only a sense of fury kept my consciousness going.

Your Dreams Taste Like Candy

"Well!" I shrieked, ignoring the increasing shock of the guests around us, "Are you going to call an ambulance?"

"Ah, don't worry, sir," he responded, relieved. "You will be fine. The FDA allows a certain amount of arachnid parts in food. In fact, you consume spiders all the time. The only thing different about today is that you've seen how it happens."

YOU'LL NEVER HEAR THIS SONG
THE SAME WAY AGAIN

Day One – Holy shit! A partridge in a pear tree! I can honestly say that no one has ever done this for me before. Thank you so much for the thought! I will admit that it is an unorthodox gift, haha. Since I live in an apartment, there's no place to plant a tree and limited space to raise a bird. But it's the thought that counts, and your true love has come through loud and clear. Merry Christmas.

Day Two – Two turtle doves! Along with the partridge, I now have three birds. It's quite the change! They are noisy, to be sure, since the apartment is only so big. But it symbolizes the true love of your heart, pushing against all constraints to let me know how much *I* am loved. Thank you, my sweet.

Day Three – Well, well, well! My bird collection has doubled, and so has my cleaning bill! Who would have guessed how much three French hens poop? If your answer was "a lot," you'd be correct! And it turns out that turtle doves and partridges don't get along very well. Who knew? It turns out that the neighbors in apartment 1913 do now!

Day Four – Okay, come on. When I saw the note that read, "four calling birds," I foolishly wondered what that meant. Obviously, I was naïve to imagine that the answer might be anything other than literal. As soon as one of them finally shuts up, another starts calling! And if you're wondering how French hens, turtle doves, and a partridge react to the calling, I have an answer for you: they poop.

Day Five – Damn, I underestimated you. Five golden rings mean I can wear a different one on each weekday, or all five on one hand. I... I don't know what to say. I'm sorry that I gave you flak about the birds. This is just an emotional time of year for me. Thank you for the rings, and thank you for showing me your true love.

Day Six - And we're back with the birds. Are you trying to send me mixed messages? I thought I was pretty clear about what does and does not constitute a truly loving gesture. The game changer here is that it's apparently goose egg season, which means they're extra angry. I don't know why you've done this to me, but please know that my apartment floor has been reduced to an avian shit receptacle. The neighbors are threatening to eat some of the birds, and I'm not inclined to stop them.

Day Seven - I apologize, because apparently I'm not explaining myself *very fucking clearly*. When I said things like "avian shit receptacle" and "threatening to eat some," you must have interpreted my words as "this is a good thing, please keep doing it." So to be perfectly clear, please fucking STOP. Consider my new life motto to be "twenty-three birds is enough for a one-bedroom apartment." I honestly did not think this needed to be spelled out, but your 'gift' of seven swimming swans has proven that you truly do not understand how Christmas works. Please note that swans do not get along with geese. Additionally, there is a baffling amount of shit in my apartment. How can they poop this much? I don't even know what to feed them, which stems from the fact that I am NOT EQUIPPED TO RAISE BIRDS.

Day Eight – Did I do something to hurt you? Is that what this is about? I get the fact that my bird complaints were not well received, but there must have been some underlying factor to initiate this whole process. I get it. Fine. But what's the deal with sending these cows for Christmas? Sure, it would hypothetically be nice to avoid paying for milk in the future. But that fact is MORE than offset by the damage done to my home. I had to pawn all five rings just to pay a company to take care of a single day's mess (apparently the maids you sent me are not the cleaning type). That brings up another point: it seems the eight WOMEN were the gift, which raises some alarming human trafficking concerns.

Day Nine – I see that you took "alarming human trafficking concerns" as some sort of a compliment. There are now nine ladies dancing around my apartment. They all refuse to speak with me, and only say, "We can never stop dancing!" every time I try to interact. With seventeen people and twenty-three birds, my apartment is officially filled to the brim and sounds like a barn dance. The toxic odor of B. O. and bird shit is absolutely unbearable. You know what? You win. Whatever you've been trying to accomplish, please take the victory and leave me alone.

Day Ten – You seem to have taken the kidnapping allegations as concern over a gender imbalance within the hostages. I now have a gift of ten human men who appear to be bound by some kind of indentured servitude. This raises a slew of additional ethical concerns, and I am terrified for my legal standing. Will the District Attorney think I'm forcing them to stay here? On another note, just who the fuck *are* these people? They will only ever say "We're lords" before prancing away in their leotards. What the fuck is a "lord"? And what sequence of events led them to believe that leaping between points A and B was the most efficient method of travel?

Day Eleven – Oh, *fuck* you. Why. Why? Eleven guys forced their way into my apartment today. I'm hiding in the closet because there is No. Physical. Space. I screamed at them to leave, to get the fuck out and never return. What did they do instead? They pulled out their pipes (not meth pipes, which would actually be preferable at this point, but goddamn tooting pipes) and started an infinite loop of piper music. This has, of course, antagonized the absolute fuck out of my ridiculous bird collection. Did they respond with shrieking? Did they attack the people? Did the river of guano flow onto every object in the apartment, creating the visage of a landscape of new-fallen snow if it were designed by Satan's five-year-old child? HOW ABOUT ALL THREE? This is it. I am officially in hell.

Your Dreams Taste Like Candy

Day Twelve – The drummers you sent all came topless, and fuck me – every one looked like Jason Momoa. Their pecs jitter like marionettes when they bang on their little drums, and for a moment the unholy chaos inside my apartment seems to drift away. You nailed this one. After their performance, we got to talking. It turns out that all 50 human "gifts" really just got involved because they're into weird swinger shit. One thing led to another, and, well – I'm now madam of the newly formed 23rd Bird Lounge, which I'm running out of my apartment. Thank you for opening me to this new and exciting lifestyle.

You and I are done.

Merry Christmas.

-Your (Formerly) True Love

AND THE GORILLAS WENT APESHIT

I GOT TO WATCH THE SLOTHS NAP AND THE GORILLAS FLING shit, tasted the world's *best* frozen banana, and felt the excited bounce of a hundred thousand dollars in my backpack all day long.

No, you just can't beat a day at the Delaware State Zoo.

But it's the nighttime that *really* gets my motor running.

I tucked into a corner by the fennec foxes as the crowd started to flow lethargically toward the exit, convinced by their baser instincts of an obligation to cease activity with the setting sun.

"Our species are not too different, you know," I explained to a sleeping fox as I slurped down the last of my banana. He was snuggled against the bars in the far corner of his cage, leaning on the unyielding metal for comfort. He felt safe.

I smiled.

The zoo was empty by the time I stepped out from my occluded corner. No one had noticed me. No one ever did.

It is *so easy* to deceive people if you act like any given activity is your designated role. People don't like questioning order.

I walked, alone, to the farthest corner of the zoo. Some of the animals stared at me as I passed, but most had already gone to sleep for the night.

Upon reaching the empty polar bear cage, I opened it, walked inside, and disappeared through the small door in the rear.

"Mr. Bennington," the doorman said gravely as he shook my hand, "It's so good to see you again. We have a new menu waiting for you. Right this way, please."

Your Dreams Taste Like Candy

I followed him, wordlessly, through the hidden passages that no one ever sees. It smelled of animal waste and human sweat, but tonight would be worth the unpleasantness.

It always was.

He seated me in a private room with just enough lighting to read my personalized menu before retreating silently to the corner.

Crocodile

Kangaroo

Gorilla

Elephant

Rats

Lion

I looked up at him in surprise. "Rats?"

"Yes, Mr. Bennington, our newest addition. One course consists of many rats, as they are so much smaller than our usual fare, but it has proven to be a very popular choice amongst our clientele seeking a more exotic experience."

I chuckled. "Different strokes, I guess. I'll be skipping the rat tonight." I put the menu down and smiled broadly. "Did you know that gorillas can learn human sign language? We're first cousins, just a few million years removed." I shivered with excitement. "Ah, I just can't get that thought out of my head. Definitely gorilla for me tonight."

"Excellent, Mr. Bennington. And the back menu?"

A giddy thrill shimmied down my spine as I turned the custom menu to the rear and looked at my options.

Twenty counts of spousal abuse

Manslaughter — driving while intoxicated

Your Dreams Taste Like Candy

Forcible rape

Attempted planting of an explosive device on an airliner

Elder abuse resulting in negligent death

Sexual battery of a prepubescent minor and subsequent homicide

My breath caught in my throat. "The last entry on the list-"

"Ah, yes," the man responded with a hint of nervousness. "That is a unique acquisition that came in just this afternoon. I can tell you more about the specifics, but please note that specialty items are market price."

I lifted my backpack into the air without looking up from the menu. "I've seen it, and I must have it. Take what you need from here."

The man took the pack silently.

"Now what can you tell me about the particulars of my order?"

"Very good, sir," he said as he stepped in front of my seat. "A thirty-year-old man was tasked with babysitting a six-year-old girl. They disappeared on the 19th of January. Three months passed before her body was found in a horrifying state of-"

"Stop!" I yelled with a wave of my hand. "Just stop." I fought back the nausea. "I don't want to know anymore." I took a deep, calming breath.

"Let it begin."

The man nodded and stepped out of the room.

The lights above me dimmed. They were replaced by spotlights that illuminated a stage in front of me that had heretofore been hidden in shadow.

The loud *chunk* of an unlocking cage resonated from behind the stage.

The curtains rustled.

A hand peeked through the fabric. It wasn't human.

Slowly, it pulled aside the cloth.

Standing before me on the stage was a 400-pound silverback gorilla. We stared at one another for a frozen moment.

Chunk. Another cage had opened just offstage.

This time, the curtains burst forth as a terrified naked man stumbled onto the stage. He collapsed to his knees in tremulous terror.

The gorilla screamed in fury.

Your Dreams Taste Like Candy

"I hear you like six-year-olds," I shouted over the composite plastic barrier that I could not see, but knew protected me. The man snapped his head in my direction before involuntarily pissing all over the stage. "Well, you're in luck. Cappuccino here is *also* six years old, and he's just *so* excited to play with you."

The man leapt to his feet and sprinted for the curtain.

He made it two steps.

Cappuccino caught the fleeing man's right arm and lightly tossed him ten feet upward.

Funnily enough, the man didn't possess that arm for much longer.

I spent $100,000 at the Delaware State Zoo that night, and the show was worth every penny.

I'M REGRETTING THE MILE HIGH CLUB

"VENEREAL DISEASE SUCKS TWICE AS BAD ON AN AIRPLANE, because you can't scratch your balls without some cranky passenger bitching to the flight attendant that 'A terrible man is fondling himself in the aisle seat!'

"And it's not even my fault that I have to sit by the aisle. That's just the nature of my job."

The man sitting next to me blinked awkwardly, as though still getting used to a body that wasn't entirely his. He kept his eyes very wide behind his round spectacles, first staring at the seat ahead, then pivoting to face me. "While I appreciate the insight into your genitalia, I fail to understand how it pertains to my current condition," he responded with a robotic softness.

I sighed. "It's called 'making conversation,' Millard. We're stuck sitting next to each other until we get into Atlanta, so we pretend to be interested in mundane shit that would otherwise get left unsaid. It, you know, prevents people from being alone with their own thoughts."

He tottered his head back and forth on his thin neck, looking for all the world like he was trying to balance the damn thing on a stick. "What's wrong with your own thoughts?"

I shrugged uncomfortably. "If we really think about it, we end up realizing that no one truly *knows* us, which makes us wonder how long the world will remember our presence after we die. Look, Millard, don't be a fucking downer. Either come up with a better topic of conversation, or hear me out when I talk about just how badly it burns when I pee."

He rotated slowly around to the empty window seat next to him. "We could have had more companionship, but you were the one to arrange a vacant seat between me and the wall," he slowly said as he lifted his hand to point.

I snatched his wrists and quickly stuffed them under the coat on his lap. "What did I *just* explain to you?" I hissed in a furious whisper. "Don't let anyone see those cuffs! People will freak out!"

I looked down at the rigid carbon fiber bonds on his wrists, then hastily wrapped his gray jacket around them. "People freak out when they hear that prisoners are being transported on their flight, so *please* keep a low profile." He stared at me, expressionless, before offering an excessively wide smile. Paired with his perfectly hairless head, the effect was quite chilling.

I grunted. "No offense there, Millard, but you suck as a travelling companion. Did you know that I used to play baseball for the University of North Carolina? The team traveled all over the country. Those guys were great. They would listen to stories about my genitalia."

"Did those stories also involve venereal disease?" Millard licked his lips softly.

"Of course they did, Millard. Where do you think I learned to pronounce 'Trichomoniasis'?"

We were somewhere over Texas when it became unbearable.

"Hey. Millard. Wake up," I urged as I poked his forehead.

He had been sleeping with his hands folded neatly on his lap, his head pointed upward, and his eyes wide open.

It really did give me the heebie-jeebies.

His eyes rolled around like an old record player before he found me and focused one pupil at a time.

"What is wrong, Jonathan?" he asked robotically.

"I don't know what I picked up from that chick, but my bladder feels like it's ready to unleash a demonic horde of sulfur ants."

"But how does that-"

"It affects you because I cannot leave you alone, even to piss!" I shot back in exasperation. "We have been *over* this, Millard!"

"But the average airline bathroom only has sixty cubic feet of-"

Your Dreams Taste Like Candy

"And I am *not* looking forward to sharing those sixty cubic feet with you. But this piss is coming *now*, so I can either wet in my pants like that creep Jimmy Fischer from middle school, or we can find a toilet. Considering this fire urine just *might* burn a hole in the fuselage, I've decided that it's wisest to deposit it in the proper receptacle."

I unbuckled us both and stood, trying my best to ignore the tiny explosions of pain in my crotch, and led my companion by his hands on our journey to the restroom.

As I opened the door to slip inside, I noticed a woman gawking at us in repulsion. I stared right back.

"Don't judge us like you know us, sister," I snapped before pushing Millard toward the toilet.

"It seems that there is not sufficient space for us to occupy this room without continuous physical contact. Is it customary to engage in this endeavor with my buttocks or with my genitalia pressed against your posterior?"

"*Nothing* is customary about this, you freak! Now pretend you can't see me while I piss!"

"Why would I pretend when it's obvious what you're doing?"

"Because shut the fuck up, Millard!" I pulled out my dick, *tried* to relax, and then it came.

Have you ever imagined what it would feel like if a scorpion wore a suit of broken glass while scurrying through your urethra?

I hadn't, either.

It was that particular moment, with my dick spouting fire, a bald weirdo pressed up against my ass in an airplane bathroom, and my glory days of college athletics now four years in the rearview mirror, that I realized my life was at its lowest.

That's when the announcement came through the speakers.

"Ladies and gentlemen, this is your captain speaking." He sounded muted. Defeated.

"The men you're seeing in the aisle have infiltrated the cockpit."

It was too painful to stop mid-stream, so I whipped my dick back inside my pants while I was still going. "How the fuck did they do that?" I whispered to Millard. "The cockpit is supposed to be iron-clad!"

He stared back at me without any noticeable change in his vacant gaze.

Your Dreams Taste Like Candy

The speaker crackled once more. "Please remain calm while we re-route the flight. We will be cooperating fully with these individuals."

Nothing made sense.

Then they forgot to turn off the speaker.

"-because they have my daughter, Sid! She's eight years old and I know that we're breaking protocol-"

The speaker cut off instantly.

"Shit," I whispered.

"Do you need me to stay in here while you defecate?" Millard asked innocuously.

"Fuck, man, *how* do you not get what's happening outside that door? Of all the flights to be hijacked, I'm here with you-"

I stared at him, slack-jawed.

Then I re-focused. "Do you want to die today, Millard?"

"All options considered, I'd rather not."

I took a deep breath. "If I do this, you *need* to cooperate. You want to be on good terms with my bosses, right?"

He furrowed his brow. "I don't think they like me very much. I can assure you that the feeling is mutual."

I sighed. "Millard, my man," I said as I pulled the key from my back pocket, "There's no greater friend than the person standing by your side when you're both neck-deep in shit."

I unlocked the cuffs with a *click* and took them in my right hand. He looked down at his wrists in apparent shock.

Leaning in, I pressed my face up against his. "You've got a choice between helping us out, thereby putting yourself in the good graces of my employers in the process, or dying in a fiery crash over Texas." I cracked open the bathroom door, because I wanted to rush his decision before he had time to think about it.

"Looks like life has thrown you a curveball."

He stared at me for a second longer.

Then his eyes turned pure white.

Millard stepped out of the bathroom, and I followed him.

"You! Why are you out of your seat?" the authoritative voice of a hijacker bellowed from down the aisle.

Millard raised a hand. As I watched, the fingers elongated – first seven inches, then two feet, then longer. The joints disappeared as his digits bound together and wove themselves into a thick, writhing tentacle that wiggled in the air above the seats.

"What the fuck-"

Millard launched his arm forward, the appendage lengthening beyond my view and cutting out the voice of the man who had yelled.

Everyone in the cabin screamed.

Millard smiled a large, genuine, *hungry* smile as he walked away from me.

A cacophony of voices drowned out what happened next.

I dove to the floor and crawled after Millard, praying that I hadn't just made the worst decision of my life.

Of course, I was feeling the damp swashing of a trapped urine pool with each movement of my pants, so I greatly doubted my own judgment in that moment.

I don't know *exactly* what that freak was doing, but I managed a pretty good guess once my crawl brought me to a dead hijacker.

His head had been crushed like a walnut. Gray and white brain coils squeezed through his shattered temples like dropped rotten spaghetti. One eyeball had popped clean out of his skull, and the other was reduced to a globby white soup on his wrecked face.

Millard was a special little duck, that's for sure. It's why I'd been stuck with him. The veterans never have air transport duty with the uber-freaks.

A scream tore through the cockpit, then was immediately cut off by what sounded like a water balloon filled with tomato sauce exploding against concrete.

Okay, Millie, I thought. *You need to be done now.*

That's when he emerged at full Millard.

His eyes were now *glowing* white, and his right arm had grown into a tendril that was ten feet long. He was holding the head of another hijacker like a trophy, and his jaw hung eight inches down in what was *clearly* his version of an evil laugh.

I expected screams to tear my eardrums apart – but everything got very quiet.

"Millard!" I shouted. "You've done enough! Come back to me! Now!"

He was either unwilling or unable to hear my demands. Instead, he reached his tentacle across the aisle and let it slither along the headrests behind the passengers' necks.

Your Dreams Taste Like Candy

He looked down at them hungrily.

Then he raised his appendage to strike.

Strike

I was a good twenty feet away with a four-inch target.

Which put me right in my element.

The anticipation of movement is ingrained in the windup, and reaction comes before thinking if accuracy is at stake. I whipped my wrist forward and watched the cuffs fly along the arc I knew they would travel.

The carbon fiber band caught the edge of his tentacle, curled around, and snapped tightly shut.

Millard's eyes instantly switched back to normal, and he watched helplessly as his tendril shrunk back into a regular human arm.

Seconds later, he stood looking like an (almost) normal man, albeit a bewildered one.

I rushed over to him and grabbed him by the neck. "Good work on the hijackers, Millie, but you really, *really* should have quit while you were ahead."

He blinked awkwardly, then stared back at me in mild confusion. "If you'll remember correctly, I gave you the same advice when that young lady approached you yesterday. Perhaps your pants would be clean if you'd heeded *my* words."

I scratched my damp balls. "Yeah, well you wouldn't be in cuffs right now if you'd kept your own wild snake at bay, so let's just have a seat and ride out this flight in peace. Are the pilot and co-pilot still alive?"

"Yes," he responded calmly. "It certainly did not seem wise to hurt those who control our collective fate. Only the hijackers were killed."

"Great," I answered in exasperation. "Now the 197 people on this plane will need to have your actions wiped from their memories so they don't go insane, and then we can pretend this fifth-degree fuckery never happened."

We walked past the woman who had judged us on the way to the bathroom. If she were staring at us any harder, her eyes would have actually popped out of her head.

I smiled at her. "At this point, ma'am, you can cast all the judgment you want. Hell, I had sex with five strangers in three days, picked up an exotic disease, and learned *nothing* in the process. Doesn't matter what you think, because Flight 1913 is making an unscheduled stop in New Orleans so that my people can make you forget everything before we hit Atlanta."

She was speechless as I turned to Millard. "Hey, you ever been to the Big Easy?"

He licked his lips.

"You'll love it. Or at least, you'll love the hotel room I'll chain you up in while I hit up Tinder. Don't worry, we'll still be in Atlanta by tonight. The mind-washing process usually takes about three hours for a group this big, which is just enough time to have my kind of fun." We settled back into our seats.

The plane was quiet enough to hear a pin hitting the floor.

Or maybe a splash of infected urine on an airplane toilet seat.

My name is Jonathan Hush, and I'm an air marshal for supernatural prisoners.

CLAUSTROPHOBIA

Patient Name: McGuffin, Dusan

Age: 37

Sex: Male

Diagnosis: Claustrophobia, fear of being unable to escape small spaces

---

The following is a transcript of a stolen Foundation video recording. It contains the Interview conducted by Excalibur on Dusan McGuffin, age 37, previously of Belfast, Northern Ireland. The subject was extracted from his home on behalf of Excalibur at 7:13 p. m. local time on Thursday, 18 October, and moved to an Interview location at [redacted]. The Interview commenced at 12:02 a. m. local time on 19 October, and was conducted by Agent 19 and Dr. M. Carmichael.

It is believed with a high degree of certainty that MD3301913 is one of The Twelve.

Your Dreams Taste Like Candy

Agent 19 is a tall, muscular man with a tire iron in one hand. He is standing over Dusan with a cold look on his face. Dusan looks back at him with intense fear.

Agent 19: You called your wife just before we took you, Mr. McGuffin. You told her to "run where it's safe." We need you to tell us where that is, Mr. McGuffin.

Dusan is looking up at Agent 19 with pleading eyes.

Dusan McGuffin: No. Please, don't do this.

Agent 19 kicks Dusan hard enough to knock him into a small metallic compartment in the floor. The trapped man scrambles in an attempt to escape. He grabs onto a folding edge of the compartment.
Agent 19 hits the man's arm with the tire iron. An audible snap is heard, and he screams. Agent 19 moves the man's limp hand into the compartment and closes the door over him.

Dr. Carmichael: We can watch his progress on the monitor, Agent.

Dr. Carmichael pushes several buttons on a nearby keypad. The two then turn their gazes to a low-resolution video feed of the man in the box. He is rocking back and forth in growing panic, but his movement is restricted due to the confined space.
With a sudden jolt, the walls start to close on Dusan. He screams. Pounding commences.
The walls soon close tightly enough to contort his head, neck, and legs to unnatural angles. Dr. Carmichael pushes several more buttons.

Dr. Carmichael: The key is to stop short of permanent damage in the first stages of the Interview. Panic, when nurtured, grows like a well-tended flower.

The two say nothing as Dr. Carmichael punches several more numbers. The monitor displays a reading of 104 degrees Fahrenheit. The screams get weaker, but persist to a near-continuous extent.

Your Dreams Taste Like Candy

Dr. Carmichael: Do you know how we learned that MD3301913 is so afraid of being trapped?

Agent 19 looks uneasy.

Agent 19: I assumed that anyone would be uncomfortable in his position. He can barely move.

Dr. Carmichael smiles.

Dr. Carmichael: There's a difference between "uncomfortable," Agent, and truly phobic. The mind of MD3301913 has a severe panic-inducing aversion to being trapped and unable to release himself. He avoids closets, busses, crowds, and airplanes because of this, but has managed to hide it well.

Agent 19 shifts restlessly.

Agent 19: None of that was in the case file.

Dr. Carmichael: No, it wasn't. We found that information the same way that we discovered the man himself, who was hiding so inconveniently on the other side of the world. Were you aware that the human brain is the most complex item in the known universe, Agent? And that it emits waves? What do you think we could learn, then, if we could read those waves? What secrets would it tell, what secrets would it *hide*?

A glob of drool falls from Dr. Carmicael's lips and onto his lab coat. He does not seem to notice.

Rather than abating, the screaming has gotten worse. Dusan is smashing his forehead against the roof of his chamber. Since his neck is forced into a bend, the hits are weak.

Dr. Carmichael: The answers to so *many* questions lie within, Agent. Yet we are so *unwilling* to split it open and look inside. If we only had the courage to push the boundaries…

Agent 19 is staring at the video feed. Dusan is trembling uncontrollably and gasping for air.

Agent 19: Is… is he going to suffocate in there?

Dr. Carmichael looks at a different video monitor.

Dr. Carmichael: He's at 120 breaths per minute. We want him awake for this.

He pushes several buttons. The monitor drops from 104 degrees to 102 degrees. The walls slacken by less than an inch.

Dr. Carmichael: The initial treatment will be twenty minutes in duration.

First segment of video terminates at this point.

Second segment begins while framing an ashen-faced Agent 19.

Agent 19: Subject's first round of treatment has concluded. He will be extracted for further Interviewing.

He turns and walks over to the hatch in the ground. With some effort, he unlatches the handle, opens the door, and pulls Dusan from the chamber.
Dusan flails wildly, but is indiscriminant in his actions. Agent 19 secures his arms and drags him from the cavity in the floor.

Dusan McGuffin: No no no I can't (loud weeping) please don't put me in there it's breaking I can feel my mind breaking just kill me please don't put me back (loud weeping) please

Your Dreams Taste Like Candy

At this point, Agent 19 wraps one hand around both of Dusan's wrists, and clamps the other down on his mouth. In his weakened state, Dusan is unable to resist the restraint.

Agent 19: You are a *sweaty* son of a bitch, you know that?

Dr. Carmichael approaches the pair. He is beaming.

Dr. Carmichael: Good to see you again, MD3301913. Do you want to go back into the box?

Dusan writhes fruitlessly against the restraints of Agent 19.

Dr. Carmichael: Tell us where your wife and son are, MD3301913, and you don't have to.

Dusan's eyes grow wide with terror, and he shakes his head fervently.

Dr. Carmichael: We know just how agonizing it is for you to be trapped in our hurt box, MD3301913. We know so much about you. We know *exactly* what your breathing, sweating, and pulse rates need to be in order to prevent a loss of consciousness. This means that we will continue to bake your mind indefinitely, and you will not have the sweet release of passing out.

Here Dr. Carmichael kneels so that he is face-to-face with Dusan. He strokes the man's face with his fingertips.

Dr. Carmichael: We're never, ever, ever, ever going to stop. The torture does not cause any physical damage, and we can give you an IV that keeps you alive for as long as we'd like. You need to understand, MD3301913, that we will torture your mind for years if we need to. Twenty minutes was more terror than you've experienced in your entire life, according to the readouts of your brain waves. Which means that there is one very, very important thing that we need to get into that very *special* brain of yours.

Your Dreams Taste Like Candy

Here Dr. Carmichael gently grabs Dusan's head, leans forward, and lightly kisses his scalp.

Dr. Carmichael: You *will* break, MD3301913. It's only a matter of how much you suffer before that happens. Spare yourself the unnecessary pain and accept the inevitable. Now. Where are your wife and son?

Dusan's face is white. His eyes are fully dilated despite the bright light of the room. He moves his lips, but no sound comes out at first.

Dr. Carmichael: I couldn't hear that, MD3301913.

Dusan McGuffin: Sis. Sis. Sister's... house.

Dr. Carmichael: Your wife and son ran to her sister's house, and are staying there right now?

Silent tears start to fall from Dusan's face.

Dusan McGuffin: Kill me. Please. Kill me.

Dr. Carmichael smiles, then nods to Agent 19.

Dr. Carmichael: Okay, Agent. Put him back in the box.

Dusan whips his head back to Dr. Carmichael, masked in panic and covered with tears. Too weak to resist, he simply trembles and stares as Agent 19 lifts him like a baby and gently places him back inside the box.

Dusan McGuffin: Please kill my wife and son instead of doing this to them.

Agent 19 latches the box and stands back to watch the video monitor.

Dr. Carmichael: We'll keep the temperature at around 100 so that he doesn't pass out. But I think we can bring the walls in tighter.

He types several numbers into the keypad.

Dr. Carmichael: I've estimated that continued compression at the current angle will snap the fifth vertebra after an additional seven centimeters. That will be the maximum constriction allowed on the airway while preserving respiration.

A mechanical groaning is heard. After several seconds, an audible crack resonates throughout the room.
At this point, Dr. Carmichael begins typing furiously.

Dr. Carmichael: We'll keep him here for the time being.

Agent 19 is staring, vacantly, at the latch on the floor.

Second segment of video terminates at this point.

Third segment begins with Agent 19's face in center frame. He looks to be holding back tears.

Agent 19: That's enough, Dr. Carmichael.

Dr. Carmichael looks furious, and advances quickly on Agent 19.

Third segment of video terminates at this point.

Fourth segment of video begins with Dr. Carmichael looking agitated as he stares at the computer monitor. He is furiously writing information into a blue notebook.

Dr. Carmichael: *Now* is when we remove him, Agent. Things happen on my time, not yours.

Your Dreams Taste Like Candy

Stiff and disjointed, Agent 19 kneels down and awkwardly removes the lock. He flings open the doors, then reels back in reaction to the sudden wave of heat.

After a difficult struggle, Agent 19 is able to pull Dusan from the tight squeeze of the box.

Dr. Carmichael: Be careful, Agent. Remember that his neck is broken.

Agent 19 lays Dusan on the ground. He appears to be dead. The color has drained from his skin, his eyes stare blankly without blinking, and his appendages roll freely with no regard for balance. The lower half of Dusan's face, as well as the front of his shirt, is covered in a copious amount of gelatinous, yellow-white chunks.

Dr. Carmichael: Looks like he had eggs for breakfast!

Dr. Carmichael laughs. Agent 19 cups his hand to his own mouth and runs from the camera. A retching sound is heard in the background.

Several seconds later, Agent 19 returns, wiping his lips on his sleeve.

Agent 19: Dr. Carmichael, he's dead.

Dr. Carmichael: How could he be dead, Agent? I've been monitoring his pulse, respiration, and body temperature. The break to his neck was *very* carefully calibrated to leave all blood vessels and nerves undamaged. There was simply nothing *to* kill him.

Agent 19: But Dr. Carmichael-

Dusan reaches a shaking, vomit-covered arm out and grabs Agent 19's leg with a loud groan.

Agent 19: GOD FUCKING DAMN IT!

Agent 19 shakes his leg free and runs to the corner of the room. Dr. Carmichael's grin grows bigger.

Your Dreams Taste Like Candy

Dr. Carmichael: As I was saying, Agent, there is simply nothing to damage his body in any significant way, as long as we're careful with his neck in the coming weeks. But his *mind*, Agent... well, look at him!

Dusan has made no effort to clean himself, sit up, or speak. His face sheet-white and slack, a fleck of vomit pivots rhythmically in and out of his left nostril, the only outward sign that the man is breathing.

Dr. Carmichael: An egg is worthless until the protective outer shell gets shattered. Only then can the nutrients inside be made available for consumption.

Dr. Carmichael licks his bearded lips, then approaches Agent 19 and regards him paternally.

Dr. Carmichael: We opine ceaselessly about the difference between burial and cremation, but no one asked the swine if he wanted his pyre to be your griddle or his funeral to be your morning meal. And no pig ever stopped to consider that his cosmic purpose was to be manufactured into your shit. You're never upset by this balance, and that's the only reason we can all have breakfast.

Dr. Carmichael steps within an inch of the taller man's face.

Dr. Carmichael: If you're afraid to partake in a more *elegant* dish, your contribution to this project can be a downward move on the food chain.

For a moment, the only movement is the continued trembling of Dusan.

Dusan McGuffin: Please kill my family.

Dr. Carmichael turns away from Agent 19 and gazes almost lovingly at the quivering mess of a man on the floor.

Dr. Carmichael: And what a prize pig we have here.

Your Dreams Taste Like Candy

He squats next to Dusan, then gently runs his fingertips across the shaking man's cheek. He either does not know or does not care about the streaks of vomit that now soil his skin.

Dr. Carmichael stands up and looks back at Agent 19.

Dr. Carmichael: His brain waves, detected while he was sleeping a continent away, are everything we've been seeking for *so long*. We're nearly *certain* that he's one of The Twelve. We've worked on this for more years than you can imagine, Agent. And it's almost here. The time is nigh.

Agent 19: But why... why all this?

Dr. Carmichael regards him stonily.

Dr. Carmichael: Two reasons, Agent. The first is that we believe the nature of his beautifully unique brain will only truly be accessible once the conscious mind has been fundamentally broken. Would you risk making love to a woman who was physically strong enough to fight back, Agent? Certainly not. And we won't gamble on a similar venture with such a precious asset. It's a funny thing, isn't it? We both control and *don't* control our own minds at the same time. The itch on your leg is only real because it's in your head, and psychologists make a fortune by explaining to a brain just what the mind really is. So powerful, but so tragically malleable.

He looks at Dusan, who is silently crying and shaking.

Dr. Carmichael: No man truly knows what is best for himself.

Here he turns back to Agent 19.

Dr. Carmichael: And the second reason is because I fucking said so. If your mind is too dull to comprehend that, Agent, I've got a recently vacated box that can explain things much more clearly.

Agent 19 regards Dr. Carmichael with an unmoving stance that could be interpreted as either stoicism or fear.

Your Dreams Taste Like Candy

After several seconds, Dr. Carmichael turns and walks away from Agent 19.

Dr. Carmichael: Get an orderly in here to move MD3301913 into an incubator.

Dusan makes several frantic noises and gestures, but they are barely audible.

Dusan McGuffin: My family-

Dr. Carmichael quickly turns on Dusan.

Dr. Carmichael: Your family was picked up four minutes after you were, MD3301913. Did you not realize that your sister-in-law's house was the most obvious place to 'hide'? I hope that the more peculiar aspects of that brain are keener than your dearth of logical reasoning abilities.

Dr. Carmichael squats so that he is once again close to Dusan. When he speaks, it is in a much lower tone.

Dr. Carmichael: The pain you endured in the belief that you were protecting your family was engineered to serve no purpose other than our own. You couldn't have saved them, and you failed in your doomed attempt. It was always hopeless in more ways than one, and your wife and son were damned long ago by virtue of knowing you.

Dusan lets out a high-pitched "eep," but says nothing more.
Dr. Carmichael rises and walks toward the exit.
His erection is prominent.

Dr. Carmichael: Come with me, Agent. The mind is a predictable quarry, and the hunt has reached its next stage. The family of MD3301913 is bound and waiting in the adjacent room. Shattering a man's psyche is a delicate task, and we must continue with the utmost precision. We will truly destroy MD3301913 as he watches what we do to his family.

Your Dreams Taste Like Candy

Dr. Carmichael opens the door and disappears from the camera's view, but can still be heard.

Dr. Carmichael: This is how the next part begins.

HELL YEAH, I GOT INVITED TO THE HALLOWEEN *SEX* PARTY

THE INVITATION CAME IN THE MAIL, ALL LINED WITH GOLD FOIL and shit. That's right, bitches, my connections paid off. Chad Durslop FTW (mic drop)

I wore a leopard costume, because I'm a sexy beast. Rawr.

It was about 8:00 p. m. when I pulled up to the house, which was nice as fuck. I untied my robe as I walked in the door so that everyone could see my hot, beefy manhood.

Damn, there were some beautiful people. I made eyes with this hottie in a peacock costume without any top on. You *know* that we were going at it on the couch not three minutes later. She was on her hands and knees while the feathers from her mask tickled my chin under my own disguise.

Halfway through, some costumed zebra came by and started licking my taint, but I was way too invested to slow down.

I put my thumb in the peacock's butthole. She groaned and started *slamming* her petite little frame into my thighs so hard that it knocked her mask right off.

I looked down at her and went flaccid almost immediately, but that still wasn't quick enough.

"MOM?!"

BIG MAURICE AND THE MYSTERY OF THE SECRET ROOM

-1-

THE CAMERA PIVOTED VIA REMOTE CONTROL, EFFICIENTLY zooming in on my most vulnerable parts. It was unnerving to watch the machine observing me while I was otherwise alone in the room. But it was so fucking *hot* to know that my husband was ogling me while he should have been working.

We're still in that "thrill" stage of marriage that comes during the first twelve months after the nuptials. He loves his role as doting husband, I adore being a doting wife, and we're still helplessly in love.

And yes, we're both hot, and we both know it. But I didn't marry Ravi because of the way a fitted suit hugs his waist, or simply for the decadent paycheck he brings home every two weeks.

Those things just make life *nice*.

But there's nothing on earth that compares with fucking someone you're truly, desperately in love with.

Which is the only reason I signed up for his "web cam" fetish plan in the first place. Allowing myself to be videotaped while masturbating took me way, *way* outside my comfort zone. Of all the men and women who had ever requested it of me, I only said 'yes' to Ravi.

Besides, he was going to make it up to me with the rope thing tomorrow. I've wanted to experiment with *that* forever.

Your Dreams Taste Like Candy

We intend to indulge every one of each other's most private fantasies before our second anniversary.

"Oh hello there, husband," I teased into the camera with a voice that dripped feminine sweetness. "You've left me here *all* alone."

I felt ridiculous talking that way, but Ravi loved it. I knew I had met my match when every weird trait that I'd learned to hide suddenly seemed alluring.

"Oh my, look at this." I pulled Big Maurice out from the blankets behind me. "I just happen to have this *big* dildo. What do you think your wife should do with it?"

The monitor next to the camera spouted an eager message: "PUT IT IN"

Take a note, men: the magic can disappear in a nanosecond, and you have less time than that to course correct.

I frowned. "Um. Can you ask *nicely*?"

The next response was even faster: "PUT IT IN YOUR ASS"

Another note: the road to ass play exists, but it is a *delicate* path to that hallowed ground.

I calmly placed Big Maurice behind me and closed my legs. "This isn't making me feel sexy and safe, Ravi," I explained calmly but coldly.

The computer screen took just a second to reply: "YOU ARE SAFE. DON'T WORRY. I'M WATCHING YOU."

Strike three. I covered my breasts.

That's when my phone started buzzing, and I saw that it was from Ravi. I braced myself to be curt enough to let him know that he needed to work to win me over, but that he would be successful if he understood that *he* needed to come up with a solution based on my tone when I responded with "It's fine" to everything he said.

I took a deep breath and read his message.

<Heya, Cinnamon Buns>

Not fair, he knows I love that nickname.

<I'm supposed to be working for the next twenty minutes and I reeeeeally don't want to. Why haven't you started the camera? ☹>

Your Dreams Taste Like Candy

Pretending that he hadn't seen me was a mood-killer.

My stomach dropped.

Ravi *never* knowingly risked losing a sexual encounter halfway through.

I stared up at the camera, horror etched into my face.

The camera pivoted upward.

I scrambled toward the edge of the bed.

Who was on the other side of that camera?

A burst of shattering glass rang through the house.

I froze. The sound of my own pulse thundered in my ears.

In the strained silence, I could hear my back door lock turning.

The hinges creaked as it opened. A man's heavy boot steps walked in.

Terrified, I sprinted from the bedroom and ran, stark naked, down the hall. I was on the second floor and turned away from the stairs as a strange man stomped through the house.

I ran into Ravi's upstairs office, closed the door, and dove into the closet.

The harder I tried to contain my breath, the louder it sounded.

I had to call 911.

Shit. I'd left the phone in the bedroom. Did I have time to run back into the room?

Clomp. Clomp. Clomp.

No, he – whoever he was – had already gotten halfway up the stairs. I'd have to pass right in front of him to get to the bedroom.

I briefly considered using the room's landline before remembering that it was 2019.

Could I use anything for a weapon? Dammit – I'd left Big Maurice on the bed. He might not be a traditional weapon – but if I was about to die, I'd relish the opportunity to bludgeon my killer with an oversized dildo on my way out.

But even that was out of reach. For fuck's sake, I didn't even have clothes.

I held my breath. My eyes burned as tears pressed through my tightly-closed slits.

Finally, I softly gasped for air.

"I think I foooooound you," an unfamiliar voice sang from the hall. It was full of joy but no mirth.

The handle turned, and the closet door creaked open.

Your Dreams Taste Like Candy

"Come on out, I can *smell* you," he grumbled.

I reached desperately around the dark closet for something – anything – that I could use to defend myself. I had no idea what I might find, but there's no *way* I would have predicted a doorknob. I turned it and prayed.

A tiny trapdoor opened inward.

The boots came to a heavy stop in front of the closet door.

"Your eyelids are going to feel so titillating on my tongue."

I plunged headfirst into the cramped darkness, shutting the trapdoor behind me as the closet door opened.

-2-

I didn't think that things could get worse. Then they got worse.

SSNNNNIFFFFFF "Come on out, Brown Sugar. I can *smell* the sex on ya."

The purest terror of my life was consuming ninety-nine percent of my mind, but the tiniest sliver wanted to scream that *this* type of line is exactly why he's an incel.

Slam. He punched the wall, which reverberated behind me.

The tiny trap door creaked.

Shit. It was only a matter of time before he found it and came after me.

I crawled a few feet through a dark tunnel. A change in the echoes and temperature told me that a large room opened up in the darkness ahead.

My hand reached the lip of the tunnel, and I realized that a steep drop lay in front of me. My head spun as I considered how far down this chamber *in my own house* must be.

Thump "I'm gonna find ya, you bitch!" He groaned in deep satisfaction. "I wanna smell your hair."

Frantically, I felt around the wall next to the chamber opening.

And I found a ladder.

It was actually a series of rungs bolted to the metal wall. Would they hold me?

Creak "Oh, ho ho *ho*, lookee what we have here! A secret door!"

Your Dreams Taste Like Candy

I had swung onto the ladder before I realized what was happening, legs working overtime as I powered downward.

It took nineteen seconds to descend thirteen steps. By the time I hit the ground, I must have been at basement level.

I could feel dirt below my bare feet. What the fuck was this place? I couldn't even see my hands directly in front of my face, so I waved my arms wildly around as I took several tentative steps forward.

The air was frigid and still on my nude body, and I felt nothing but dirt as I walked across the ground.

The grunting sounds from above informed me that I had minimal time before the intruder discovered the ladder. I had to stay hidden.

That's when my hand bumped against a wall and flicked on a light switch.

Several things happened at once.

I winced in pain at the sudden light, but immediately realized that I didn't have time to dwell on ocular discomfort. I quickly scanned the room.

Knives. Chains. A table with leather restraints. A fucking human-sized *cage* that was suspended from the ceiling.

This was a torture room.

"Oh, my!" cackled the voice from above.

I looked up.

I was anticipating a horrible face, but even *this* took me off-guard. I thought it was a mask at first, but quickly realized that it was his actual skin. His sunken, sallow flesh somehow clung tightly to his skull while drooping in all the wrong places. The man's beady, black eyes receded far too deeply into his skull. He licked his thin lips excessively, as though he was unable to get them sufficiently wet. His balding scalp retained just enough long, greasy, gray hair to give the appearance of sun-parched weeds in fallow soil.

Drool dangled from his lip, trembling before it fell along the ladder and splashed to the dirt below.

"I like your video," he gurgled in a voice that sounded like dog shit smells. "I wanna taste your ears from the *in*side."

He turned to climb down the ladder. As his body emerged, it gave the appearance of a skeleton.

Could I fight him off?

He rested a hand on the first rung, revealing a large chef's knife.

Fuck.

Your Dreams Taste Like Candy

What the fuck.

Nothing about the world around me made sense.

Until something clicked, and *everything* made sense.

I looked across at the table, and then up at the cage above it.

Yes.

The man hit the ground with a soft thud as I leapt onto the table, rolled to the other side, then hopped off and landed on the dirt behind it.

He turned to sprint toward me. I was in the corner with nowhere to run.

He gurgled his saliva.

I turned around with a huge, cheery smile on my face as he jumped onto the table.

"Don't you like my breasts?" I asked warmly as I spread my arms before him.

He froze in shock.

Perfect.

I knew that I'd only have one shot at this, but I'm a gal who thrives under pressure. So I confidently reached to the wall behind me and snatched the edge of the rope tied there. That loosened the tension on the cord. The rope's other end, which had been tied to the ceiling, descended to the table.

He was wrapped in the lassoed end before he could say, "The fuck?"

I loosened a second part of the rope, freeing a counterweight. The lasso tightened around his knees, flipping him upside down and smacking his head – hard – against the table. The knife hit the wooden surface with a *clang* before clattering softly to the dirt floor. The asshole flew upward as the counterweight pulled him high.

Right through the open bottom of the cage.

He screamed as he slammed against the bars of the cage and the rope constricted tightly around his thighs.

I quickly and efficiently stood up on the table, then reached for the underside of the cage. Ignoring his pathetic cries, I pulled the bottom shut and latched it in place.

The man's screams turned into groans as he realized that he was trapped by both the rope and the bars in his claustrophobic cage.

And the rope was still pinching his legs.

And he was upside down.

Your Dreams Taste Like Candy

I looked up at him and grinned.

He spit. The thick loogie fell through the bars and splashed onto my cheek.

It smelled.

I wiped it away and continued to smile. "Man, this must suck for you at the moment. But after ten minutes in this position, you're going to know what true hell is."

He screamed like a little boy.

"Now," I said mostly to myself as he continued to blubber incoherently, "I need to have a *very* serious conversation with my husband about this room that he's clearly built for me."

-3-

My, did the man bang hard against the metal bars.

"Save your energy, Sweetness," I offered in my best saccharine voice. I hopped to the dirt floor and plucked his knife from the ground. "You've got a *long* road ahead of you."

I flicked off the lights, then groped around until I found the ladder once more. I delicately held the knife in one hand as I climbed back out of the room, leaving my would-be attacker caged, upside-down, alone, and in darkness.

I emerged into the natural light of Ravi's office. My first goal was to get to the phone I'd left behind.

No, that's not true. My *immediate* priority was to find some clothes.

But the sound of a man sprinting up the stairs put even that plan on hold.

I slipped behind the door, gripping the knife tightly in one hand. I held my breath.

Then my husband burst into the room.

I pounced.

Your Dreams Taste Like Candy

Using his own momentum, I shoved Ravi from behind and pressed him up against the wall. I held the blade to his throat and stared into the eyes of the man who had promised to love me forever.

"Priya!" he screamed. "Are you hurt?"

I raised an eyebrow. "Oh, Ravi. The hurting hasn't even begun."

"You're merciless," Ravi panted from the table below me. The next words were garbled as he struggled to catch his breath.

"Shouldn't your primary concern be your wife's happiness?" I asked sweetly. "I got what I needed." I rolled across his nude body, slipped off the table, and stood on the dirt floor. "You can always take care of yourself, Ravi. You know I love to watch."

He flashed an exasperated look. "Priya, I can't move because of how tightly you've made these ropes."

I shrugged. "*You're* the one who wanted to be on the table first, Ravi." I sighed. "Besides, you could have it much, *much* worse."

Here I looked up at the cage suspended above us. The mysterious intruder still dangled inside, but it was getting difficult to tell when he slipped in and out of consciousness. Hanging upside-down for that long was surely bad for his health, but it was such a *thrill* to know that we were being watched.

"Ravi, I don't know how many times I've said it, but this room is just..." I bent down to kiss him. "It's perfect. Thank you for giving me everything I want. Thank you for *knowing* what I want."

I looked up. "Of course, what I *really* want is to try that rope thing myself. That cage looks so *cozy*, and I need you to put me in there as soon as..."

Ravi strained to see me, but the ropes restricted his movement. "Did you have an idea, honey?"

I smiled.

I chewed thoroughly, following the bite with a sublime Chianti Bellavista. I stared across the wooden table at Ravi.

Your Dreams Taste Like Candy

We had decided to stay naked for dinner.

"I never, *ever* thought we'd be bold enough to try this. You dirty talk in ways that would make Ron Jeremy blush, but I can't believe that you actually convinced me."

I swallowed. "We live, and then we die. What does hesitation preserve?"

Ravi pursed his lips.

I reached across the food and grabbed his hand. "What choice did we have?" I asked gravely. "You found out how the video feed was being pirated, so there's no chance that another intruder could find our home. But if we let him go, even to the police, people would find out about us."

Ravi squeezed my hand and nodded gravely.

"You'd be ruined professionally if people found our sex tapes, and I'd never be safe if people knew how to get into our home. We had to end this now. Besides," I continued coyly, "When will we ever, *ever* get a chance to try this again?"

I winked and picked up the carving knife. The intruder moaned pathetically in protest, but what little physical strength remained was easily restricted by the ropes that held him firm. Delicately, I moved the knife and carved off another sliver of his penis, quickly dropping it onto the hot plate with a satisfying sizzle. Ravi covered the stump with a bloody cloth as I tended to the frying penis chunk. The temperature was just right to start a delicious crisping effect on the fatty tissue as I flipped the deliciously marbled meat for an even grilling. The aroma was one that neither of us had ever encountered before, and I sadly reflected on the fact that I might never smell it again.

"It seems that nineteen grams of meat contains thirteen ounces of fat, so this will be a rare treat if we want to keep our slender figures," I explained to the intruder.

He groaned a deep, pain-infused gurgle. With his mouth gagged, only the lowest moans came through.

"You just don't get meat this fresh anywhere else," Ravi noted as he swallowed his portion. "I think that's the difference."

I pulled the chunk off the hot plate and quickly cut it half, handing one to Ravi before dressing my own. We were using a white wine-infused black truffle mustard, which was the perfect pairing for a meat whose size was small but flavor was powerful.

Your Dreams Taste Like Candy

"Mmmmm," Ravi moaned as he took another bite.

"Rrrrrrrgth," the man mumbled as he dipped toward unconsciousness.

I leaned back in utter contentment. "Ravi, we've pushed the sexual boundaries further than I could ever have dreamed." I sighed. "Thank you for sharing every weird experience that I've ever imagined."

He winked at me.

"So," I asked eagerly, "Do you have anything planned for after the meal?"

He shot back a boyish grin.

"Just desserts."

MY NEW HOUSE HAS REALLY STRANGE HOME OWNERS' ASSOCIATION RULES

WRITTEN BY GUEST AUTHOR BLAIR DANIELS

"THIS — THIS HOUSE HAS AN HOA?" I STUTTERED.

The real estate agent nodded.

No. I'd heard the horror stories. Fines for walking your dog. Fines for the wrong color curtains. Fines for obscenely shaped stains in your driveway. A Home Owners' Association was just about the worst thing a house could have.

"Do you have a copy of the HOA agreement?"

The real estate agent avoided eye contact. "How do you like the house?" she asked, trying to change the subject.

"I'd like to read the HOA agreement, please."

After rooting through some drawers, she pulled out a thick stack of papers. "Here you go."

With a heavy heart, I began to read.

PELICAN PEAK: HOME OWNERS' ASSOCIATION RULES

1. Your garage must be kept closed at all times, unless you are currently entering or exiting the house.

2. The community has a strict curfew of 10 PM. You may not make any noise between 10 PM and 6 AM, and you must also keep all the curtains closed during this time.

3. Food scraps cannot be mixed with regular trash; we have a compost bin. Discard food scraps in the red plastic bin provided to you, and leave it on the curb on evenings shortly before curfew. We will pick it up and bring it to the compost bin. Do NOT attempt to bring it to the compost bin yourself.

4. You must always wear neutral-colored clothing when exiting or entering your home, and when walking around the development.

That's where I raised an eyebrow. What? Neutral-colored clothing? I looked down at my own outfit – aqua-blue jeans and a hot pink, fluttery top. What is this? Some kind of dystopian nightmare? Making us conform, so we can all look the same in these cookie-cutter townhouses?

"So I wouldn't be allowed to wear this outfit?" I asked the real estate agent.

She hemmed and hawed. "Uh, well… probably not. But, you know, you can just get one of those long duster cardigans, or a jacket, in a neutral color and wear it when you go out. It's not a super-strict rule – you can have some color showing –"

"Not a super-strict rule," I repeated, pointedly nodding in her direction. "I see."

I continued to read.

5. Never knock on a neighbors' door unannounced. Similarly, never answer the door if you aren't expecting anyone. As a community, Pelican Peak values privacy and safety above all else.

6. When walking your dog, keep him or her away from the cul-de-sac on Petunia Lane. The compost bin is back there, and sometimes animals are triggered by the smell.

7. Never leave children that weigh under 50 pounds playing unattended outside.

Your Dreams Taste Like Candy

8. The homeowner's dues are $150/month, due on the first weekday of every month.

I stared at the sheet. "This is pretty restrictive."

"But look at what you're getting for the price," she said. "Granite countertops and mahogany cabinets. Stainless steel appliances. A rain shower in the master bathroom. All for under two-hundred thousand!"

I did love rain showers...

I made an offer the next week. Several weeks later, I was moving in – along with several new black cardigans and jackets. My corgi, Buff, seemed to like the place well enough. She liked watching the squirrels run by – something she couldn't do from the window of my 11th-floor apartment.

That first night, I followed the rules to a T. At 9:47 PM, I put my food scraps out – chicken bones, kale stems, and an apple core. At 9:58 PM, I locked all the doors, drew the curtains, turned down the radio, and settled into bed.

(I wasn't going to sleep, of course. It was time for my three-hour Seinfeld marathon before bed.)

Around 10:15 PM, Buff started growling.

Rrrrr!

I groaned, paused the episode, and walked into the second bedroom. "Buff! Shhh!" I hissed, remembering the association rule.

She didn't even turn around. She just sat at the front window, her head poking around the curtain. Hackles raised, staring out into the darkness, growling like mad.

"Buff?"

My fingers fell on the curtain's edge – but then I stopped. Keep curtains closed after 10 PM. That was the rule. But does that mean I'm not even allowed to take a peek?

And what if it's some crazy guy sitting on my porch or something? Or a rabid squirrel?

I pulled back the curtain.

Your Dreams Taste Like Candy

At first, I just saw darkness. Amorphous blobs of townhouses stuck to each other, speckled with blocks of hazy golden light. Everyone had their curtains drawn. The street was empty. No cars, no people, no squirrels.

Wait.

The street wasn't empty.

A tall figure stood on the sidewalk, right in front of my house. The light from my window barely illuminated his form, but I could still make it out.

He picked up my red plastic bin.

But there was no garbage truck, or wheelbarrow, or anything else around to dump it in. 'Where's he going to empty it?' I thought. 'Is he just going to carry the bins one-by-one to the compost? That's really ineffic—'

He hoisted the bin up.

His mouth stretched open – far wider than I've seen any mouth open.

Then he poured the contents in his mouth.

A light cracking sound emerged from the darkness as he chewed up the bones. I stared, horrified, and Buff did too.

Then she began to bark.

Ruff! Ruff!

The thing froze.

"Sssshh!" I said, patting Buff's head. "Please, be quiet –"

Ruff!

He snapped around and ran towards the window at full speed. A flash of a gray, wrinkled face. Hollow, black pits for eyes. A gaping mouth with, somehow, no teeth or tongue.

I let the curtain fall. I backed away, hugging Buff, my heart pounding in my chest.

That's when the knocking started. And I remembered, perhaps, the most important rule of them all:

Never answer the door if you aren't expecting anyone.

HOW I LOST MY VIRGINITY

I AWOKE AT 9:57 A. M. TO FIND THAT I HAD MORNING WOOD AND three minutes to get to class.

I made the best of a bad situation by spurting against the wall near the corner of my bed.

The sheets are very crusty in that corner.

After I finished, it dawned on me that I should see if my roommate was around. Thankfully, he wasn't.

Rory never seemed to spend any time in our room. I was used to it; the more people get to know me, the more they stay away.

I got to my 10:00 class 19 minutes late, which was 13 minutes after rolling out of bed. I saved time by wearing the same gray sweatpants to class that I had slept in. As I burst through the door, the other students looked my way and the professor looked disappointed.

I found a seat in the back row and tried to catch my breath. That was a challenge, because I'm extremely out of shape. Jerking off and *then* rushing to class really hurt my chest, and I quietly gasped while spending the next several minutes fighting off dizziness.

I *hated* how the sweat would collect in twin crescent shapes under my breasts. I endured enough judgmental glances simply for *having* c-cups as a dude, but the sweat marks looked like two smiling mouths caressing my nipples.

Your Dreams Taste Like Candy

I knew that going to college in Arizona was a mistake. The heat caused my sweat glands to work overtime while my erection glands gave no mercy as skimpily-clad women pranced about on campus.

Neither fact was kind to me.

Normally I can get away without showering for a couple of days (at least I think I can, but maybe that's part of why people avoid me). But even *I* can smell myself after sweating that much, and I know I'm gross.

Everyone makes me feel gross.

So why try to change anything? It's not like I have any friends to appreciate my accomplishments. I'd cry at the thought, but people only shed tears when they lose things.

And believe me, the guy with no self esteem has absolutely nothing else to lose.

I thought on this as Professor Higgs cast a thinly-veiled stare of disgust my way. I tried, and failed, to subdue my wheezing.

I looked away in order to return my sense of shame back to the 'default' setting.

Unfortunately, my eyes landed on Ophelia.

She'd worn shorts today, meaning that her legs were stretched out in all their shiny bronze glory. I felt my attention get sucked into her soft skin like the Death Star pulling the Millennium Falcon up its tractor beam.

I broke away from the sight, and my eyes landed slightly northward.

Ophelia had Resting Bitch Face if I ever saw it. That was one of my biggest turn-ons. Her raven hair framed a cream-white face that screamed "you're shit and I hate you" even when she didn't realize it.

Ah fuck, I was losing control. I focused on her hairband instead. It was thin and red.

Too late. I was rock hard.

Why did that do it for me? Why did a red hairband push me over the edge? I hated myself, and with good cause. I was a disgusting virgin whose only real companion was my computer. The four terabytes of porn I owned were my best friend and biggest enemy.

Right there, in the middle of class, I wiped away a tear.

I correctly anticipated that no one would notice.

But the fart was unexpected. I'd been so focused on other bodily functions that I'd left my bowels overlooked. It was a powerful bellow of depth and resonance, loud enough and long enough to erase any hope of masking its owner.

You know when you *know* it's going to reek just by the feel of it?

It smelled even more rancid than I'd imagined.

They all looked at me. It was *so* much worse than being ignored.

I couldn't wipe the tears away fast enough, so I sprang out of my chair and raced for the door.

Unfortunately, my boner was on full display at that point. The semester was four months old, which meant that *both* pairs of my underwear had gotten too dirty even for my slovenly tastes, and I had been going commando for a week. With only loose sweatpants covering my lower body, my dick protruded nearly past my gut.

I burst outside. Adjacent to the building, I slipped into some bushes that I had *thought* were hidden and started masturbating. It was the only way to stave off the coming storm of tears and self-loathing that would crush me before I could race back to the safety of the dorm room.

It had seemed like such a good hiding spot. It had worked before.

But I stopped myself mid-pump when a voice shouted from above me.

"Get up, you disgusting pig."

This was bad.

I looked up to see Ophelia staring down at me like she'd just found an elephant turd in her orange juice. "You've got two choices, you piece of shit. I call the cops, or you come with me right now."

Her authoritative tone put me half a jerk away from painting the bushes with a coat of gentleman's glue, but I steadied myself with a deep breath and thoughts of walrus mating rituals.

"Follow me. Behind, not next to."

I obeyed.

The shame prevented me from asking where we were going. Or why it was below the art building. Or what possible reason she could have for leading me underground.

When we finally got into the sub-basement, I decided that it was time to start asking some questions. "Ophelia, I'm so sorry for who I am. But what-"

She whipped around and grabbed me by the throat. I didn't feel like I deserved to stop her, since I was such a piece of shit.

Your Dreams Taste Like Candy

But it quickly became apparent that I couldn't have done anything, even if I'd wanted to.

Her hand turned ice cold and locked into an iron death grip around my neck. My breathing stopped instantly. Then she lifted me, all 330 pounds of disgusting flesh, and my feet left the floor.

She was using one hand.

The last thing I saw before passing out was her eyes turning a bright, flaming red.

I woke up with my hands cuffed to a metal pipe.

Which was unfortunate, because I had a raging erection and no way to address it.

Upon further reflection, I realized that it was also very important to deal with the fact that I was imprisoned and alone. I thought about how long it would take for someone to notice that I was gone.

I cried again, and stopped wondering.

Clack, clack, clack.

Click.

Ophelia towered over me, illuminated by the menacing glow of a single bulb above her head.

She wore red velvet high heels.

They red matched the color of her eyes, which still blazed a supernatural crimson hue.

"You're going to be quite a meal, big boy." She licked her lips. "Fortunately, I've got a hell of an appetite."

She reached under her skirt, then yanked her panties down. They landed at her heels, and she tossed the g-string onto my stomach.

oh shit oh shit oh shit oh shit

Good moments are planned, but great moments come unexpected. I realized that I was about to have the most wonderful dream in my life come true with six seconds' notice.

My boner needed less time than that.

"WAIT!" I screamed as she straddled my waist. "It's... my first time. Um. How do I, ah, do the sex with my hands above my head like this?"

Your Dreams Taste Like Candy

She cocked her head to one side, then peeled her t-shirt off and stuffed it in my mouth.

Her eyes returned to normal once we finished, and she got dressed in a new set of clothes. I grunted through the shirt as she was turning to leave.

She looked back in mild confusion before plucking the garment from my mouth. "Can you still talk?" she asked in surprise.

"Well, yeah. It's just that... did I do it right? I've only seen this happen in videos, so I assumed there would always be four or more people."

She cocked her head to the other side. It was really cute.

"How are you still moving after ten hours of sex?"

My stomach did a series of cartwheels. *Ah shit, I sexed wrong,* I thought. "I'm really sorry, I've never done this before. I guess I sort of assumed I was supposed to spend as much time on the sex as I do jerking off."

So I wasn't masturbating long enough. This confirmed it. I was a failure at every aspect of life.

"You don't feel like you're going to die?" Ophelia asked in surprise.

"Well, my arms are pretty numb. If you're going to leave, can you undo the handcuffs?"

Her eyes flashed red for just a moment. "Once I choose a meal, I consume every bit. You're not going anywhere."

I didn't know what that meant, but it sounded better than returning to an empty dorm room. "That's fine," I explained. "But could you release one hand?"

"Why do you want one hand free if you're still chained to the pipe?"

Well *that* was an awkward silence.

She looked at me like I had two heads. "I just finished ten fucking hours on you!"

"Look, I'm really sorry!" I sputtered. "I don't know how long the sex takes!" With my arms chained, I couldn't wipe my eyes.

Instead, she walked over to my side, sat down, and dried the tears for me.

Somehow, it was even more intimate than the fucking had been.

"You don't care about going home?" she asked softly. "Why are you so eager to masturbate?"

Your Dreams Taste Like Candy

I shifted uncomfortably on the mattress. Normally, I hated opening up to people, and that fact suited the rest of humanity just fine. But in that moment, Ophelia seemed genuinely interested in what I had to say, and I found that talking to her was actually easy. "Well, what do you think I'd do when I got home?"

She looked up at the handcuffs. "Wow, your right arm is *much* more defined than your left."

I smiled. "Thanks."

"Listen, you seem like a nice enough guy, so I'm going to level with you." She still had Resting Bitch Face when she talked. That made it hard to focus, because both of my heads were demanding a lot of blood from my circulatory system. "I'm leaving this school. Soon. I have to move a lot, because there are people who think my type should be eradicated."

I frowned. "Wow, I'm really sorry."

A tear shined in her eye, glinting red in the ruby glow of a sudden flare of supernatural hue. "Oh."

"What's wrong?" I asked in genuine concern.

She wiped away the tear, and I swear that steam hissed lightly as her finger brushed her eye. "Nothing. Um, no one has ever asked me that before." She cleared her throat. "Anyway," Ophelia continued, now business-like, "I have a few errands to run. Then I'm going to come back here, fuck the life out of you, and move onto the next city." She smiled. "You do seem like a really nice guy."

"Thanks," I said, happy for the compliment.

She turned to leave.

"Um. Ophelia?"

She looked back at me, and my stomach spun like a helicopter.

"So… would you be able to release one of my hands?"

She frowned and sat down by my side once more. "I don't think you understand. Let me explain it very plainly. I'm sorry if this hurts to hear, but you need to know what's going to happen. When I return, I'm going to fuck you until there's no energy left in your body. I will use your dick, face, hands, even your elbows as I please. You'll be chained up the entire time. Eventually, I will extract so much energy from you that I will stay young for another month, your cells will cease to function, and you will die. This is how I have been able to stay alive since the year 106 A. D."

Your Dreams Taste Like Candy

"Yes," I responded with growing frustration, "But is it so much to ask for you to let me jerk off until your return?"

Her brows crinkled in the cutest way. "Do you have anyone who will notice you're gone?"

That was the most awkward silence of all.

She put her soft, tiny hand into my cuffed one and sighed. "Humanity eats dead animals three times a day, but they think I'm the monster when I take a life for my own survival. I know what it's like to feel hated."

I nodded. "Most people don't even want to sit next to me in class."

Ophelia offered a half-frown. "That's... because of the smell. You really need to scrub under the folds when you shower."

I blushed.

She raised an eyebrow. "I'm now sensing that the bigger issue is you really need to shower."

"What's the point if people think I'm gross no matter what?"

She wiped her eye again with another *hiss*. "You're right. No matter what we do, some people will always have a lot of hate." She sniffed. "Did you know that even guys who *don't* know about my... proclivities call me 'resting bitch face girl'?"

"Well," I offered, caressing her arm with my protruding gut since my hands were indisposed, "Do you want to talk about it?"

She sobbed.

We talked.

And the conversation never really did end. She ran her errands while I jerked off, we talked again, she fucked me for another ten hours, we talked *again*, she decided to kidnap me, and then we talked some more.

I had never learned how to start a relationship, because I had never really had any friends. So one day I asked her.

"Ophelia, am I your boyfriend?" I inquired from the makeshift cage under the bed of her new dorm room.

She crinkled her nose, sending my heart aflutter. "You're... the person who makes me feel normal."

"Oh," I responded. "Um, is there a difference?"

She smiled. "Don't make it weird."

Your Dreams Taste Like Candy

And that's pretty much how I ended up here. Ophelia gives me computer time while she's out harvesting human snacks, and I take occasional writing breaks between jerkoff sessions. She pulls me out of my cage for a "full meal" between midnight and 10:00 a. m. each day. Ophelia drifts from college to college, enticing men but never making friends, until she has to run away from people who suspect her true nature.

Apparently, other guys can't survive more than five hours of Ophelia's "feasting." I don't know what's so weird about me. But I've accepted that 'different' and 'wrong' are two very separate concepts, despite what I'd assumed my entire life.

I never would have imagined a relationship to be quite like this. But we're both happy, and the rest just kind of gets made up along the way.

We're two very lonely people, but we're lonely together. I don't know if there's any way to be happy besides that.

WHAT ARE YOU THANKFUL FOR?

FOR ME, EVERYTHING CONNECTS BACK TO MEMORY. THAT'S what I'm thankful for most of all.

Scent is so fundamentally intertwined with memory that the concepts become indistinguishable from one another, like two different strands of flower that bind themselves to the same vine. I can smell the richness of gravy wafting through the aroma of potatoes, and part of me *is* a child again. I'm home, wrapped in a feeling of *belonging* that can only be experienced by a child.

"What are you thankful for?" I ask across the table. Cora smiles back at me, and my heart flutters just a little. "For me, it's the fact that my wife is still my crush, three years after our wedding."

She's grateful for the fact that we've gotten more out of life than life ever promised, Cora says. Because we're assured that everything will end one day, but no guarantee was ever made that life was going to start.

"That's happy and sad at the same time," I offer. "Is that really what you want to choose?"

She tells me that there's no better choice, because what she said was real. I reach across the table to take her hand in mine, but she is just beyond the reach of my fingertips. Instead, I cut two slices of pie. I take one for myself. She asks me if that's a bit much, but I tell her no. "We all know what 'too little' tastes like," I explain. "I'll take 'too much' when I can."

Cora says she's thankful that she can take care of me. "I need that," I explain as she points to my lips, and I wipe the food away with my napkin. She shakes her head, and explains that I should never *need* her, but only *want* her. We grow to love the things we want, but our needs become unappreciated parts of who we are. I should be a whole man without her.

I feel the tears before I know that I'm crying. "It's too late for that, Cora." They drip down my nose and onto the two slices of pie that really are excessive for a Thanksgiving of one. "I'm not whole."

The seat across from me remains silent.

"You're more than just *you*. When flowers weave themselves through the vine, one life becomes dependent on another. One death kills more than just itself." My tears were flowing freely now. "Choosing to live today means choosing to die tomorrow. It's a good thing we don't understand the consequences when we decide, isn't it?"

I finish the last of the wine.

"Your memory is more painful than your death, Cora, but it's the most precious thing I have. That fact seems impossible, but so does every great thing I've ever felt. For me, everything connects back to memory. That's what I'm thankful for most of all."

PUS

I SAW A BEAUTIFUL ONE. RIGHT THERE IN THE CROOK OF MY nose. It was gorgeous.

I leaned into the mirror and squeezed. An extremely thin, squiggly, jagged string shot off like a rocket, twirling, spinning, entwining in on itself with lightning speed.

My mouth watered.

I scraped it onto my fingernail and gazed down at the delicious tendril. I wanted another. I *needed* another.

I found another.

Just to the right of my nose, I discovered a blackhead. I leaned in again and squeezed gently. Imagine my delight when not one but three pores erupted, dancing slowly this time as they emerged from *terra firma* and greeted one another.

I wiped the snakes on my fingernail again, and was immediately back in front of the mirror.

There was a nice, fat whitehead on the tip of my nose (how could I have missed it?), and I dug in. It took some teasing, but I was rewarded in the end as a thick, fat worm emerged like a July 4th black snake. This one had a lot of meat to it; I kept pushing, and it keep oozing more and more pus out of the pore.

By the time it had given everything to me, my nose had a two-inch tentacle dangling from the tip. It wiggled, it jiggled, it fell into the sink.

Plop.

I needed more.

Your Dreams Taste Like Candy

There was a perfect zit hiding in my eyebrow hairs. The surface was white and glossy, almost gem-like, begging to be picked. I obliged it lovingly.

The skin around our eyebrows is easy to move around like putty. It's not for the use of expressing emotions, oh no. It moves like that for us. It moves like that for pus.

I pinched a glob of eyebrow skin between my two index fingers and felt a knot. 'That's where the good stuff lives,' I thought. 'But not for long.'

The right way is to squeeze on the knot from between and behind. It resisted any explosion at first, and I pressed firmly inward. The glossy sheen of the pimple remained unbroken, and I began to sweat as I pushed harder.

I was finally rewarded with a burst of whiteness. It left a splash mark on the mirror. I smiled, and left it there as a trophy.

I had to get it all.

The chin is a perfect spot. It took some more coaxing this time, but with a lot of pinching and squeezing, I was finally able to get something out.

More.

The nose. I couldn't overlook the gold mine! There are so many itty bitty clogged pores on the schnoz. I got to town. Every square millimeter was waiting to be a mini volcano, and I made it happen over and over and over and over again. When they started to seem empty, I just squeezed and pinched harder, and more came out. There was always more.

All over my face, there was *always* more. It was just a matter of squeezing harder. Once I got the white serpents to squiggle their little dance, I would just dig my fingernails deep, deep into the flesh and there would be more to emerge. More and more and more and more came out the harder I pushed. I was in bliss. It was amazing. There was no limit to what came out, so I just kept digging and digging and digging into every pore on every piece of my face until every skin cell had been eviscerated.

I woke up in a hospital bed very heavily bandaged. They saved my life, but there is nothing left of the skin on my face. My life will never be the same.

Never pop zits while on acid.

YOU DON'T REALIZE JUST HOW MANY PEOPLE ARE LIKE THIS

MY VALENTINE IS BEAUTIFUL.

Auburn hair pulled back in a ponytail. Little buds poking through the front of her sleeveless t-shirt (*clearly* braless), short silk boxers, and pink ankle socks. It's erotic in a *cozy* way that belies an intimacy that is far beyond superficial erotica.

I wiggle my ass to sit more comfortably, and tiny waves of pleasure remind me that I won't be needing a little blue pill tonight.

She's sitting at the desk in her bedroom, long, slender legs spread out before her. Fuck, she's gorgeous.

The sliding glass door faces the tiny patio outside her bedroom. Three feet past the apartment's edge, a short wall supports the steep, ivy-covered hillside beyond. I am sitting in the ivy again tonight, once again covered in darkness as the light from her bedroom puts her on stark display.

I'm directly across from her, but she can't see me.

She never sees me.

She picks up her phone and looks at the number. Her face wrinkles in disgust, and she silences the call.

I take a gulp from my thermos (it's chilly again tonight!) and reach for the Vaseline.

The jar is almost empty; I have to buy a new one each week.

There's a rustling from behind and above me, and I instantly freeze. I'm very well hidden when it's dark, but anyone with a flashlight would find my nest immediately.

87

Your Dreams Taste Like Candy

Slowly, I turn around.

There's a shadowed figure walking in the darkness. My pulse races, and I can feel vomit's finger tickling the back of my throat.

crunch crunch crunch

He's walking down the hill, and he's getting closer to me.

Then he stops.

He pulls something out of his pocket. It glows, and I can see the outline of his scowl.

Her phone rings. She gives it half a glance before immediately hanging up.

The man's phone light turns off. His call has been terminated.

Then I understand. It's that fucking guy Ned, who must be the pushiest asshole in Salt Lake City, Utah. He's been asking her out for six months now, and my Valentine is simply disgusted by his advances.

I know all about her life, because I thoroughly catalog what I find in her trashcan each day.

I look at him with such fury that I nearly shatter the Vaseline jar in my white-knuckle grip.

Ned is *such* a creep.

Then the light from her apartment glints off the blade in his hand, and my heart stops.

He's holding an *enormous* hunting knife.

I want to cry. I cannot imagine anything bad happening to my sweet Valentine! She deserves the very best! After months of me licking her silverware while she's at work to make sure it isn't poisoned, fucking Ned is going to kidnap her!

He takes a step forward, and I act.

Of course, I have my Nikon D7500 DSLR camera at the ready (I've taken 1,913 photos just tonight). But the flash attachment is rarely used, for obvious reasons. This time, however, I turn it on.

Then I point and shoot.

Ned is negotiating the tricky hillside right as the flash blinds him, and the effect is perfect. I catch an instant of pure shock on his face.

He tumbles.

And comes to a rest at the bottom of the hill, right where the short retaining wall meets her patio.

All is still.

Your Dreams Taste Like Candy

I crane my neck slowly, surely, to see why he isn't moving. And from my angle, it's obvious.

The hunting knife has come to rest deep in his left temple. One eye has popped, and the socket is filled with nothing but white jelly.

He's dead.

She glances outside with a look of concern and a furrowed brow. She might have noticed the flash from the corner of her eye, but she hadn't been facing me at that exact second.

And her door is fucking *soundproof* (trust me). Moreover, from where she sits, it's impossible to see the pitch-black hillside.

It's okay. When the morning light comes, it will illuminate my gift to her. She will see Ned's fresh corpse in her backyard, and she will know that there is a love all around her that she cannot see.

Always watching.

Happy Valentine's Day, my sweet.

YOUR CHILDREN ARE BEAUTIFUL.
NOW GET THOSE HELLIONS AWAY FROM ME

CHILDREN AREN'T ALWAYS INNOCENT.

There. I said it.

The last five months of my life have been spent teaching second grade at the Crespwell Academy for Superb Children, and my life is forever changed. I know that I don't ever want to be a mother (which has made the lack of activity in my bedroom actually seem nice), and there are days when I'm disgusted just by remembering that I'm the same species as certain individuals.

Every possible explanation has been offered. Maybe this whole town is a cult. Perhaps there's a hidden burial ground beneath the campus. These kids could be demons (plausible), or I might be on drugs (no, but that option might help me deal with everything in the future). It's not what I'd planned on doing with my life. But if I'm being honest, I didn't really plan *any* of my life after graduation. It had seemed so far off, so unreal, that the thought of preparing for a world without college was like asking what I wanted to pack for the afterlife.

In the end, I don't have any realistic option other than to stay at the one place that hired me after college.

-What's really getting to me is the fact that there's no time to decompress. My four years at Brown were stressful, but I could always look forward to returning to my apartment at the end of the day and drinking a glass of wine, taking a hot bath, or indulging in both at the same time. I tried that yesterday, but it doesn't work when work follows me home. I had turned the lights down low and sunk up to my chin when things started feeling *wrong*. The viscosity of the water was entirely off, and the whole bath smelled of copper instead of lavender. I decided to hold my eyes closed as I stood up, ran the shower over my body, clutched blindly for where I knew the maroon towel lay, and dried off. Even though it had been just 7:13 p.m. when I went into the bath, I decided to go to sleep. Eyes still closed, I walked to my room and crawled into bed. I slept naked that night. In the morning, I walked back to the bathroom (eyes still closed), and I took the hottest shower I could endure. When I finally allowed myself to see again, my skin looked normal (if not medium-rare pink from the heat of the shower). But there was a reddish crust in my fingernails, and I get a distinct whiff of copper every time my arm gets near my nose.

-At the end of every school day, after the kids have left, there is always a small pile of dead maggots on my desk. Every attempt to find the culprit has proven unsuccessful. The maggots will disappear again at some point during the disposal process. It's simply impossible to keep an eye on them at all times. The disappearance will only take place when I am not looking at the maggots. They only ever appear in groups of prime numbers.

-The finish of class is proving to be a light at the end of a daily tunnel. The tension subconsciously flows out of my body (even if just a little) when the last child closes the door behind them. I've slipped a flask into my purse on a couple of occasions. After a particularly rough day, I slipped my hand deep inside without looking (I know every nook and cranny of my Coach handbag by feel alone), but couldn't find it. What I grasped instead was both familiar and *wrong* at the same time. And while a tongue against my flesh can feel thrilling in the right setting, that setting was not the bottom of my purse. Several more tongues licked my skin on the way out as I yanked my hand back like it had been burnt. I left the handbag in the classroom that night. It was gone in the morning.

-Ms. Malbone is the school's lone science teacher. Elementary schools rarely have intensive science programs, so she sojourns from classroom to classroom, spreading the gospel of dispassionate critical analysis. So naturally, she has the greatest emotional impact on the students. When she announced that the class would be performing dissections, most of the girls winced while the boys grinned maniacally.

It took her presentation of a human liver to start my stomach churning, but the rest of the class was suddenly subdued. Was this really appropriate? The class seemed to think so as boy and girl alike dove eagerly into the donated organ. But it was the brain that really pushed me toward the brink. Ms. Malbone was explaining the roles of the different lobes (and how to tell them apart once the children carved them up with a scalpel) when the first wave of nausea hit me. The kids were clamoring for the brains when she announced that they would need to split into pairs, since there were only seven specimens to be shared among thirteen students. It was big Benjamin, whom the others mocked for his girth and his gas, who got one brain entirely to himself. Ms. Malbone dropped the tiny organ from her tongs onto his tray and explained, "It's so small because the victim was so young." That's when I finally ran to the bathroom and puked.

-I had been afraid of Tristan because he seemed so different from the rest of the children. That changed during a history lesson. We were discussing World War I, and several of them were curious about how *angry* people would need to be in order for millions of men to be dragged to war. It was the most interest they'd ever shown in a lesson, so I went with the enthusiasm. I *almost* screamed when the lights went out, but kept my cool. So did the children. It was presumably just a broken circuit, because the room was illuminated once more shortly after. I was not comforted; every single child was staring at me. Every single one had milky white eyes, with neither pupil nor iris to be seen. Every single one was silent and grinning just slightly. I felt my spine melt. My throat was too paralyzed to say anything more than "Eep." Then the lights went out again, and they turned on once more a moment later. All of the eyes had returned to normal.

-I hate rats. So when I switched on the classroom lights at 7:00 a.m. and sent one scurrying across my foot (on the day I chose to wear open-toed sandals, no less), I nearly had a panic attack. I can still feel its little claws scraping and wormy tail slithering across my skin, no matter how many times I wash my feet. I called Mr. Crillins, the janitor, who gave me a leery smile as he lurched into the classroom and checked behind some cabinets. "There's a whole family of 'em in here," he explained while flicking spit at every "s." "Mama just had li'l babies. You'll have to relocate to room 1913 while I take care of them." We stayed there until lunchtime, and I saw the students right after they'd gone through the cafeteria line. They all looked sullen as they smacked their mouths in disgust. "Thanks a *lot*, Ms. Q," Emma pouted. "You just *had* to complain to Crillins, and now our lunch is really gamey."

-During a lunch break last week, all of the "teacher" bathrooms were being used. I had four minutes until class started again, so I told myself that protocol could be broken in emergency situations, and I went into a "student" bathroom. The door had closed behind me before I realized that all of the lights were off. Unable to see the switch, I noticed that candlelight was flickering from within one of the stalls. That door slowly creaked open upon my arrival, but it was still too dark to tell which child stepped out. I held my breath, but I could *feel* them seeing me. The shadow took three quick steps in my direction before another voice from within the stall shouted, "No!" The shadow froze, and the voice spoke again. "She doesn't smell like she's ready." My stomach spun faster than a pinwheel. I fumbled for the light switch. When that proved too elusive, I barged out the door. I still have no idea who was in the bathroom.

-Teachers have a sense for trouble brewing, so I was keeping a close eye on the energy between Tristan and that skinny Herman who seems to fear him. When Tristan opened the coat closet and shoved Herman inside, I reacted instantly. I had grabbed Tristan by the elbow and pulled him (gently) aside within three seconds. There wasn't time to question why Tristan's arm was ice cold. I opened the door to find – nothing. A five-minute search of the twenty-square-foot closet revealed that it was filled with nothing but coats and an exsanguinated rabbit (which I chose to ignore). Panicked, I called Principal Apachaya to my room and confessed. His expression changed from 'concerned' to 'relieved' as my story concluded. "Don't worry about it, Ava. He'll be back." He left without another word. As the day wore on with no sign from Herman, I decided that I would call the police if he didn't return by the 3:30 bell. At 3:27, the closet door flew open, and Herman collapsed onto the floor. He had grown even more gaunt, wore medieval-style rags, and looked like he had been gone for several months. I tried to speak, but he made the most severe type of eye contact with me as he shook his head. Tristan followed him out of the classroom, and no one spoke of the incident again.

-I didn't realize how much I was dreading the children until a wave of physical tension hit me after I returned from my lunch break yesterday. Every one of the kids was gathered in a circle. I quickly saw that little Oscar was in the center, and everyone was giggling or gasping. My teacher's instinct immediately went into high gear, and I knew without seeing it that I had to break up whatever was unfolding. Since Oscar was so much shorter than the rest, I couldn't tell what was happening until I stepped inside their little ring. I really regret that choice. Because there's no way to expunge the image of Oscar's unbuttoned shirt spread wide, revealing a rogue, wiggling index finger protruding from his bare chest.

-I try to keep my distance from the children during recess. But as I sat in my classroom yesterday, watching them play soccer on the asphalt, I had a sudden realization: there are no soccer balls available. I chose to ignore the internal voice screaming at me to let things alone, and I quickly found myself out on the playground. A large mass of children was concentrated on the obscured ball in the center, each child rushing to kick it in an excited frenzy. Mason slid across the blacktop and booted it in my direction. I knew right away that something was very, very wrong. *Flop flop flop flop SPLORCH.* Something heavy smacked against my ankles with a red spatter. I could do nothing but stand in frozen shock as I stared down at the battered human fetus they had been using as a soccer ball.

THE CURE FOR HOMOSEXUALITY

I WAS FIVE YEARS OLD THE FIRST TIME THAT MY FATHER CALLED me a faggot, and thirteen when he first truly meant it.

I had watched President Obama's "It Gets Better" speech about a dozen times in a row. I had cried, stopped, cried harder, stopped again, and walked slowly to where my father was sitting in the living room. I'd rehearsed a hundred different ways to say it, and finally settled on the strongest one.

"Dad, I want to talk to you about something. I'm gay."

Mom was usually terrified of Dad's wrath, but she saved me a trip to the hospital.

She picked up a bag of frozen peas from the AM/PM and took it to the fleabag motel where she and I spent the next week. It was painfully cold against my face, but she held it firmly in place even as I struggled to push it away.

"I know it stings, Pumpkin, but it's the best way to treat a black eye. Trust me on this." She uttered a sigh so delicate that I was afraid it might break. "The cut Dad's ring left under your eye will take about two weeks to heal. I'm so sorry."

I cried then. The tears pressed hard against the frozen bag, and icy drops ran down my cheek.

When all the cold had melted away, I leaned against my mother's shoulder while she pulled me deep into her blouse. The smell of Tide, knock-off Mary Kay perfume, and Virginia Slims embedded itself so deeply into my memory that night that I'm perpetually one whiff away from a flashback.

My tears were no longer frozen, and they flowed unabated. "Why did God make me gay, mom?"

"I don't know, Pumpkin," she squeaked through her own gentle tears. She rocked me back and forth.

"I don't want to be like this anymore." I heaved, trembled, regained my voice. "Can we fix it? I don't want anything else, anything at all."

She was silent at first. After several painfully tense seconds, all she could say was, "I'm sorry."

My crying stopped then. Something had deadened inside of me, and it flipped the tears like a switch. "Mom," I prodded quietly, "why is love so fucking complicated?"

Her fingers slipped unconsciously to the thin wedding band on her left hand. She spun it slowly, but kept it in place.

"I don't know, Pumpkin," she heaved. "I'm so sorry, I just don't know."

I didn't miss having my father in my life.

Other people, however, took close note of my condition.

I tried to hide it. But teenage boys could practically smell it on me, and they were all too happy to ridicule the fact that I admired them more.

I had assumed that joining the freshman football team would be the perfect plan to make new friends at a new school. It seemed like an ideal way to prove my highly-doubted masculinity.

I was wrong.

Chad Vraag, slender and athletic, was the freshman quarterback. He had frosted tips (the look was popular then), dressed like Gianni Versace, and carried himself with the confidence of an asshole who had earned his arrogance. To be honest, he would have been exactly my type if he weren't such a dick.

Chad would always have a loyal squad of fellow football players around him, even in the locker room. And contrary to many assumptions, it was not an erotic experience to be around a bunch of pubescent boys changing their clothes. They smelled like shit, and most of them had the looks to match the odor.

But the most important part about the locker room is that no adults ever came inside.

I immediately knew that something was wrong when the door slammed shut. The sound was just *off* as it reverberated about the room.

I looked around, and quickly realized that I was alone.

And then I wasn't.

Chad and six other teammates of varying size and intelligence quickly positioned themselves around me.

I became hyper-aware that I was only wearing my underwear and a t-shirt. My locker was open. I wasn't ready. I was surrounded. My heart hammered, and I tried to think, but could only focus on the growing panic.

An enormous lineman named Gage picked me up. He was strong enough to restrict my breathing.

He threw me face-down on the floor. Four different boys grabbed each of my limbs as Gage sat, painfully, on my back.

Chad got on his hands and knees, then leaned toward me with a smile. I could smell Listerine and Excite Axe Body Spray on him. His face was an inch from mine.

"I know what you like, Phillips. I know *who* you like." His grin showed a veneer of straight, white teeth. "Did you think you'd be out of place here? Don't worry, kid. I've got *just* what you want."

I had two blissful seconds of complete ignorance before the boys holding my legs began to pull back my underwear.

Chad's grin split wider as he pulled a broomstick from behind him and pointed it in my face.

"Phillips, this welcoming ritual will make you feel *right* at home."

I understood what the broom handle was for.

As Chad stood up to walk behind me, I screamed.

They laughed.

Every step on the walk home was agony.

I drifted past my mother without a greeting, headed straight to the bathroom, and closed the door behind me. I turned on the hot water.

Your Dreams Taste Like Candy

The razor blades were on the top shelf of the medicine cabinet.

My hands shook.

Tears blurred my eyes, but I told myself to hold on, *hold on* just a few more minutes, and I wouldn't have to carry the pain that was too much for one boy, that the wrongness would all spill out, it would finally pour into a vile world that hated me from the inside.

My fingertips turned white. The blade was unsteady.

I wanted to cut it all away, every piece of the hate and filth.

My vision tunneled.

I wiped the tears away and saw Mom looking back at me in the mirror. She spoke to my reflection.

"Don't you do it. Don't you pretend your life is just your own." She was sheet-white and expressionless. "One of the worst things about living is that you can't choose how deeply you affect those most vulnerable to you." She breathed heavily. It trembled and rattled. "But that's why I get out of bed on the days when I can't find any other fucking reason. Don't you *dare* forget that."

The water gurgled down the drain.

I stared at her reflection.

She stared back.

The razor shook in my hands.

Then my mother turned around and left the room.

The blade held my vision until tears made it too difficult to see. I closed my eyes and listened to the gentle roar of the drain's endless thirst.

Mom had already started eating when I joined her at the dinner table that night. We ate without conversation. Only the soft sounds of chewing interrupted a silence that was heavy as a lineman crushing my back.

I didn't quit the team. After closing the razor back inside the medicine cabinet, it became impossible to imagine doing so.

I lifted. No one would stand near me in the weight room, so I worked out on my own.

Years passed.

Your Dreams Taste Like Candy

It's dangerous to max without a spotter, but I felt safest when alone. Most of my lifting took place on my own, late at night, at the nearest 24-Hour Fitness.

I cried when I hit 330 in the bench press.

I stopped the tears when I realized they had been the first since my freshman year.

It made sense to ask my coach about starting. He gave me a wary eye.

"I think you're safest on the bench, Phillips."

My uniform remained starch-white that season.

But I still returned to the locker room after every game and changed. The world set me up for failure, but I chose to decline the offer every time.

I had to watch Chad win the adoration of student and teacher alike. He spent his time surrounded by an ever-changing harem of women, and seemed more comfortable socializing with them than with any of the boys on the team.

I never really understood the attention, but had learned long ago to stop trying to comprehend human affection. He completed nineteen passes on the season (only thirteen of which gained yardage), and we went 3-7 against a weak schedule.

I had been tasked with extra equipment cleanup after our game against Ogden High School (the game with Ogden was supposed to be a very big deal around my school; it was supposedly one of the biggest rivalries in the state). So I was the last one in the locker room, and the second-to-last one to come out.

Chad was waiting by the door with a smile on his face but no shirt on his chest. "Hey, Phillips," he said coyly, poking my arm. "I bet you think that no one has seen what you've been up to." He gave me a half-smile and steady eye contact that he *clearly* didn't know was discomforting. "Well, *I've* noticed," he continued, flashing a grin of straight, white teeth. He brushed the hair away from his face with one hand and touched my biceps with his other.

He leaned toward my face with his eyes closed.

I was surprised by how light he felt as I pushed his frame against the wall.

He stared at me in shock, one hand gently clasping the other wrist.

"You're not used to hearing 'no,'" I said, mostly to myself. "You're just the saddest thing."

Your Dreams Taste Like Candy

I paused right before the door closed on me. Without looking back, I shouted rearward.

"Being gay doesn't mean I'll like every asshole."

Chad wasn't the only one to *notice*.

As we walked off the field of our final defeat, the luster of high school football drew away with a physical pull. We herded into the locker room and finally understood that it was nothing more than a metal clothes receptacle filled with long-dried sweat.

And when the last Division III college had rejected Chad's application, it finally became obvious that God had granted teenage notoriety as consolation for an insignificant life ahead.

After we were six months removed from football, even Gage turned on Chad.

And he didn't care who knew it.

The Last-Chance Dance was an annual tradition, steeped in the high school ritual of finally being rejected by a longtime crush.

I don't know why I went, but I didn't regret leaving early.

The parking lot had seemed empty until I saw Gage.

He was standing next to Damien, who had played nose guard on the football team. They had cornered Chad between two cars and a cinder block wall.

Chad was terrified.

"Fuckin' A, man," Gage grunted. "You can't go one goddamn night without making a pass at another guy? We warned you about this shit."

Chad pressed himself against the cinder blocks. His efforts to conceal the tears were utter failures.

He looked down at what Gage was holding in his fist and gasped.

Chad didn't even try to hide the tears that came next.

What should I have done in that situation?

If justice and goodness are at odds, the only choice is to accept brokenness in a world designed for imbalance.

I chose to stop the *fair* thing from happening. I'd been denied justice for too long to feel beholden to the concept.

Your Dreams Taste Like Candy

Damien threw a right cross against Chad's pretty face. His skull bounced against the cinder blocks, and a bloody cut opened under his eye. Damien grabbed Chad's throat.

Gage closed in on Chad, and I descended on them both.

I tossed Gage with more ease than either of us expected. I enjoyed a moment of his frozen helpless shock as he spun through the air and realized who was responsible for his dominance.

Gage collided violently with Damien, and the two fell to the ground in a heap.

A very *bloody* heap.

The district attorney had no interest in charging me. Gage had been holding his own knife, and I was acting to prevent a crime.

Damien's grieving parents *did* blame me for the death of their son. To be perfectly honest, I'd judge them if they didn't.

Gage didn't take his own life in the strictest definition. The guy never went to college and didn't get a job. I often wondered how it would feel in the exact moment when he finally realized that he had pissed away his entire fucking life.

As for Chad – he didn't hesitate to show me gratitude. The two of us had waited, side-by-side, until my mom came to pick me up at the police station.

I didn't brush his hand away when he laid it on mine. I let him speak.

"Phillips, man… I've done some bad things. I'm sorry." He looked at me with the passion of a drowning man reaching for a receding chance at hope. "After all this shit…" he squeezed my fingers, turning them white, "…could you give me a chance? Could you be the bigger man?"

I looked down at our interlocked fists, then placed my free hand on top of his.

Then I pried my hands away.

I stood and walked toward the door before turning around to face him.

"Don't be fucking stupid. The past doesn't go away, Chad." I threw on my jacket. "I can't change it, and I can't ignore it. You know how I deal with the past, Chad?"

Your Dreams Taste Like Candy

He looked at me with a sadness that evoked sympathy, but was useless against my resolve.

I smiled.

"Pride."

THERE'S SOMETHING WRONG WITH MY WIFE'S THIRD NIPPLE, BUT I CAN'T PUT MY FINGER ON IT

I DIDN'T THINK IT WOULD BE SO *PROMINENT.* OBVIOUSLY I'D noticed Quinn's breasts before (all the boys had), and obviously it's a sin to think about them. But I had no way of knowing about the third nipple until I saw it for myself.

And what was I supposed to do? Ask my wife about it?

Besides, there was so much to learn after getting married. Sex is weird, but fun! I really think Quinn likes it, too.

I wish I had learned what sex was *before* marriage, though, because I feel like I'm screwing it up.

And I still don't know what to do with that third nipple.

It's *weird* to see my boner as a duty instead of a source of shame. I actually feel like it's both at once now. Does that make sense?

I know that thinking about sex before marriage is sinful. Reverend Smetter did a good job of explaining that. But how are we supposed to know what to do without learning about it?

Quinn is teaching me, which is exciting. Girls' bodies are much more complex than boys' bodies, which are about as straightforward as light switches.

I'm not complaining. EVERYONE in the Compound was jealous when I got assigned Quinn as a wife. I'm pretty sure that even some of the older Parishioners were staring at Quinn! She's always been the prettiest in our Class, and now that we're both eighteen, she's my wife!

But it turns out that there's a LOT to learn about women that they didn't teach us in our Lessons. For example, how am I supposed to know why she's upset if she doesn't tell me? How is it reasonable to know what she wants for dinner if she keeps it a secret? When she says what's bothering her, and then I tell her how to fix it, why does she get MORE angry?

I was super excited when Reverend Smetter divined that I was supposed to marry the most beautiful woman I'd ever seen, but I'm starting to wonder if my wife is broken.

And I *really* think that third nipple might be unusual.

There are other weird things, too. Every time she says "it's fine," I actually end up in a whole bunch of trouble! It's like it's always "opposite day." Then there are times when she says, "We don't need to have sex tonight," but when I'm about to fall asleep, she just jumps on me and gets started! She basically controls my boners.

And it turns out that she wants me to do things to her nipples, which I *never* saw coming. But when the third one glows bright green, and I feel like I'm floating, why does the room get so hot?

I think that Reverend Smetter is displeased with her, because he always looks angry when she walks near him. He called her into his office for a Conference yesterday, and when she came home, she ate ten pizzas and fifteen grilled chickens.

Could someone explain how common that is?

I also have a lot to learn about that "time of the month." Why do her teeth become razor-sharp? I love her just the same, but it seems like she doesn't want to talk about the changes that happen to her body.

I did *not* know that women can climb walls with the adhesive powers of their fingertips. Women are SO much more complex than men! I really wish that my Class had been taught more by Reverend Smetter.

I wonder if people who live in other Compounds have such limited knowledge before marriage. I really would like to visit the Outside one day, but I don't know anyone who's ever gone past the 2.989 square miles within our walls.

Your Dreams Taste Like Candy

Internet phones are rare enough as it is. Reverend Smetter doesn't know we have them. We didn't ask permission, though, so he didn't say "no."

Learning new things is important. I really do want to be a good husband to Quinn. It's not just that it's my Holy Obligation, and it isn't only because she's basically the most beautiful woman I can imagine. What's most important is that I really do love her, even though we've only been married eight weeks.

Even on her "changing" days.

Which brings me to another point. When a woman's eyes turn jet-black, and her tongue protrudes two feet out of her head, does that mean "have sex with me" or "get the heck away"?

Because sometimes, I think it means both. I don't understand how my wife can want two opposing ideas at the same time. Is this a normal thing?

And when she talks about "The Reaping" in her sleep, should I be worried? Or do all women say that? Because lately I hear her mumbling about it during the daytime, too. She keeps saying things like "The Reaping is near" under her breath. But when I ask her about it, she gives me that smile that makes me feel all funny and then she hugs and kisses me and I forget what I'm thinking about.

I also found a map of Reverend Smetter's manor hidden in the closet. That place is strictly forbidden, but there are all kinds of markings on the map, like she's planning to break in.

I want to support my wife. Is there anything I can do to help her?

Or should I just smile and agree with whatever she's saying at the time?

I'LL LICK HER EYES WHEN I'M DONE

Her eyelids flutter as she begins to swim back up to the shore of consciousness. She rolls a glassy pupil my way, seeing but not understanding. I open her mouth, place a forkful inside, and she chews stupidly, like a cow on its cud. She swallows.

Another forkful. Chew. Drool. Swallow. More.

She's a hungry girl, isn't she, folks? I keep feeding her, well past the point when I thought she'd be full. I sneak some bites as well, of course. The juicy meat nearly melts in my mouth. I bite on a forkful and suck, letting the flavor wash over my tongue. So *fucking* succulent.

I don't want her to vomit. I'm not opposed to it in general, of course, but I need to know that she's digesting it, that the pepsin in her stomach is breaking things down to the molecular level and absorbing it back into her bloodstream. I need to know it. I need to know it.

So I stop feeding her when she's had her fill. Between the two of us, it's almost all gone anyway. The thought of it sends waves of ecstasy through me.

I pull out a syringe and slam it into her abdomen. She reacts almost instantly, lurching her head forward, eyes no longer glassy, staring around the room.

She stares down at her chest and realization dawns almost instantly. She screams. Oh fuuuuuck, she screams and it's like warm tears trickling down my spine and tickling my ass like a pig's tongue. She stares in horror at the stumps where her arms used to be, flapping the ghost of what's left in a fruitless endeavor to gain control. Her life is in no danger, of course, because I'm an excellent doctor. But she realizes right away that her life will never be the same again.

I wait for the next scream. God help me, I'm not disappointed. When she looks down and sees that there's nothing left of her *legs* but nubs, her desperation reaches new lows. The screaming dissolves into miserable gurgling. She is beginning to accept the fact that she went to sleep as a whole person, but woke up as nothing more than a head and a torso.

She looks at me with a stare that lies somewhere between pleading and anger. "Please, put them back," she blubbers, drooling down her chin. "Put my arms and legs back on."

She sees me as both her tormentor and her only hope. Quite the contradiction. My head swims with carnal pleasure. It's nearly more than I can bear.

"I can't," I say simply.

Her head wobbles dangerously before she can re-focus on me. I chuckle as I watch her struggle to re-learn the concept of balance with no limbs. "Why not?" She's trying to sound forceful instead of terrified. She's failing.

"Why, my dear, what do you think we've just eaten?" I don't hide my smile.

She looks around and sees the bones on the floor for the first time. Two femurs, picked clean. A pair of tibias, fibulas, humeri, radii, ulnas, and a smattering of hand and feet bones. She understands. *She gets what happened.*

It takes a lot of effort, but I'm able to keep my cool at this point. I don't want to orgasm just yet.

She screams again. It's all so much for her. It's this moment, the last scream, that I've been waiting for. So guttural. So base. So human. She's realizing that she wants to die right now, to end it all and be free of the memories, and she's realizing that she can't. She'll be at my disposal for as long as I want. And it will be long. So long. She must know that now. She must. Now.

Now is the time. The scream is unending. It sounds like it's going to rip the air.

I'm such a bad boy. So bad. I need to know I'm a bad boy. I grin maniacally and reach for the sandpaper. The coarse sandpaper, because I want this to be *real.*

Elm Grove Police Department

Evidence Item No. 103120191913

Incident Type: Suspected homicide

Coroner's Conclusion: A complete set of bones from both arms and both legs was mailed to Elm Grove Police along with the included note [Evidence Item No. 103120191913]. DNA analysis confirms that all bones came from the same individual. The victim is female, Caucasian, probably between 20 and 30 years old.

It is suspected that the victim could be Sandy [redacted], 25 years old, who has been reported missing by her father, Dennis [redacted].

Forensics evidence on the bones indicates a skilled removal. It is possible that the victim survived the dismemberment.

Notes: Along with the bones and attached message [Evidence Item No. 103120191913], a single piece of sandpaper was included in the package sent to Elm Grove police.

That sandpaper was covered in blood and semen with matching (yet unknown) DNA sequences, leading EGPD to believe that it was used for masochistic masturbatory purposes.

IT'S EASIER NOT TO THINK ABOUT IT

DYING HURTS LIKE HELL.

Losing your life is painless, because that was part of the deal at birth. No, it's what comes *next* that really burns. No one knows the day or the hour when these things will happen; but when the veil is finally lifted, we are forced to confront what is *after*.

I don't even remember the car hitting me. Even if I had, everything passed too quickly for me to be afraid of the crossing.

And all physical agony is temporary. If it can't be used to keep us alive, the pain is simply worthless.

Then it's over. The moment, all moments, cease.

We're forced to confront the fact that everything which had seemed *way* too important was really worth nothing at all to the Greater World.

The journey we take in that moment is redemption of the *sole* promise that we were bestowed upon birth. And in that moment, we realize that *every* good thing was a gift.

And we realize that the reasons for being selfish have disappeared forever.

As have the opportunities to be self*less*.

Everything we've ever done is etched in stone at that moment, completely irredeemable for all of all. Whatever has been done can never be undone.

Your Dreams Taste Like Candy

Whether that's heaven or hell varies based on the individual.

"Who the fuck are you?" were the first words of my afterlife.

A bored-looking woman sat watching four monitors that were arranged in a two by two pattern. "I'm Morta, you're Tim, and you're dead."

"Oh," I responded flatly.

She sighed and rolled a six-sided die. Even from across the room, I could see a man's vibrant visage moving across the face of the die that landed upward. As I cautiously crept forward, I recognized him as the man in the upper left screen. He was older, maybe in his eighties, and was sitting calmly on a couch.

Morta allowed another soft sigh and pointed at the monitor. The man slumped, then calmly rolled onto the couch cushions.

I wanted to speak, but so many words tried to rush out at the same time that I could not figure out what to say. I realize now that I wanted to cry for the man. He had spent his entire life, perhaps eighty years, working ceaselessly to race to that particular moment.

And all that moment gave him in return was a mundane death in front of daytime TV.

"Why?" I demanded.

For the first time, she turned to look at me. Morta had the face of a woman in her forties, but the wear etched in her countenance could not have been won by a being younger than a thousand.

"Look at the other three."

A man sobbing over a picture of what appeared to be his wife dominated one screen. A boy of about ten stood at the edge of a steep embankment on a second one. The final image showed two parents hugging a teenage girl in a hospital bed.

"These are horrible," I responded, aghast.

"These are hope. And hope is nothing without the horrible," she explained dismissively.

I wanted to explain to her why she was wrong, but I opened my mouth and no words came out.

She waved her hand and the monitors reset.

Your Dreams Taste Like Candy

One of the new pictures showed a dark-skinned, emaciated teenage boy sprawled on a street corner. He lay next to several other skin-and-bone bodies that looked too lifeless to move. People hurried by without giving him a second glance. The adjacent monitor revealed a soldier in an American military uniform crouching behind a short wall as explosions rocked his meager shield. The third view was of a hospital patient too bandaged to recognize. The fourth was another starved boy on another forgotten street corner.

Morta rolled her die. The face of the first boy appeared. She raised her finger.

"Wait!" I yelled.

She waited.

I said nothing.

She pointed at the screen.

The boy had already been so still that I hardly noticed a difference.

"Why do you roll a die when you just end up choosing in the end?"

"It's the same reason that every person blames the Fates," she responded calmly. "It gives me the illusion of pretending it's *not* all my choice."

She waved her hand, and four fresh screens popped up. She rolled, then picked up the die and looked closer. "Roll again," she explained. "That's one of the six options, along with 'none of these.' The other four sides correspond to the people on the monitors."

She rolled once more.

It landed on the face of a starving child in what appeared to be Sub-Saharan Africa. I tried to find him on the screen, only to discover that three individuals fit that description.

"Why do you choose so many poor people?" I asked in horror.

"Why do all of you choose to put me in that position?" she responded. "Even if I only selected people from the Third World, humanity would still line them up faster than I could act."

I felt compelled to change something before remembering that I was dead.

Three of the next four images were of young children. The fourth was an old man cradling an infant.

Morta rolled her die.

It stopped on one of the children. She continued to stare, and it suddenly gave one final turn.

It came to rest on the man.

She pointed at the screen. The targeted man placed the infant on the couch next to him, grabbed his own chest, and flexed the fingers in his left hand.

Morta waved, and the screens changed once more.

"Why even have the option of killing children?" I asked accusatorily.

"People would not believe in death if any group were exempt," she droned. "I press my influence too much as it is. Do the majority of children you know survive into adulthood?"

"Well – of course," I stammered.

"The 'of course' is my influence. It was not guaranteed. You're welcome."

She waved her hand. A new crop of faces emerged. Morta rolled.

"None of these," she read from the die, and waved them all away.

"Why rely on chance for the opportunity to dismiss death? Why don't you save them all?" I demanded.

She shrugged. "Now I'm behind schedule. Someone lives because another dies. Was the last result worthwhile? Can you describe any of the four who were saved?"

I searched my memory, only to find that I had not cared enough to look closely at their faces.

My head swam. "So why me? Why am I stuck here?"

She pointed to the edge of her desk without looking. "The die got lodged in the corner. It was stuck halfway between your face and 'none of these.'" She turned to look at me. "You are stuck in between."

I was overwhelmed with the sudden realization that my soul was in a *very* precarious balance. I hyperventilated.

"You're terrified for your life when facing death, but rarely worried for your soul when facing life. That is the one thing that I will never understand about people, no matter how many of them I see."

"Please," I begged, cutting her off. "Please give me my life back."

"Why?"

"Because."

"That's weak."

"Because I love my life!"

Your Dreams Taste Like Candy

She regarded me stoically. "You spent 31 hours and 53 minutes playing video games in the last week alone," Morta noted with clinical assuredness. "This is an average week for you. What would you be gaining with new life?"

I floundered. I had expected her to ask what I would be losing in death.

"I'd... be gaining my self," I responded without emotion.

"I mean, what would you be getting that justifies a different person dying in your place?"

I wanted to argue for the superiority of *my* life, but that suddenly seemed like a foolish choice when my soul was on the scale.

"Well, if I endured this, I would experience the greatest moment of my existence. It would permanently answer the question of whether life is a comedy or a tragedy."

She gawked at me in disgust. "You just watched me take the lives of several people. You know that thousands more will face death immanently. Yet you have the arrogance to think that the nature of all things hinges on what happens to you?"

I had once visited an amusement park with a ride that shot people up and down sans warning. I felt that sensation now.

I chose to be calm. Then I reached deeper into my mind than I had thought possible.

"Um. You, ah, said that the other option on the die was nobody at all?"

She grinned with one half of her mouth and frowned with the other. "You're right. Also, I'm thirty seconds ahead of schedule. Might as well tilt things in your favor. Enjoy your redemption; five people died so that I could get those thirty seconds." She reached her hand toward me and was about to flick her wrist when I interrupted her.

"Wait! That's it? But this is – thank you! – this is too huge! It will change everything!"

Morta raised an eyebrow. "Will it?"

"Yes!" I screamed. "Not just for me, but – well, you can't expect me to keep this knowledge secret!"

She shrugged. "Tell anyone you want."

My eyes nearly bugged out of my head. "But won't that ruin everything for you?"

Morta rolled her eyes. "Tim Goin, if you tell this exact story to everyone willing to listen, I guarantee that no one will believe you, and no one will change their life." She snorted. "Trust me. I've known more humans than any man has."

She waved her hand.

"Just a bump on the back of your head," the doctor explained dismissively. "And you're extremely lucky that's all you have to show for a car accident. A few millimeters lower would likely have severed your vertebral artery. There's no coming back from that place." He turned and walked away without ever making eye contact. "But you're completely fine."

There are two fitness centers in Battleboro, Vermont, and I joined them both. Every video game I had found itself on Ebay, and I actually felt cleaner after donating an entire paycheck to For the Love of Dogs.

Life was deeper after I met Morta.

But here's the terrifying thing.

Last week I skipped a day at the gym. I watched TV for three hours yesterday.

I am completely certain that my old patterns will slowly creep back.

I am also completely certain that it will be due to my own free will.

Dying is the *only* guarantee. Absolutely everything else is a gift.

Unfortunately, I will never stop taking that fact for granted.

You see, it was always assured that Morta would choose me one day.

And to be honest, my meeting with her never actually changed anything.

Am I wrong?

MIRANDA'S RIGHTS

NOTHING IS MORE DANGEROUS THAN A PARENT IN FEAR FOR their child's safety.

The divorce was horrible; my ex-wife Miranda was merciless and unrelenting. The endless legal wrangling and custody battles took a toll on Eric that no five-year-old should have to endure.

But things turned out for the best. Miranda showed her true colors, I showed mine, and I won complete custody of our son.

With patience and faith, things have a way of working themselves out.

Of course, Miranda could never accept that.

It got to the point where I couldn't even let her know where Eric and I lived. The police had gotten involved more times than I could possibly count, but the cycle never seemed to end.

Miranda just could not deal with the fact that she wasn't getting custody of our son.

The situation had gotten dangerous.

I enrolled Eric in kindergarten at Hill Street Elementary on December 19th (thirteen new schools since the divorce is just absurd, but I had no choice). I could not drop him off without constantly looking over my shoulder.

Waiting for the worst.

Praying that Miranda wouldn't find us again, and hoping that things wouldn't turn ugly if she did.

If it weren't for my son, I don't think I would have had the strength to keep it up. I did it for him.

Your Dreams Taste Like Candy

And yesterday, my paranoia paid off.

I was dropping him off at HSE at 7:55 that morning. "Have a great day, Champ," I offered as I hugged Eric and kissed his scalp. He wriggled away from my grasp, opened the door a crack, and then I froze.

Miranda's 1999 blue-green Toyota Corolla was parked half a block away, facing me head-on. I could see the furious glare etched on her unstable face even from a distance.

"Get back in the car," I whispered to Eric as I grabbed his wrist. "Now."

He wasn't moving fast enough, so I yanked him forcefully back into the seat and punched the gas pedal. The sudden momentum slammed the passenger door shut.

Miranda's car roared to life.

She was going to make this difficult.

I gunned the car in her direction, taking her off guard. I caught a glimpse of unbridled fury on her face as I zipped by.

She wasn't expecting me to drive *toward* her. She wasn't planning to need to turn her car around. That bought me some time.

And every second was crucial.

I turned left, right, and left again before looking into my rearview mirror.

I experienced a brief moment of elation when I saw that the coast was clear.

My heart sank when her car peeled around a corner in hot pursuit. I was thankful, at least, that her mode of transportation was a distinct enough color to recognize instantly.

This was going to be bad. At these speeds, involving the police seemed inevitable.

And Miranda's increasingly intense behavior told me that she wasn't going to back off this time. She was done chasing, and was finally ready to push things to their breaking point.

I figured that getting away from the suburbs of Pullman, Washington would be the quickest route to safety. We could shoot deep into the rural parts of the state at ninety miles an hour and pray that she'd be unable to keep up in her shitty car.

Apparently, however, she had already considered that possibility.

Your Dreams Taste Like Candy

Flashing red and blue lights appeared behind her. It looked like half a dozen of them.

I ripped my eyes away from the rearview mirror to take in the sight ahead of me. Another six cop cars were barreling down on us from ahead, prepared to end this insanity for good.

A quick scan of the fields around us revealed no side roads, driveways, or exits.

The police had both sides completely covered.

They had been waiting for her.

Calm washed over me as I pulled the car to the side of the road. This was it; we were in the moment that we had been planning for since Miranda had made it clear that she would never stop hunting us.

I rested my hand on Eric's cheek and kissed his scalp. He remained calm.

"Remember what I taught you, Champ. It's time to be brave."

He nodded.

I reached to the back seat of the car, grabbed my AR-15, and put the Glock 42 into his little hands.

"My gun has more power, but you can keep Daddy safe by firing at the police. They don't want to hurt a child, so you're the only way to keep me alive. This is all on you, Champ; I'll only survive if you do a good job. Are you ready?"

A single tear fell from his eye as he nodded firmly.

"Atta boy, Champ. That bastard of a judge said I was too dangerous to have any contact with you, but here I am keeping you safe from anything that might hurt you."

I looked over at the police cars, which were now stopped in a line across the middle of the street. Gun barrels were aimed at us from both directions.

I smiled at Eric.

"What these idiots don't realize is that nothing is more dangerous than a parent in fear for their child's safety."

THIS IS HOW THE GORILLAS WENT APESHIT

DROOL AND PUKE SPILLED FROM MY MOUTH AS THE MAN removed the ball gag. The fluid mixed with the slick cocktail of tears and sweat that covered my face.

He smiled. "You, my friend, are the best fifty dollars I ever spent."

I coughed, gasped and sniffed. "Why?" I asked meekly as I stared around the dark room.

He snorted. "Why not?" Here the man squatted down so that he was eye level with me. His breath smelled of cheese and rot. "Listen," he continued in a low, rumbly voice that would have been seductive if I were the type of person who got hard upon hearing Pennywise the Clown, "I got no beef with you. All I know is that two days ago, some guy tells me the Delaware State Zoo has a torture room for fifty dollars. I get to mutilate a stranger into little pieces, they clean up the mess!"

He leaned over and licked the tear off my cheek. His tongue felt like soil and sadness. I shuddered.

"No," I whispered, "Why did you let *yourself* become this way?" I pulled against the handcuffs that kept my arms wrapped around the metal pipe, but they didn't budge.

His eyes darkened. "You really want to know about me, little man?"

"I recognize you," I went on, quieter still. "I already know who you are. They arrested you for killing little Annie Tibbets, but there wasn't enough evidence."

The resulting silence had a nearly tangible weight.

Your Dreams Taste Like Candy

"You're never leaving this room," he finally responded. "So it doesn't matter." He plucked a rusty spoon from the ground and examined it. "I want you to know the type of man I am. I want you to be afraid." He looked up and made intense eye contact.

I looked back at him, but saw nothing behind his eyes.

"Two things," he went on. "First, they have *no idea* what I did to that girl before she died." He smiled, and the stench of his breath wafted over me like a mist. "It was far more than they possibly suspected. And secondly," here he caressed my neck with long and dirty fingernails, "I can do things with this spoon that will make you beg for death *days* before it's over. Welcome," he grumbled deeply, "to my rodeo."

"That's all I needed to hear," I responded in the lightest voice possible.

I flicked the false link from the handcuffs, freeing my arm.

He was frozen in utter confusion as I whipped my wrist around the pipe and brought the edge of the metal cuff down on his temple.

He was unconscious before he hit the ground.

I stood, spit the excess drool onto his face, then wiped my lip.

"You should know that this," I heaved in exhausted satisfaction, "is not *my* first rodeo, either."

The customer looked up at me in surprise. "Rats?"

"Yes, Mr. Bennington, our newest addition. One course consists of many rats, as they are so much smaller than our usual fare, but it has proven to be a very popular choice amongst our clientele seeking a more exotic experience."

He chuckled. "Different strokes, I guess. I'll be skipping the rat tonight." He put the menu down and smiled broadly. "Did you know that gorillas can learn human sign language? We're first cousins, just a few million years removed. Ah, I just can't get that thought out of my head. Definitely gorilla for me tonight."

"Excellent, Mr. Bennington. And the back menu?"

I knew what he would say before he said it.

"The last entry on the list-"

Your Dreams Taste Like Candy

"Ah, yes. That is a unique acquisition that... *came in* just this afternoon. I can tell you more about the specifics, but please note that specialty items are market price."

He lifted a backpack from the ground. "I've seen it, and I must have it. Take what you need from here."

I accepted the pack without a word.

"Now what can you tell me about the particulars of my order?"

"Very good, sir. A thirty-year-old man was tasked with babysitting a six-year-old girl. They disappeared on the 19th of January. Three months passed before her body was found in a horrifying state of-"

"Stop!" he yelled. "Just stop." He looked ill, and I smiled inwardly. "I don't want to know anymore. Let it begin."

Drool and puke spilled from his mouth as I removed the ball gag. "Up and at 'em, champ," I explained cheerfully. He looked up at me in foggy confusion, then stared down at himself. "Wh... why'm I naked?" he asked dully.

"It's almost showtime!" I responded enthusiastically as I adjusted my bow tie in the mirror. "You're going to be the star attraction!"

He farted, burped, then stared up at me in confusion. "Why'm I chained up when you're dressed in that fucking monkey suit?"

I stood straight, admiring my reflection.

Perfect.

"I have some bad news for you, old sport. I was never the victim, and you were never the client. If you had been, the cost would have been *much* higher than fifty dollars. We've been watching you for some time, but we don't put anyone on the menu unless we're one hundred percent sure of their guilt. So please accept my sincerest thanks for your confession." I turned to face him and frowned. "Sometimes, I do have to get my hands a little dirty." I flipped my expression into a smile. "The things we do for a paycheck, am I right?"

He stared at me stupidly. "What? You're not making any fucking sense."

I patted his cheek. "Don't worry. My friend Cappuccino will explain everything."

Your Dreams Taste Like Candy

I turned to walk out of the room before looking over my shoulder once more. "Oh, and do play nice. He doesn't like mean people, and he won't hesitate to twist your arm a little."

THEY TOLD ME I WAS EVIL

"WHY CAN'T ANYONE BESIDES ME SEE THE NAGUAL?" I ASKED. Xolo smiled at me, but he was sad. "Invisible people are everywhere. Most choose to close their eyes and not see them."

Mamá was screaming. I peeked my head around Xolo so that I could see her better.

She was holding Herminia's head in her arms, rocking back and forth like my sister was still a baby. But Herminia was four year older than me, already twelve, and Señor Coyote said she looked like a woman.

Señor Coyote was sitting next to a rock. "Chíngame, it's hot." He curled up in the tiny patch of shade. "We have to move, Mamacita, decide what you gonna do."

Mamá was still screaming, still rocking Herminia's head back and forth, back and forth. White foam covered my sister's lips like she had spilled milk, but we'd had nothing to drink all day. Then her head rolled to the side, and I saw that her eyes were wide open, and she didn't move no matter how hard Mamá shook her.

Xolo touched my chin, then gently turned my head around. He smiled again, and it was sad again. "Look away, Felicidad. Look away, and you can be safe."

We walked faster without Herminia. She had been getting slower every day.

Your Dreams Taste Like Candy

"She will be happy?" I asked Xolo.

"Callate!" Señor Coyote yelled at me. He was walking ahead of us because he knew the way, but he could still hear me. "Stop fucking talking to yourself."

He didn't get angry when Xolo responded. No one else reacted when the nagual spoke.

"Herminia doesn't hurt now," he answered.

I didn't understand, but I asked no more questions, because I did not want to make Señor Coyote angry.

He stopped walking and grabbed Mamá's hand. She leaned away.

Xolo stopped walking and grabbed my hand. I leaned in.

"Espera," he ordered. Mamá held still. "This is Anima. The safe house is right there." He smiled at Mamá, but it was an angry smile. "Págame."

Mamá hardly moved. She had barely spoken at all since we started walking faster. "$191.30 took me five years to save. We paid you everything, we owe nothing."

He pulled her close and smiled bigger, but it was still not a happy smile. "Págame. You or your daughter."

I understood that Mamá had broken after Herminia stayed behind, though she still stood tall. But she broke again when Señor Coyote took her behind the rocks, yet I didn't understand why.

"You don't need to understand why," Xolo said as he appeared. "You're almost done walking. Look away and tell me about your new home."

I talked with Xolo for a long time before Mamá returned. Then she snatched me by the hand so hard that my shoulder hurt.

She was angry, but I didn't understand why. I asked her, but she didn't say anything, and I realized that she was too broken to speak.

"Is it safe for me to sleep?" I asked Xolo, who was curled up in a ball next to me on the floor.

"Shh," he said.

"Will it ever be safe for me to sleep?"

"Close your eyes," he responded softly.

A woman screamed on the other side of the safe house.

Your Dreams Taste Like Candy

"Close your eyes," he said.

"Hielo!" a man yelled.

There was noise.

The house had been filled with strangers before I went to sleep on the ground, and now new strange people were coming inside. The new strangers were afraid, just like the old ones had been, but they were afraid in a different way.

A man picked me up and I did not like it. "Don't worry," he said, but I worried.

"Espera!" Mamá screamed from the other room. "Wait! Please let me say goodbye!"

The man took me outside. Mamá did not tell me goodbye.

"Don't worry, little girl," the man said as he squeezed me and I felt sick, "you're safe now."

I never saw Mamá again.

The boys and girls around me did not have parents either.

I was glad to have Xolo with me.

He lay down next to me when Officer Fallar made us get on the ground and face the floor. "God fucking damn it!" he liked to scream. "If you would just *behave*, you wouldn't be in this situation. What's it going to take?"

Once, he stopped in front of me, and I could feel him staring. I looked up, even though I wasn't supposed to.

He smiled at me, but it wasn't a friendly smile.

"Just you wait, pretty girl," he said in a voice like Señor Coyote. "Once the Flores decision gets reversed, we'll be able to take care of you."

I put my head back on the floor.

The other people on the floor were crying softly.

I covered my eyes with my hand and Mamá hugged me close.

"What's it going to take?" the man shouted. "Barrio 18 will treat you well if you show us respect. Do we need to teach you respect?"

Your Dreams Taste Like Candy

He bent down and grabbed Francisco by the shoulder, then lifted him to his feet. Mamá pulled me closer, but she stayed on the ground.

I was scared for my brother, because he was only fourteen, and I wanted to stand next to him so that he would not feel alone. But Xolo came to me then and rested his paw on my shoulder. "Don't upset the man with a gun," he whispered. "Always remember that."

"Does this boy need to be taught a lesson in respect so that the rest of you learn?" the gunman yelled.

Mamá's hot tears burned into my neck. She asked the Virgen de Suyapa to hold her, because she needed someone who would understand a mother's pain.

Xolo rested his paw gently on my face.

"Close your eyes."

"What's it going to take?" Officer Fallar repeated to the group of children assembled on the floor. "If you just show proper respect, we will go easier on you."

Two men lifted the boy who had been resisting and pulled him away from the rest of us.

"God damn it," he yelled in a quieter voice. "The problem is that you need to learn the fucking boundaries. *None* of you would be here if you hadn't chosen to break the law in the first place."

Abuelita stroked Mamá's hair as she rocked her daughter back and forth. Mamá wasn't a baby, but I understood that she was Abuelita's baby, so I said nothing.

"We need to leave," Mamá whispered. Her voice was so frail that it sounded ready to shatter like clay.

"Please wait," Abuelita begged. "Follow the rules, wait your turn."

"Francisco followed the rules. I can't spend two daughters to follow the same path."

"You can take them when there is room. Be patient." Abuelita stroked her hair. She was trying not to cry.

"They tell us there is no room unless we win a lottery," Mamá whispered, "but they are playing a game with us. There is always room in a place filled with hope." Mamá wiped her eyes. "There are so many jobs working in the fields that they cannot fill them

all, and only immigrants will take them. But if I wait for someone to tell me it's my turn, I'll die first." She turned around and looked at Abuelita with sad eyes.

"They want us to come, just not as equals."

"Be careful," Xolo warned me.

"What for?" I asked in confusion. "I'm just getting out of my cot to use the toilet."

He looked scared. "Be very careful, Felicidad."

I got up and awkwardly walked through the maze of children on the floor. It's easier to find my way to the bathroom when they keep the lights on, but it's harder to sleep.

No one wanted to use the bathroom at night – at least the girls didn't. So there was no line for the toilet.

The flusher was broken, so I left everything sitting in the bowl when I finished. I was thirsty, so I stood up on the toilet. The sink was part of the seat where we pee and poop, but I was too small to reach it, so I always had to stand on the toilet seat to get water.

I tried to put my face in the sink, but someone had pooped on the seat and not cleaned it, so my feet slipped. I fell and landed in the toilet, and it soaked deep into my socks. I didn't like how warm it felt.

But I remembered Herminia, and I felt very, very thirsty, so I reached my head as far forward as I could to get to the sink.

Slow footsteps walked up behind me. That didn't make sense, because no one liked using the bathroom at night.

It was the soft *click clack* of a man's shoes.

I was still trying to drink. But Xolo grabbed my hand.

The footsteps stopped behind me.

I turned around.

It was Officer Fallar.

He smiled, but it wasn't friendly, and I wasn't happy.

"Looks like the Flores restrictions end tonight," he whispered.

Xolo was weeping.

No one else was nearby.

Officer Fallar walked toward me.

Your Dreams Taste Like Candy

"Look away, and close your eyes," Xolo said as Officer Fallar stroked my cheek.

Xolo sobbed openly, warm tears falling down his distant cheeks, as he let go of my hand.

"Close your eyes."

THE MILE HIGH CLUB IS REGRETTING ME

"IF I'M OBEDIENT WHILE WEARING THE HANDCUFFS, THEN I can't adjust my bra. Have you noticed that I can't adjust my bra?"

I tried not to look at her chest, and then I looked at her chest. "Yes, I noticed."

She smiled. It was cute. "Can you adjust my bra for me?"

"No. I'm not supposed to."

"Well then my nipples might fly *right* out. You wouldn't want that, would you?"

I sighed.

She jiggled her chest. Yep, she was at risk of exposing her nipples.

"I know what you're doing, Prisoner 91."

She looked at me innocently. "And what's that?"

"You're taking advantage of the fact that I can't drink while on the clock, so it's going to be much easier to wear down my patience."

She offered a pouty lip. "Why would you say that about me?"

"Because this isn't my first rodeo. I've seen this one, 91. Three minutes into the flight and you're trying to distract me with what you believe will cause me to lower my guard."

She cocked her head. "Am I wrong?"

I involuntarily looked at her chest, then turned quickly away. "No. I mean, yes, you're wrong."

She glared at me. "So you're gay?"

"No."

"You sound gay." She jiggled her chest again.

Your Dreams Taste Like Candy

I turned sharply around to face her. "Look. I've just finished wrapping up the paperwork for a clusterfuck of a thwarted hijacking that had to be hidden from the public eye after I unleashed a disguised monster on a bunch of assholes, with the former turning the latter into silly putty. I *tried* to have the kind of fun that you're advertising during my layover in New Orleans, then found out the hard way that my "dates" were both hookers. I do *not* want to talk about what it took to get out of jail. So can we please, *please* have a peaceful plane ride where you don't try to take advantage of me? I have a job to do."

Her facial expression immediately went from "pouty" to "bitchy."

This was going to be a long flight.

And my bladder was still waging an unholy war against itself. Protocol forbade me from sharing a bathroom with any female prisoner, so I was just going to have to piss my pants if the insatiable urge arose.

I sighed.

"Okay," the prisoner relented. "I'll leave you alone."

"Thank you," I responded softly, closing my eyes and scratching my balls.

"It's just that we're in the back of a red eye flight that's headed from Atlanta, Georgia to Louisville, Kentucky. This 747 is half-full, the row next to us is *completely* empty, and most people are sleeping."

I looked over at her in exasperation. "And?"

"And these handcuffs render me totally docile." She smiled coyly. "I'm completely unable to use any of my... *unnatural* abilities. So what you have before you is an utterly tame woman going unnoticed into an airplane bathroom in a sleepy, empty plane."

I laughed. "Oh, no. That would break approximately eight million different rules." I shook my head. "There is absolutely no way, whatsoever, that you could successfully Mile High Club me in that bathroom." I smiled and folded my arms. "I'm made of stone."

The bathroom was cramped with both of us in it, but that's part of what makes the Mile High Club so exciting.

"Wait," she asked breathlessly. "Do you have a condom?"

"I'm Catholic," I lied.

Your Dreams Taste Like Candy

"Are you saying that you never wear condoms when you have sex with strangers?" she shot back.

"Hey, these handcuffs prevent you from using any and all supernatural powers, right? It's never come up before, but you don't have any, like – special vagina abilities, do you?"

She smiled.

I was about to cum when a jolt of pain shot through my waist. It felt like the lava urine that had been erupting from my dick decided to change course and re-visit my bladder.

I opened my mouth to yell in protest. But when I dropped my jaw, no sound came out.

And I couldn't put my mouth back into place.

She turned around, smiled at me, then slid herself off of my dick.

I watched helplessly as she pulled her skirt back into place, then lowered her cuffed hands to the pants that were sitting in a puddle at my ankles.

I was completely paralyzed.

She quickly found the handcuff keys and freed herself. "These carbon fiber manacles are quite the technological marvel, soldier. They *nearly* muted all of my abilities. I didn't know if any activity restricted to my nether regions – instead of my hands – would *also* be out of play, but it looks like you found out the hard way."

She glanced down at my immobile waist.

"Be sure to call a doctor if that lasts for more than four hours. Just because I like you so much, the paralysis *probably* won't kill you."

She bent down to kiss me, then hovered in place six inches from my nose. She grinned – but the edges of her lips spread past her cheeks, under her ears, and around the back of her head. Her nose grew three inches, four inches, then ten. Her skin turned ashen gray and then jet black as her eyes narrowed into slits.

Her teeth were even worse. They elongated into a series of crooked spines; the inside of her mouth looked like a cactus.

Except the spines were jittering like spider legs.

Your Dreams Taste Like Candy

So she was a shape-shifter with paralytic abilities. God damn it, I wish that they had put that in the prisoner dossier.

And I wish I had read the prisoner dossier.

Then she talked to me. Her new voice sounded deep and vile, like an unholy kraken fart bubbling up from the depths of the North Sea.

"Thanks for the ugly bump, Sugar."

I almost vomited, but I barely held it back.

Barely.

Then she bent down to kiss me. I had no power to resist as the wiggling spine teeth caressed my lips hungrily while her mouth closed over mine.

Her lips were bone-dry, but her tongue was hot and wet. It was long, thin, and felt uncannily like a sentient earthworm that poked between my lips, tickled my gums, then caressed my uvula. My gag reflex was clearly still in order, and I realized that I very realistically might end up dead in an airplane bathroom with my pants around my ankles after having choked on my own puke.

Shit. Three years ago, I'd made a promise to myself I wouldn't go out like that.

This was turning out to be a really shitty flight.

Then Prisoner 91 melted once more, took on a more human shape, and formed its skin into what appeared to be clothing.

But before I could see its new final form, it opened the door and stepped out. It then shut me in, and somehow turned the lock *from the outside*.

There are moments that cause us to take a major pause and re-evaluate our life choices. As I sat there, staring at my unsatisfied erection, unable to look away due to paralysis, I reflected on the fact that I clearly never re-evaluate my life choices.

I stayed like that for some time.

A few people knocked, but what was I going to do? Even if a response were physically possible, there's really no easy way to tell anyone that I was stuck in the bathroom because I'd accidentally let a monster loose. No, they'd have to assume I had diarrhea, was getting high, or couldn't make it the entire flight without masturbating.

They could always try another bathroom.

I, however, had bigger problems.

Your Dreams Taste Like Candy

Because once this plane landed, an unauthorized shape-shifter would be unleashed on an unsuspecting Kentucky.

I breathed deeply and focused.

I stared intently at my dick.

Just slightly, it moved.

I probably knocked down six people as I raced to the front of the plane, but I didn't bother to check.

"Wait!" I hollered as the flight attendant pushed open the door.

She turned to me in shock, looking for all the world like *I* was the crazy one.

"Fought off the paralysis! Faster than the monster thought! My dick's been through more than that before…"

She seemed ready to scream.

"Manifest!" I shrieked. "Check the flight manifest before anyone gets off the plane!" I pulled out my badge.

"Officer," she responded shakily as a second flight attendant slowly moved between us, "you can look at the manifest if you're an air marshal, but we have to deplane these people."

My mouth was still too numb to explain myself fully, and standing upright took the lion's share of my energy, so I didn't protest as the second flight attendant opened the plane's door to let the stream of people walk past me. As she did so, I got a strong, negative vibe of the "we fucked and you blocked my calls, even *after* I did all that weird shit you requested" variety.

I'm sure she was judging me because I knocked down all those people, but part of me wondered if we'd met before. I tried to smile at her, but the paralytic was still doing its thing, so I just leered and drooled.

One by one, the passengers shuffled past me on their way out the door. I watched them go, trying frantically to guess which one might be the rogue shape-shifter.

The plane was nearly empty and my panic was nearly full when a mustachioed man in a gray jacket walked past with his eyes glued to the floor.

I pounced.

Your Dreams Taste Like Candy

"Get off of me!" he screamed. "Help!"

"Sir!" the first flight attendant yelled, "sir, please release that-"

"Check the manifest!" I shouted back. "He won't be on it!"

He curled around to stare at me. We locked eyes and had a silent moment that can only ever be experienced by two people who have shared anonymous bathroom humping.

"How'd you know?" he whispered.

"You smell," I grunted as I whipped out the handcuffs and snapped them into place, "like sex and shame." I hoisted the shape-shifter to its feet. "And I am a seasoned veteran of both."

The flight attendant rushed over to us with the manifest. "What name is on this man's ID? We have to confirm-"

"He's got no ID," I shot back.

'He' dropped his head in defeat.

We walked across the tarmac with no one else nearby. "How'd you fight off the paralytic?" Prisoner 91 asked.

I grunted. "That was really fucked up. Did I tell you about the week I've had?" I sighed. "Two things you should know. First of all, I was a collegiate baseball player with a significantly higher muscle density than the average man my age. It takes a hell of a lot more to affect me than you'd expect. I once drank thirty beers in college. They had to pump my stomach, but I didn't die."

A black SUV was racing toward us through the wet Kentucky heat. I stopped, then reached out to hold the prisoner in place.

"And secondly – my dick has been through a lot. I mean a *lot*. I can fight off a genital invasion faster than you'd believe. I knew that once my dick got moving again, the rest of my body would follow. I just prayed that it would happen before we touched down."

The SUV screeched to a halt in front of us.

"One more thing. You'll be happy to know that I didn't regain muscle control in time to stop from pissing myself. That's the second time in as many flights that I soaked my own pants in urine. You're an asshole. Fuck you."

"So everything went according to plan," Mr. Dufresne explained from across his desk.

"Actually – not quite," I confessed to my boss.

"Oh, really?" He asked reservedly. "Everything appears to have been in order."

I sighed. "Not exactly. You'll find out sooner or later, so it's best you hear it from me first." I closed my eyes. "It's not a big deal, really. Just a couple of procedural errors."

"Procedural errors?" he asked, raising one gray eyebrow.

"Nothing huge. It's just that I fucked Prisoner 91, was incapacitated, then nearly lost her. Or him, I'm still not clear on that. And I'm eighty percent sure that I knocked over a little kid and an elderly woman. Ninety percent sure. But all's well that ends well, I suppose."

I held my breath as Mr. Dufrense nodded slowly. "I was wrong about you."

I lowered my head.

"I didn't think you'd do it, but we have the test results in black and white. Your shape-shifter has the clap."

I looked up.

He tossed a medical report across his desk. "Experiments on the subject's cells suggested that it would be extremely sensitive to human sexually-transmitted infections – potentially enough to render it sufficiently docile to manipulate and control it outside of our facilities *without* handcuffs. The only problem is that it has the ability to eradicate any known infection through yet-indeterminate means."

I stared, slack-jawed, at my boss.

He leaned forward. "It means that your shape-shifter could somehow kill bacteria before we injected it." He put his hands behind his head and leaned back. "This was a tough nut to crack, but we asked how it might be possible to get the subject to inject *Neisseria gonorrhoeae* into itself without realizing it."

I gaped at him numbly. "So you used my dick."

"So we used your dick," Mr. Dufrense smiled.

"You knew the subject and I would fornicate in the bathroom."

"Actually, the office pool predicted that you wouldn't bother to leave your seat. There's a reason the row next to you was empty."

I rested my head in my hands. "So I'm not fired?"

"Fired? You're not fired. I fire people who are useless to me. We have a lot of plans left for you, Mr. Hush."

I stood up, relieved. "So what next?"

"You'll need to head to the company pharmacist in the sub-basement, there are some specialty requests that only she'll have. We've already forwarded your prescriptions."

"What am I taking?"

"It's… better not to ask."

I groaned. "Does she have condoms?"

"We have a budget, Mr. Hush. I'm not going to waste money on something you'll never use."

I opened my mouth to respond, then nodded quietly.

"So – then what?"

"Well," he answered with a genuine smile, "our records indicate that you've never been to Tajikistan, which is important, because you *cannot* be recognized. There's a bottle of snake venom, a pair of fishnet stockings, eight psilocybin tablets, and a rubber ducky. Don't ask any questions," he added as I opened my mouth.

I nodded silently, then turned to exit.

"Oh, and Jonathan," he added, just before I left.

"Be sure to use your best judgment."

#VACCINE EDUCATED

I WAS FIRST IN MY CLASS AT JOHNS HOPKINS MEDICAL School, and I'm an idiot.

I thought much more highly of myself at the time, of course. I was the smartest man in the best school at the dawn of a new millennium, ready to lead a brave new world.

The official eradication of the measles in the United States was little more than a bump in my rearview mirror. We didn't think much about those things back in 2000. I was giddy with the knowledge that the first survivor of Alzheimer's was *somewhere* on earth at that very moment, and that I would bend the nature of the human mind to my will.

For the greater good, of course.

It was easy to connect myself with the right people.

And the *rightest* of people was Dr. Nigel Crad.

At forty years old, he had spent the last fifteen years living the life that I *knew* waited for me. He was faced with the difficult predicament of whether to leave his position as chief of medicine to become partner at a top pharmaceutical company.

Seven figures a year, or eight? It's an important choice.

I can't tell you which hospital or company, of course. I *can* tell you that ten percent of Americans live within 150 miles of the hospital, and fifteen percent of us will use that particular insurance at some point in our lives.

But Dr. Crad was a man who could make bold decisions and never look back in doubt.

So I knew not to question him when he pulled me into an office. It was just me, him, and a scared-looking girl of about six.

Your Dreams Taste Like Candy

"Hello, Lizzy," he said to the shaking child in his best 'doctor' voice. "I'm Dr. Crad, and this is Dr. Provato. Can you be brave while we give you an injection?"

She wiped her eye. "But I'm not sick. Why did you tell my mommy that she couldn't be in the room?"

Dr. Crad laughed. Suffice it to say that the sound chilled my latissiumus dorsi. "Don't worry, Lizzy. She's just filling out some paperwork for the insurance company. Now," he continued in a lower voice, "Can you be brave for me?" He plunged a needle into a vial that only had a black label.

Alarm bells rang in my head. I thought it best to silence them.

I'm so sorry.

I was in the room two weeks later when Lizzy rolled back and forth in her hospital bed, forcing an orderly to hold the frame in place while it shook. Her mother sobbed uncontrollably, crumpled in a heap at the end of her daughter's bed.

Lizzy died of measles encephalitis at 7:13 p. m. on November 18th, 2000.

But her mother didn't cry as Dr. Crad broke the news. Tears are a way of dealing with tragedy, and she simply didn't deal with it. His words crushed her like a steam roller, and the withered husk of a woman left behind was simply incapable of giving voice to the remaining fragments of her broken spirit.

It was the first time that I truly saw a soul tear apart.

Lizzy's body was lost in a tragic mix-up at the morgue. Her already distraught mother collapsed to the ground upon hearing the news. Since Dr. Crad and I were the only other people in the room at the time, he kindly prescribed her a powerful sedative to cope with the pain.

Unfortunately, she overdosed on those pills that very night, and the mistake was lost to time.

"Do you hear that, Dr. Provato?" he asked me as he lit my cigar in his office that night. He leaned back, took two puffs on his own Cuban robusto, and regarded me gravely. "Lost to time."

I nodded.

No one ever discussed Lizzy or her mother again.

Your Dreams Taste Like Candy

"Congratulations, Chief of Medicine," Dr. Crad effused warmly this week. His hair was grayer with nineteen years gone by, and all but seven of them as chairman of the board. He looked fondly around the office. "Some of the best years of my life were spent here." He turned to lock eyes back on me. "Use them with discretion." Without another word, he marched out of the office and snapped the door crisply shut behind him.

I looked down at the desk.

My new desk.

I could *feel* the change running through me. Outside of this room, people would be hired and fired, would *die* or *live*, all because of the choices I made. Nothing would happen without my oversight.

I hadn't noticed the folder on my table. It hadn't been there before.

I looked up at the door that Dr. Crad had just closed behind him.

Then I quietly sat down and opened the black folder.

A chart showed decreasing rates of measles in the United States with a profound drop defining the 1960s. After 1992, the rate essentially flatlined.

I turned the page.

The next chart showed the levels since 1992, with a long red mark in 2000.

The line had been climbing steadily upward. The final entry on the list was the only year to top 1,000 cases.

It was this year.

I turned the page once more. Before me was the case study of a young boy. He had died earlier this year. My heart felt what you could call sympathy, but I had seen too many deaths over the years to be shaken.

The next two pages were similar case studies.

But I did a double take on the final one.

Lizzy Pliff, age six, had died on November 18th, 2000.

She had contracted the measles.

I thought again to the first child that I had watched die. Was the medical community aware of a measles-related death in 2000?

I had known not to ask the question at the time.

I flipped the page again. It was just a picture of Jenny McCarthy. At the bottom was a handwritten note: "Will people follow McCarthyism again?"

I scratched my head and turned the page.

The next was a picture of a Facebook group. It showed several discussion threads talking of the dangers of vaccinations.

Your Dreams Taste Like Candy

A knot slowly began to tie itself in my stomach.

I turned to the next page.

Before me was a chart of various medications. Separate bars showed results for acetaminophen, ibuprofen, and a type of immunoglobulin treatment.

They were charted based on corporate profits derived from units sold.

My world slowed down as the pieces all arranged themselves.

I caught Dr. Crad just before he slid into his Maybach.

"Dr. Provato!" He snarled at me. "Why have you taken that file out of your office? It was left because you have the *discretion* to-"

"Treatments!" I yelled at him, ignoring the flecks of his spit that had landed on my face. "All of the treatments in this chart are very common ones made by your pharmaceutical company, which means an increase in billions per month if there's a measles outbreak!"

He looked at me like I was a smear of shit on the leather seat of his Mercedes. "For fuck's sake, man, I vouched for you!" I couldn't ignore the spittle on my face this time, and wiped it away furiously. "I never thought that *you* would possess the subtlety of a baboon!"

I wanted to say every word in my head, but struggled to articulate a single one. Finally, I forced out a semblance of rational thought. "But – no! – you don't *need* to sell more! The folder only predicts a maximum nine percent increase in sales-"

"Which, as you said, is billions per month," he shot back coolly as he snatched the report from my hands. He stepped so close to me that I could feel his hot breath inside my nostrils. "Tell me, Dr. Provato," he asked in an icily dangerous tone, "Were you idiotic enough to show this to anyone else?"

I took a shaky breath. "You'll succeed so easily," I whispered. "Parents will do *anything* to treat their suffering children. If you tell them that vaccines are responsible, if you give them a culprit, you can't blame them for believing the lie. They'll stop getting vaccinated by the thousands. They're not stupid, they're just desperate."

He narrowed his beady eyes at me. "*We're* not the ones telling them. It's Facebook and celebrities out spreading our message."

I took a fearful step back. "With enough cases, people will start to die. Mostly children."

Your Dreams Taste Like Candy

He lowered his head at me. "That's the goal of treatment, isn't it, *Dr. Provato?*" He stuffed the folder into his jacket. "Besides, corporate estimates are optimistic that we can keep deaths to a minimum. The majority will just suffer for a bit." He breathed in deeply. "Every known disease risks eradication by the end of the twenty-first century. An entire sector of the global market will collapse if nothing is done."

Dizziness was setting in. "But, Dr. Crad – the world will hate the pharmaceutical companies!"

He climbed into his car and started the engine. "Sorry, I couldn't hear you over the sound of my Maybach. And Dr. Provato," he continued with a final glance in my direction, "be sure to take care of your health."

I coughed as his tires kicked dust into my face.

It had always been for the greater good.

Life and death had been my business for so long that it took a life-changing revelation to see my work in a new light.

But that kind of mental and emotional removal is necessary to do a job like mine.

In fact, removal is indispensible. No great task can be accomplished without sacrificing that which poses a danger to the system.

And those decisions have to be made with a strong stomach.

My stomach is weak right now. Both ends of my digestive track are leaking, and there is a concerning amount of blood in the fluids.

But it was the first signs of gangrene on my fingers and toes that told me it was time to drive out of the city.

I'll spread this message to anyone and everyone who will listen before the information gets taken down. *They* have enough power and influence to keep it away from social media; I doubt you will read this account on more than one internet source.

And I'll never be able to tell you in person. I'm sending this out from the edge of the desert with spotty reception and not another human in sight. I won't be heading back into the city again.

They've found a very effective way to silence me.

I have a synthetic, untreatable form of the bubonic plague.

MASKING THE SMELL

BECOMING A PARENT CHANGES EVERYTHING.

We have implicitly accepted the notion that all things in life should be regulated for orderly consumption. I expect to know *exactly* how much manganese is in my Froot Loops, thank you very much, because a bureaucratic sub-sub-committee in Washington wrote it into Agricultural Bill 3301913-B, just as God intended.

Then life hands you this tiny, squirming ball of pre-developed human, and you are responsible for literally every ticking second of its life.

So why did we spend so much time regulating Froot Loops when the staircase is quite literally one step away from murdering a child?

Life itself suddenly becomes *extremely* fragile. We learn that everything we had *thought* kept us safe was actually just there for illusion, and things are never quite the same again.

Fortunately, kids are much more resilient than we are.

So by her second birthday, Felicity was riding gleefully on my shoulders as I sprinted across the backyard.

How did I know she'd be safe?

I took it for granted.

She had more stamina at two than I did at thirty-seven, so we would often take breaks to look at the sights while Daddy caught his breath.

On the fourth break of a particular evening, I decided that Felicity really wanted to look over the neighbor's fence while the spots slowly receded from my vision.

Your Dreams Taste Like Candy

"What do you see?" I asked, blinking furiously. "Is it the neighbors' chickens that wake us up every morning at the asscrack of dawn? Do you see chickens? Chick-ens?"

"Tik-hinz!" she announced triumphantly. Felicity grabbed the edge of the seven-foot fence and hoisted herself higher, coming just slightly off my shoulders.

Then my daughter turned back to look at me, and smiled.

Every time she was riding on my shoulders that week, she would squeal for me to stop so that she could look at the "Tik-hinz!" I was all too happy to oblige the break in running around, even if it forced me to stare at the wall while she reached over my head to gawk in fascination at poultry.

Things continued like that all week. When I decided that the mosquitos were getting too aggressive and my beer was getting too warm on that muggy South Carolina Friday night, we headed in early. Felicity didn't like this one bit, so I turned on the TV to drown out her crying.

She quickly stopped crying.

"Tik-hinz!" she shouted with glee as she pointed to the screen. Her face was the definition of pure joy.

I nodded dismissively, threw back a sip of my Yuengling, glanced at the television, and nearly choked on my beer.

"Tik-hinz!" Felicity announced again.

Then she turned back to look at me, and smiled.

I didn't care about the spilled can of beer as I ran to pick her up, blood chilled and heart racing. That new-parent hyperfear flared once again as I sprinted with her to the phone.

The police were in and out of the neighbor's yard for the next three days. I tried to shield Felicity as much as humanly possible. But deep down, I knew there was no point.

She had already seen the worst of it.

I realized that when she pointed to the TV. I understood as I saw what she thought were "chickens" on the screen.

It had all come horrifyingly together as she pointed to a murder scene with seven mangled bodies, looked at me, and called them "Tik-hinz."

The corpses in the neighbor's yard had already begun to rot. Fortunately, their open-air disposal had reduced the impact of the smell. The police say that the disfigured, tortured bodies of the victims fit the exact M. O. as the killer whose handiwork Felicity had noticed on the news that night.

My neighbor is wanted for questioning. Unfortunately, he has recently gone missing. There are no credible theories or leads about where he might have gone. There's very little the police can say.

They do believe that he likes to stalk his victims, though. Sometimes for weeks at a time, living a fantasy based on watching people who don't realize what danger they're in. Eventually, he'll leave something horrible for specific future victims to find, because he wants them to feel vulnerable.

Afraid.

Chicken.

I'M SORRY

Monday, February 12th

I have no idea how it happened. All my windows are locked from the inside, and my bedroom is on the second floor.

And my parents would have *freaked* if a boy had slipped into their seventeen-year-old daughter's room through the house. I can't even imagine what they would do if they saw a *man* in my room.

So you can imagine how totally messed up it was when I looked up from my bed and he was just *there*. I'd been reading (well, texting, but not important) and looking down at my bed. I looked up, and he was just sitting there with his leg up on my window seat, head resting on my UCLA pennant, smoking a cigarette and staring out the window.

I was too scared to scream at first.

"Why scream at all, Stacy? I can hear you perfectly fine from right here," he said with a gravelly voice.

I started hyperventilating.

"Calm your breathing, Stacy. If your best response to panic is depriving your brain of oxygen, then you can't afford to starve it any further."

I stared at him, transfixed, as he turned around and stared back at me. He was lean, nearly gaunt, with wild sandy blonde hair that would have been cute in an emo sort of way if he weren't scaring the hell out of me. His black collar was flipped up to his ears. His cigarette had no scent.

I caught my breath. Something about his voice calmed me.

"Who the fuck are you?" I spat out as soon as I could speak.

144

I wasn't inclined to run.

He sighed deeply, blowing a thin stream of smoke from between his lips. "Why ask, Stacy? Do you implicitly trust the answer that the strange man in your room will provide?"

I shook my head silently. He smiled.

"No. The only ones that people trust are those who can hurt them the most." He nodded contemplatively and sighed. "When I lived under the Saharan sun, looking back and forth across time, they called me Aker. Use that name unless you trust me."

I called him Aker.

"Why are you here?" I finally managed to eke out. I still didn't feel like running away, but I do not know why.

He chuckled. "That's a hell of an existential question, Stacy." He ran his fingers through his hair, his long, thin cigarette still poking between them. It did not seem to be getting any shorter. "Why are you?"

I fumbled for words. "It's – we – I know we covered existentialism in English-"

He shook his head. "No, I mean why haven't you run out the fucking door?"

That was harder than the existential question.

He sighed again, and it sounded sad. "Most people have *so many* opportunities that they squander, Eustachins."

"My name is Stacy."

"That's what I said." Here he took his foot from the ledge and placed it on the floor, leaning in closer. "Untold numbers of those opportunities are chances to *run away*, both physically and metaphysically. You've thus far chosen to bypass both."

I remained still on my bed.

"Why do people run away? They're afraid of the people who will *hurt them*. Now if trusting someone means nothing more than the chance to bestow pain upon them, what would you do if I said I trusted you?"

I didn't budge. I wasn't afraid anymore.

I still didn't know why.

He responded with his own stillness. It took me a moment to realize that his eyes were very sad. He closed them.

"Terry Leech is a boy at your school. You know him?" The gusto had diminished from his words. I nodded. He showed no response.

Your Dreams Taste Like Candy

"Do you know what happened to Saint Eustachins?" he pressed softly. I shook my head. He wiped a tear from his eye.

"I'm giving you the chance to hurt me," he creaked out in a voice that was barely above a whisper.

Tuesday, February 13th

I looked around the room with a rolled cigarette hanging out my mouth like a cowboy kid.

The door creaked open. I tore out the cigarette and threw it in the toilet. No way I was getting caught by a teacher. Especially that shithead Mr. Aster.

My asthma started again. I grabbed the sink with both hands.

A student entered instead. One of the basketball assholes. I really, really needed to be left alone right now.

My breathing turned into a wheeze.

The douchebag washed his hands, looked into the mirror, and walked out of the bathroom.

Dick didn't even ask if I needed help when I was wheezing. They never cared. I wiped a tear from my eye.

My breathing slowed.

No one was around to listen.

I walked into a stall, put my backpack on the floor, locked the door, and wrapped my arms around my legs. I rocked back and forth.

I wiped more tears away.

I had actually done it. Denise Willaker had spent two whole hours studying with me. She'd laughed at all my jokes. I'd walked her back to her house, she squeezed my hand, smiled, and said we'd talk "soon."

All those months obsessing over Stacy Flowers when I never even actually talked to her. Then Denise and I actually connected in a real way, and I wondered if I'd ever think of superficial Stacy again.

Your Dreams Taste Like Candy

It was the first time a girl had touched my hand. Good thing that Denise went right back into her house, there was no way I could have hid my boner.

My hand felt permanently warm. I walked down the steps and looked up at her bedroom window.

Denise had let her hair down and changed into sweatpants. There was something so intimate about it that my dick actually started to hurt. I winced.

I remembered Bang Bus.

A surge of adrenaline ran through me. Pure excitement at the thought. I never believed that Bang Bus was real - but Denise Willaker had basically just jerked off my hand. This was a new reality! This might actually turn her on!

I climbed into the bushes beside her house, heart racing, dick aching. Was I really going to do this?

I wondered how I would feel if I found her doing the same thing outside of my window.

I nearly fainted at the thought.

Yes.

I unzipped my pants.

I was way too focused to think about anything else until I saw the blue and red lights flashing against the brick wall of Denise Willaker's house.

Three more people came into the bathroom and left as I sat there with my legs wrapped around my chest. They didn't notice me.

They never did.

Sure, everyone had gawked at me for the first week after the bush incident. I was basically a celebrity. It was impossible to go anywhere without being noticed. I had no idea how long it could go on.

But to my shock, time kept going. The outside world didn't stop just because mine did.

And then I was shocked again.

They forgot about me.

After weeks of trying so hard to be alone while I ate my lunch or took a piss, I finally got my wish. People got bored and moved on.

I didn't know what to do.

I got lonely.

Your Dreams Taste Like Candy

I told myself that I wouldn't come here today, to this bathroom, if I got one friendly text within the month. I pulled out my phone.

From Dad: *Terry, remember that the lawyer said you should stay away from the girls' bathroom.*

I wondered, after I read that, when my dad would finally pretend like this never happened. I was sick of hearing from him.

We hadn't made eye contact in a week.

Dad was sitting at the kitchen table when I got home last week. He was waiting for me. It was awkward. He was never good at pretending not to be awkward.

"Terry, have a seat," he said crisply.

I looked over at his balding head with an emotion that I didn't understand, and sat.

"The lawyer says… it's not a good idea to move into a college dorm. Not with a criminal record like yours. He says it's best to make other plans."

And just like that, the rest of my entire fucking life became "other plans."

I was crying openly but silently now. All I could think of is what *they* could have done. How extraordinarily fucking *little* would have been necessary to stop the slow hurt. How much it would have meant for someone to text me, smile at me, hang out, *talk* to me and *if I couldn't even have that then I would never hold another hand again.*

The tears and snot and heaves wracked my body. I wanted so badly to talk to Denise, to at least let her know that she was the type of girl that *made* a smart boy stupid, and wasn't there anything to that?

It took two months before I saw her again at school. Given that (for a time) everyone had been surging around me, I figured that crossing paths would have been easy. But she was a ghost.

Two months. On the day I finally saw her, I had been hiding in the bushes (as usual) by the science lab precisely to *avoid* attention. When I finally emerged 45 minutes after the last bell rang, we ran into each other by fate. The lawyer had said to stay away, but tell a drowning man to stop caring about air and see what kind of a result you get. And in that moment, when she saw me stand out of the bushes and a look of disgust etched itself onto her face, in that moment, I knew, I knew.

I made the connections in my head. She didn't have to say it for me. She had friends who were watching me, *watching me*, everywhere, and they would tell her when it was safe to come out of hiding because she didn't want to see me, and the most important thing in her fucking social agenda was *avoiding* me because the filth that my presence represented was greater in scope than the happiness that she got from her *real* friends.

My feet slipped and my head fell between my knees as I sobbed. I didn't care if I drew attention to myself now, no one paid attention and everyone did, and there was no hope it would ever get any better.

I reached into my backpack and pulled out the nine mil. The crying stopped. It felt so *consequential*.

Well folks, you had the chance to make me consequential the easy way. I just wanted to feel what *every goddamn person in this school gets to feel except for me*.

I walked, zombie-like, to the window. I twisted the latch and pressed it open. It swung out from the bottom.

I didn't bother checking the door. Plenty of people were about to notice me in a quick fucking second.

I thought about giving the folks below one more chance, the same chance that they *never once thought to give me*, because I'm not the monster that they make me out to be, but then, right then, there is that fucking Aaron Crowley in his goddamn red letterman's jacket holding hands with Ann Carter and *talking to* Denise as she walks by, and it's just so fucking easy for all of them to make each other happy all the fucking time and they can't spare one second for me to be happy even once even once even once EVEN ONCE and the cocking of the gun is something I barely notice and

"Terry!"

Spinning and shooting are the same action and there's blood.

I've shot Stacy right in the head.

I feel like I'm floating as the conscious part of my brain watches the logical part take over.

I pick up my backpack, wipe my fingerprints off the handle, and place the gun in Stacy's dead hand with my own hand tucked inside the sleeve of my hoodie.

I run out the door and see no one in the hall, and bolt. I figure I've got ten seconds to get out of sight before anyone's brave enough to follow the sound, and I take off.

-Not The Valentine's Day Ending That Everyone Wanted-

Wednesday, February 14th

COTTON CORNERS, GA – A small town was rocked by tragedy yesterday when a high school senior committed suicide in her high school's bathroom.

Stacy Flowers used a nine millimeter handgun to end her life with a single gunshot wound to her head. There were no witnesses.

The news came as a shock to the seventeen-year-old's friends and family. She had been accepted to UCLA as an early admission candidate, and had expressed excitement to her friends about the opportunity to begin her freshman year.

The mood on the campus of Cotton Corners High School was somber. Afternoon classes were cancelled yesterday, though many students chose to gather on campus as the day came to an end. Several were seen openly crying.

"She was just the best kind of person," senior president and basketball captain Aaron Crowley commented. "She was there for everybody."

Junior Denise Willaker seemed to be in shock. "You never know what's going through someone's head, or how the person right next to you could be calling out for help while no one's listening."

Stacy's family declined a request for a statement. They did, however, release a picture of the note left on her bed that morning. The word "protector" was the entirety of the message. Family members have urged any of Stacy's friends who may have knowledge of the note's meaning to come forward.

But it seems that Cotton Corners is at a loss for words.

"I don't know what to say," explained Terry Leech, who is also a senior at Cotton Corners High.

"I wish I could tell her what she meant to me. What she meant for everyone."

HOW MUCH MACE IS RECOMMENDED FOR AN EIGHT-YEAR-OLD?

THE MOST AMAZING HUMAN SURVIVAL TRAIT IS OUR ABILITY TO tolerate kids.

Most mammals find a way to walk within a few weeks of birth. They quickly discover where to pee and poop with prudent judgment, and in no time at all they can get through the day without constant surveillance blocking their seemingly endless desire to kill themselves.

Human beings have no such adaptations. Our species survives based on the simple fact that we feel obligated to protect our helpless offspring, thus perpetuating the undesirable traits that make our children annoying.

I knew this information. But did it stop me from signing up to teach second graders?

Of course not. I'm a product of this illogical human construct, and therefore prone to lifelong bouts of illogical decision-making.

So I was counting down the days until summer vacation promised the sweet release of nothingness. Being twenty-two and single, I was preparing to live every girl's dream of moving back into my childhood bedroom and spending the summer indoors.

Because there was no way that I would continue working at the Crespwell Academy for Superb Children.

I had thirty-one hours and fifty-three minutes of employment left when the cat first appeared.

We had been going over two-digit addition when I heard a low grumble from behind me.

152

Your Dreams Taste Like Candy

There was a black cat in Ronda's lap. It looked uncomfortable.

A chill ran down my spine because *there was no reason for Ronda to have a live cat*. We were in the middle of a second-grade math lesson, and it was implied that animals had to stay outside the classroom.

"Ronda," I explained calmly, "you'll have to put that cat outdoors."

She stared at me without smiling. "But Miss Q, it will escape," she responded matter-of-factly.

I forced a very stern voice. "If you let something go and it doesn't return, Ronda, then it was never really yours to begin with."

"But she already smelled me, and she knows I want to cut her open." She continued to refrain from smiling.

I had long ago learned to resist the nausea. I simply walked over to the cat, forcibly removed it from her grasp (I didn't touch Ronda, because God help you if you physically contact a student), and slipped the cat out the open window. I didn't know where the thing lived, but there was no way I would allow it to wander where the kids could reach it. Those monsters would probably barbecue it or turn it into a shirt.

That's when the lights went out.

The children remained calm and collected. I knew this because their eyes glowed white in the dark.

Have you seen thirteen children staring at you with glowing eyes in a pitch-black room?

It is *so* much creepier than it sounds.

They blinked in individual spurts. Each pair of shining eyes would momentarily disappear at random intervals.

I was too terrified to move. I'm sure they knew I was at my weakest.

If I had had the power to walk away in that moment, I would have sprinted off and never returned.

Then the knocking started.

It was immediately obvious that the pounding was malicious. The banging was aggressive, high on the door, and it wanted my attention.

I walked carefully between the rows of glowing eyes that stared me down. I was too afraid to blink as I passed through.

The children turned their heads to follow me as I passed.

I could feel them glaring behind my back.

I approached the door. It was shaking violently in its wooden frame.

"Stop," I commanded in my strongest 'teacher' voice.

Your Dreams Taste Like Candy

The knocking ceased. That caught me off-guard.

"Um. Good. Now go away."

Even *I* thought my voice sounded lame.

"I've come for the children," it responded simply. The voice was high and low at the same time, passionate yet utterly inhuman. It made my neck feel cold.

The knob turned.

I grabbed it and immediately re-discovered how weak I was as the metal slid powerfully beneath my fingers.

The door opened a crack. I threw all of my 110 pounds against it.

It continued to move, albeit more slowly.

I looked down in the darkness and evaluated my options for weapons. I'd left my keys in my purse. No part of my flip flops, skirt, or blouse could be fashioned into a weapon. My fists were smaller than lemons.

Nope. I was definitely going to lose.

The door opened wide enough for a man to fit inside. There was just enough light streaming through the windows to illuminate a hand as it wrapped around the edge.

It had seven fingers. They were long, thin, and pale blue.

A brush of fur slid past my ankle as a shadow flew across the floor.

The voice screamed.

Then things happened very quickly.

Resistance from the opposite side of the door immediately ceased. Just before my body's weight slammed it shut, the tiny shadow ran back inside the room. The lights turned back on as I fell against the door and slid to the ground.

The little shadow turned itself to face me and meowed.

I stood up, brushed my skirt, and walked to the front of the room.

"Now," I explained calmly, pretending that nothing bizarre had happened, "What is 87 plus 78?"

I sat across from Principal Apachaya the next day, heart racing. *I was finally free.* I didn't care about being unemployed; all I wanted was to be done with Crespwell.

Your Dreams Taste Like Candy

"I imagine that you want to be done with Crespwell," he explained bluntly from across his desk. "You've had quite a year."

I stared at him, slack-jawed. "Yes – I've actually come here to resi-"

"You found a cat in your classroom yesterday," Apachaya continued as he narrowed his beady little eyes at me. "You protected the animal."

I was taken aback. "Well – yes, of course. Should I have let something innocent get hurt?"

He regarded me thoughtfully. "Most people would."

An awkward silence hung between us.

"Then *he* came," Apachaya continued in a lowered voice. "Two children would have satiated his hunger."

My head spun. "You KNEW he would be there? You expected him to take *two children?*"

He shook his head. "Ava, you must know by know that Crespwell is a… special place. You've made it an entire academic year, which is more than I can say for most teachers." He leaned forward on his elbows. "And no one - *no one* - has actually stood up to *him* and won." He sighed deeply. "How did you do it, Ava?"

I was about to explain that a cat had saved the class, but decided that he had covered the 'sounding crazy' quota for this meeting.

I cleared my throat. "Feminine charm, I guess."

He gawked at me blankly. "Well, that must be an *extremely* dangerous weapon."

I nodded quietly. "I'd actually like to talk about my plans going forward. While I appreciate the opportunity, it's time for me to-"

"We need you back next year," he interrupted flatly.

You know the discomfort that comes with realizing that *both* creepy guys at opposite ends of a bar are about to approach?

Multiply that discomfort by the number 'crazy.'

"Principal Apachaya, I actually came here to hand in my resignation-"

"$250,000 to return in the fall," he said flatly.

And that's how I signed up for another year of this shit.

So I'm going to take a relaxing summer. But come August, I'll be right back in the thick of things.

Yes, there may be fetus soccer, brain sharing, and nighttime children.

But times are tough.

And it sure beats retail.

JUST SKIP THIS STORY

BEGIN AUDIO TRANSCRIPT

Man: It's time to wake up, my scrumptious little nugget. This erection is bursting at the seams.

Harold Wilson: Oh God, what have you done to me?

Man: I haven't done anything, my juicy nugget. I only get the tinglies in my fingers and toesies when they do it to *themselves*.

Harold Wilson: Both of my shins are broken! *vomits* The shards are popping out of my skin!

Man: I know, I'm also just *so* hungry.

Harold Wilson: *crying* I'm in so much pain! Why are you doing this?

Man: I've only done that to make sure you don't go walking away before making a choice!

door opens

Harold Wilson: DALIA! She's alive! DALIA, I'M HERE, DADDY'S HERE! I thought my daughter was dead!

Your Dreams Taste Like Candy

Man: No, my lumpy nugget. I took her several weeks ago, and we have been snuggling ever since. She and I like to play.

Harold Wilson: Oh God, she's alive! Is she awake?

Man: You're a silly nugget. She's so tired! That's why I've got the blanket pulled up to her chin. I'll wake her up when we play.

Harold Wilson: *crying* She disappeared 79 days and 17 hours ago. My life ended in that moment. *crying* She's only 24, she has her whole life ahead of her. Please, let her go.

Man: We will play.

Harold Wilson: *breathing heavily* What?

Man: We will play a game of choose. What happens is up to you. Either you die, or she dies.

Harold Wilson: *yelling* Then kill me!

Man: If she dies, it is with a painless injection as she sleeps.

Harold Wilson: *yelling* KILL ME!

Man: I know what scares you, Harold.

Harold Wilson: *whimpering* Kill me.

Man: You are so afraid of enclosed spaces that you can't work in an office. It makes you feel hot.

Harold Wilson: *whispers* How could you possibly know so much about our lives? How long have you been watching us?

Man: Always.

Your Dreams Taste Like Candy

Harold Wilson: *cries*

Man: This is a composite curing oven. It helps me make the most delicious chicken nuggets! It can only fit a man if his shins are broken and wrapped around his shoulders.

Harold Wilson: There's… no way that a man can fit in there.

Man: I can fit you in there.

Harold Wilson: *whispers* No.

Man: You will bake to death over several hours.

Harold Wilson: *vomits*

Man: How much do you love your daughter?

Harold Wilson: *barely audible* Kill me.

LAPSE IN AUDIO TRANSCRIPT

Man: Risey shiny, my baby nugget.

Dalia Wilson: *moans* Oh God, why am I still alive?

Man: Daddy played.

Harold Wilson: *yelling* Dalia! I love you!

Dalia Wilson: Dad? Dad! You have to get away from him! Get away before it's too late!

Man: It's too late. He chose.

Harold Wilson: You'll get to live, Dalia. *sobbing* You'll get to live.

Your Dreams Taste Like Candy

Dalia Wilson: *screaming* NO! What have you done!

Man: Off comes the blankie!

Dalia Wilson: Look away from me, Dad!

Harold Wilson: Dalia? *yelling* Dalia, what happened? Where are your arms and legs?

Dalia Wilson: *crying* He took them from me. He cut them off, and he won't let me die.

Man: She's a sad little nugget.

Dalia Wilson: All I want is to die. *sobbing* I've been begging him for weeks to let me die.

Man: But you'll live. He had the choice, and you'll keep living, for a long, long, long, long time.

Dalia Wilson: Please, Dad, tell him to kill me.

Man: Too late. Time to bake Daddy.

Dalia Wilson: What?

Man: I have a delivery to make, and he chose to die so that you would stay alive. Time to close the oven door. Say goodbye forever.

Harold Wilson: I didn't know you wanted to die. *cries* I'm so sorry that I failed, Dalia.

Dalia Wilson: No no no no no no no NO NO NO NO! Stop! Dad, I love you! I love you! Don't kill him!

oven door closes

Your Dreams Taste Like Candy

Man: This is what puts the tinglies in my fingers and toesies.

Dalia Wilson: No, please don't kill him! Please kill me instead! Please don't kill my Daddy! PLEASE DON'T KILL MY DADDY!

END AUDIO TRANSCRIPT

Elm Grove Police Department

Evidence Item No. 052220191913

Incident Type: Homicide; Missing Person

Coroner's Conclusion: Complete pairs of femurs, tibias, fibulas, humeri, radii, and ulnas, along with full sets of tarsals, carpals, and all other hand and foot bones appear to have been removed with surgical precision.

Given the level of medical skill apparent, it is very likely that the donor of these bones remains alive.

All bones were taken from the same victim. Forensics concludes that the individual was a Caucasian woman between the ages of 20 and 30.

Dalia Wilson (age 24) was reported missing to EGPD on 5 February 2019.

Notes: This audio transcript [Evidence Item No. 052220191913] was taken from a digital recording that was hand-delivered to the main entrance of Elm Grove Police Headquarters.

There were no witnesses to the delivery.

Dalia Wilson remains missing. Her father, Harold Wilson (age 69), disappeared three days ago.

Your Dreams Taste Like Candy

Along with the audio recording were directions to an Elm Grove industrial warehouse, which had formerly held the processing facilities of Most Delicious Chicken Nuggets, LLC.

The bones from the coroner's conclusion were found in the processing facility.

Blood and hair (later determined to be human) were discovered in a composite curing oven.

Most Delicious Chicken Nuggets, LLC appears to have abruptly abandoned all operations three days ago. Despite concerted efforts, no former employee has been found.

Most Delicious Chicken Nuggets, LLC has been providing lunches to Elm Grove Elementary School for the entirety of the 2018-2019 school year. The final shipment of food was delivered today, but the driver disappeared before EGPD could apprehend him.

All students had eaten lunch before EGPD could intervene.

Every nugget was consumed.

THE PENIS DANCE

IT WAS IMPOSSIBLE TO SAY WHO SPOTTED THE OTHER FIRST. They simply locked eyes from across the room, walked towards one another, and embraced in the dance.

Neither said a word as the music overtook them both, their bodies writhing in symbiotic unison. Soon, she opened her mouth and placed it on his.

He responded by opening his own mouth just as wide. He slid his mouth penis into her gaping maw. It prodded every corner – gums, tongue, palate, uvula – as her eyes rolled back in ecstasy.

Soon, the activity of the prehensile penis reached a fever pitch as it writhed and hummed almost uncontrollably.

It was time.

She opened her eyes. He did likewise, and looked meaningfully into hers. He nodded. He was sure. She nodded back.

And she bit.

Her jagged fangs tore the penis from him in one clean bite. He fell to the floor, blood spurting from his mouth, and smiled as the life drained out of him. She closed her mouth tight as the newly-liberated phallus squirmed frantically around her tongue and along her cheek. She closed her eyes in concentration, and swallowed.

It kicked on the way down.

And it didn't stop kicking when it landed in her uterus.

The crowd danced around her as she laid her hands on her newly-swelling belly, cheeks aglow with maternal love. Oh, how he kicked. She could tell it would be a 'he'! Such a strong boy. His kicks were already energetic and powerful. Soon they became overwhelming. The outline of tiny footprints pressed her abdomen from the inside. Thrust after powerful thrust nearly knocked her off her feet.

The kicks were quickly replaced by punches. Left, right, left, right - he wanted to get out! And she knew that soon, he would.

She stepped over to where the man's still-bleeding corpse lay on the dance floor. Blood stuck to her high heels as she walked through the mess that she had caused for her strong boy. So strong! So powerful! Punch. Punch! PUNCH!

She gasped as a small fist finally erupted from her uterus, ripping through the flesh and freeing what was once held captive into the outside world. The boy thrust his other hand through and ripped her apart like an exploding firecracker.

The boy found himself on the ground next to the corpse of his father and the viscera of his mother. He stared hungrily at the intestine and flayed skin which now covered the floor that was filled with dancing people. He hungrily turned and began to devour what was left of his late mother. He gobbled her guts, slithered in her skin, and swallowed what was left of her head whole.

When he was done, he licked the floor, and smiled.

Your Dreams Taste Like Candy

WHAT IF I HAD NEVER BEEN BORN?

I SAID "NO" AT FIRST.

Liam, Colin, and Troy had taken an Uber from Troy's house. I'd worked late and driven myself straight to the bar once I was finally able to leave that fucking office.

So I did the responsible thing and decided to stay sober. I sat out the first round when they accepted my decision. But I was chided on the second, and had been relegated to the status of a "faggot who should stop being a pussy" once the waitress came by a third time.

She smiled at me. Her teeth were slightly crooked, but that made her more endearing in a girl-next-door kind of way. I don't even remember saying 'yes' when she asked about a drink order. It just kind of happened.

Liam pushed me to the bar almost immediately after I was served my Guinness with a wink. He told me that I needed to get her number or get shot down, but I had no business jerking off into my own tears because I had passed up an opportunity.

I nearly fell as he nudged me, which caused the crooked-tooth waitress on the other side to stifle a flustered giggle. "Did you need something else?" she asked sweetly.

I looked stupidly into my nearly-full beer.

Then I downed it.

"Just another Guinness, please," I offered with my best smile.

She nodded and turned around. When her back was turned, Colin appeared from nowhere with a shot of Jameson. He thrust it into my hand and gave me a knowing look.

Your Dreams Taste Like Candy

I slammed back the Jameson in one gulp, leaned forward on the counter, and confidently added "and your number."

I came back to the table with a fresh beer, a bashful smile, and Kelly's contact info in my phone.

"Best of luck telling your right hand that he's got competition," Troy noted gravely. "He's going to be very jealous."

I *know* how red I must have looked.

"Well, boys, this has been fun, but I have to get back to Molly before 9:00 to have any hope of avoiding another screaming match," Liam explained coolly.

The three of us awkwardly polished off the rest of what we had and hurried outside.

The sun is setting much earlier at this time of year in New Hampshire; it was completely dark when we got outside. The three of them had to wait for their Uber, and I was driving in the opposite direction, so I waved and left.

I dropped my keys once, laughed at my own stupidity, then successfully navigated my way into the car.

I thought about texting Kelly as I drove. How long should I wait? The opening line would have to be an inside joke. 'You seem impressed with what I left you, but that was just the tip.' Ha. I'm fucking clever-

shit

I did NOT notice the red light until it was too late. I was committed to crossing the intersection and floored it. Angry honks. Heart racing, I looked behind me. Two cars, stopped in the middle of the intersection, undoubtedly *pissed*. But everyone was safe.

My heart rate was not slowing, though, and my hands were shaking. I turned back to face forward and floored it. The road curved ahead, and I didn't like speeding around it, but I didn't want to get caught by a cop for running the red light. I focused on the turn.

And realized that I was in the left lane. I had drifted while looking back at the intersection.

And now there were headlights directly in front of me. I swerved to my right, *he* swerved to my right, and we were still facing each other with twenty feet between us.

I turned *hard* to the left. The wheels rolled over the grass. I *bounced*. The car wasn't supposed to shake that hard. I lost my grip on the steering wheel.

Your Dreams Taste Like Candy

Couldn't find the brake. Pushed hard but the shaking increased and then the slamming

CRACK

thonk thonk thonk thonk

The car was completely out of my control for nearly a full second.

Then I regained my wits and slammed on the brake pedal. In that precise moment, I saw a young boy's face light up in front of my headlights. He was too centered for me to attempt a left *or* a right turn. I pushed harder on the brakes and he seemed so fragile-

crunch

And then he disappeared from view.

The car stopped. I opened the door and looked down.

Directly into his face. He was shocked, but not gasping.

No one can gasp with the front tire of a car resting on his chest.

This kid was dying.

I felt vertigo.

Screaming from a nearby house. Not pissed-off screaming – no, this was the kind of a wail that someone makes when their entire world is peeling apart.

I closed the door, then pressed the gas.

I could feel the car lower itself as I came off his chest.

I gingerly stepped out as the boy's father dove onto the grass and slid the last few feet toward him. The man grabbed his son's shoulders and pulled.

Bad idea. I could now tell that spinning the wheels on his obliterated chest had eviscerated most of the boy's skin. His ribs were a shattered mess, and when the boy's father pulled on his shoulders, it only served to split the boy's torso further in half. We were standing just below a streetlight, and it shined directly onto the carnage as his screaming father picked up splinters of broken ribs and tried vainly to replace them into the gaping maw of his son's chest.

Your Dreams Taste Like Candy

The boy's eyes drifted to his father, not understanding why his dad was inflicting so much pain.

It was his last thought.

I stood numbly as the man screamed incoherently and sobbed over his dead son. A woman whom I later found to be his mother ran out in response to the screaming. When she saw the scene, she didn't make a sound. Instead, she crumpled softly to the ground, and remained completely still.

In retrospect, I had finished all three drinks in under five minutes. In retrospect, I had skipped lunch, and my stomach was completely empty.

In retrospect, I wish I had done a lot of things differently.

But in that moment, all I could do was look forward. Nothing will ever be the same for us. I realized that no matter *what* I did with the rest of my life, there would always be three people who'd have been better off if I'd never been born.

So I hope this changes at least one mind. A final score of 1-3 isn't what I wanted, but it's the best I'll ever do.

In Memory of Charlie Williams

January 9th, 2013 – September 27th, 2018

JUDGED FOR MY SEXUALITY AND SICK OF TAKING IT

EVERYTHING ABOUT HER WAS PETITE. SHE WAS 5' 2" IN HEELS, had padded her way to a b-cup, and her slender little waist looked like it might snap in two if I could do half of what was running through my imagination.

Her face was intoxicatingly *cute* in a girl-next-door kind of way, and I didn't even realize that I'd been gawking until she stared back.

Fuck. I was just so *bad* at adjusting to the predatory role. My instincts were razor-sharp when it came to fending off even the most aggressive man-whores. Reversing that approach was new, raw, and unnatural.

Feeling unnatural had always been familiar, though.

Stacy and I had been sleeping over at each other's houses since our parents first allowed it in the fourth grade. I don't know how I would have made the transition into middle school without her.

And this was the first time that she had ever asked to go home early. It was 7:13 p. m., long before we normally dozed off together in my queen-sized bed, and her father had whisked her away after the most awkward silence of our lives.

No one can judge the tears when you're alone.

Your Dreams Taste Like Candy

We'd started the night with a movie, but had — for the first time — tentatively broached the topic of sex. I was thrilled and afraid, because like everyone I knew, my conservative parents refused to acknowledge its existence.

I had just assumed that all carnal feelings were sinful.

And that everyone felt the same indistinguishable morass of hateful attraction to our own lusts.

So in assuming that all shame was equally felt, I had had NO IDEA that my attraction to other girls was abnormal.

Stacy clarified that for me.

She never spent the night again.

Cute-girl-next-door made a beeline for me, and I suddenly realized that I had switched back from predator to prey. This woman was, *undoubtedly*, on the hunt. Confusion and excitement and doubt and *mind-numbing fear* crashed through my head like a "Three Stooges" short. I ran through a list of ten introductions and quickly rejected them all. Surely, there could be no paragraph brief enough to explain the complexity of my emotions. She would judge and dismiss me immediately.

Cute Girl stopped in front of me and smiled. "Want to dance?"

I nodded.

We did.

I was nervous each time her bare arm rubbed against mine.

I pulled back in shame when she ground her ass into my crotch.

I felt guilty and disgusting when I realized just how wet my panties became in response to her touch.

And I felt alone when she left me to go dance with someone else.

What the hell kind of a predator was I?

I walked off the dance floor and headed for the exit.

Clack clack clack clack

Someone in heels was running to catch up with me. "Wait!" she breathed, grabbing my elbow.

My adrenal glands burned badly enough to cause physical pain.

"Hey!" she gasped breathlessly. "I didn't give you my name. I'm Natalie. I need a ride."

Your Dreams Taste Like Candy

Silence hung thickly between us as I pulled the car out of the parking lot.

"So…" I offered timidly. "Where do you live?"

Instead of speaking, she hiked up her skirt. Without making eye contact, she slipped her panties out from underneath the hem of her dress, slid them over her knees, looped them past her heels, and tucked them deeply into my purse.

She ran her tongue across her teeth.

I drove faster.

I locked my apartment door behind me and she pounced.

The kiss was intoxicating enough to affect my balance. It ended far too soon, with a final pull on my lips between her teeth that flirted with wonderful pain.

Every nerve on my neck was at the complete mercy of her – well, to be honest, I couldn't distinguish among her lips, teeth, and tongue. There must be a dendrite that fires a direct channel between the space under my ear and the pleasure centers of my brain.

I felt like I was floating.

I felt like butter.

It's what she wanted.

The easiest prey is snagged with the mind.

Pleasure and pain are so closely connected that I didn't feel the bite at first. All I knew was *intensity*. But she sucked deeply, I felt the blood rushing out of my neck, and I slowly understood that the sensation rocketing through my skull was anguish.

Her fangs had split me open, and my blood was pouring freely into her throat.

She slurped hungrily.

She swallowed.

I was physically weak.

Prey.

Eaten.

Your Dreams Taste Like Candy

And this is where it got really hard.

I breathed deeply and pulled.

This time, the pain was beyond categorization. I wailed as the white-hot torture ripped through my throat and felt that surely *surely* the agony was tearing my neck in two.

I pulled again.

Blinding pain overwhelmed me once more, but it was less intense than before.

I was (barely) able to comprehend the world around me this time.

Her lips were glued to my neck. Her eyes widened with surprise.

I pulled again.

Blood rushed back into my body, fresh and revitalized with the essence of the hunter. It tingled in my fingertips and toes.

She whimpered.

"Sssshh," I offered in response. I stroked her auburn hair. Her brown eyes stared up at me in complete submission.

I pulled again. The flood of electric energy into my veins was strong enough to counterbalance the pain now, and her sallow skin collapsed against her skull like a deflated balloon. Her eyes appeared cartoonishly wide in contrast.

I stood erect.

And pulled again.

What was left of her pallid skin cracked and flaked as her eyes rolled back into their sockets. The hair sloughed off her scalp and landed unceremoniously on the floor with a *plop*.

I ran my tongue across my lips.

With one last pull, her bones cracked and splintered. The energy coursing through my muscles felt ready to climax. With a final thrust, I drove my fist into her skeleton. It burst in a white, powdery explosion against the wall.

My skin tingled.

I licked my teeth.

I was buzzing. I always had more energy afterward. I felt ready to clean the apartment and then write a novel.

To be honest, though, I wanted a second round more than anything else.

Your Dreams Taste Like Candy

"Your lifestyle disgusts me," I said to the white residue on the wall. "So you'd better get ready to accept me as I am." I reached into my purse. "I'm a predator in search of prey."

I plucked her panties from between the folds.

"And I'll only be satisfied with the best trophies that I can find."

MY PATIENT FELT SHITTY

I BEND OVER THE SPLIT ABDOMEN, A FESTERING PIT OF intestine laid out below me. It's beautiful in its raw vulnerability, able to twitch just slightly below my blade – but otherwise immobile, and at my mercy.

"The patient came into the emergency room 'feeling shitty.' There's an understatement - I've never seen an appendix look this way."

A lone bead of sweat picks its way along the creases of my brow. Nimble. Precise.

Deliberate.

Crepper wipes the sojourner from my skin with deft professionalism. Even with the surgical mask covering her countenance, I can tell she senses something is amiss.

She's a good nurse.

"I have the appendix," she responds crisply. "Extremely enlarged at 19.13 grams. I'll send it to-"

"It's fine. I – I'm fine, Nurse. Please – go ahead and take it yourself." I clench the scalpel slightly tighter.

She responds with stoic intrigue. She knows how bizarre it was for me to request just one assistant for the procedure, and this complication cannot be explained easily.

"I don't have time for discussion in the middle of surgery. Go now."

"Yes, Doctor." She regards me for a moment longer before turning around and heading out the door.

I act quickly. With the patient split open, I am able to reach inside the abdominal cavity and grab his rectum.

Your Dreams Taste Like Candy

I'm a skilled surgeon. It is short work to detach the rectum from his anus. When I am done, the large intestine sits in my hands like an empty sausage casing.

Well, perhaps not so empty. I can tell by the bulge in my left hand that the patient had clearly eaten sooner than the recommended twelve hours earlier. I can't blame him, though – he didn't know that surgery was imminent. Grabbing the colon like a withered toothpaste tube, I squeeze and pull the bulge along its track. Aiming it over a small metal bowl, I slide my gloved fingers nimbly around the contours of his intestine. My efforts are rewarded when a smelly brown eruption squirts from the end, looking for all the world like a blossoming flower in extreme fast forward. I empty the contents into the bowl, then get to work on the next part of the plan.

I waste no time, estimating a maximum of 240 seconds before Crepper returns.

But my scalpel wavers for an instant.

Then I remember the photograph. My twin son and daughter, both eight, bound and gagged. My wife next to them, face contorted in agony, four of her own severed fingers stuffed into her cheeks by an unknown assailant. A very simple message: "Follow these instructions during today's surgery, or I'll cut them to pieces very slowly over the next six months."

I thought about what was written after that.

I'm a skilled surgeon. Part of that talent is the ability to shut down both tears and vomit.

Though it's never been as difficult as it is in this moment.

Yet I begin.

I quickly make an incision on the side of the stomach. Then I pull the rectum to the opening and cover it. I take a deep breath, then reach for the needle.

I'm able to stitch the open rectum onto the stomach very quickly.

I'm sewing the abdomen shut when Crepper walks back in.

"Doctor, I-" Then she senses that I do not wish to speak. Instead, she walks to the side of the table and whisks away a rogue bead of sweat from my forehead with surgical precision.

"Good job, Nurse." I sigh. "Well done. Stand by, the patient should be waking up very soon."

I took a deep breath.

"Let's see if he still feels shitty."

THE STRANGE NEW GIRL'S NOT FOLLOWING THE HOME OWNERS' ASSOCIATION RULES

I COULD TELL THE NEW GIRL WAS GOING TO BE A PROBLEM right away.

She waltzed into the open house on Daffodil Lane wearing some obscene fluttery pink top like it was a perfectly normal thing to do.

She didn't even notice the scorch marks on the driveway.

I bit my lip until it bled. My wife used to berate me for the fidgeting.

In a lot of ways, it was easy being single again.

I suppose it's a good thing that pink top girl didn't notice the scorch marks. It means we cleaned up well.

And such eyesores are *strictly* against Pelican Peak HOA rules.

I sat alone in my room, watching the black and white video monitors.

The Willard house was quiet (finally), and was so devoid of movement that it could have been a still photo.

Wind gently swayed through the magnolias on the corner of Daisy Lane and Garden Street. A bin full of food scraps sat prominently by the curb.

There was a sallow-skinned man that I knew to be 6 feet, 3.32 inches who was standing outside the Murphy house. His face was pressed against

175

the window. Through the grainy footage, I could barely discern his tongue methodically licking the glass.

The Murphys couldn't tell, of course. Their curtains were drawn.

Everyone assumes they're safe when their curtains are drawn.

I sighed in relief.

Just another normal night.

I was about to check the footage from the other streets when something caught my eye.

Oh, shit.

The Gray Man had stopped eating garbage. He was staring at the nearest home.

Fuck. It was the new girl. I *knew* she was going to be trouble.

I looked wildly around the living room and settled on a nine-iron. It was going to have to do.

Heart pounding, lungs burning, I sprinted toward rapidly-brewing disaster.

My breath was beyond catching and I could barely see when I got to her house. There he was, pounding angrily on the door. If the fool inside had half a brain, she would be hiding in the darkest closet right now.

"Stop!" I screamed before realizing that I *had no plan.*

Slowly, the Gray Man turned to face me.

The empty black sockets were big enough to hold baseballs. Light from the half moon was just strong enough to illuminate the farthest recesses of his hollow skull.

He dropped his jaw.

It kept falling until it was two feet below his face.

No matter how many of the damn things I see on the video monitors, I *always* get icy chills when I see them in real life.

He groaned. Then he started walking toward me.

I pointed the nine-iron at him in self-defense, but knew it was like taking an umbrella into a hurricane.

AAAAAAAOOOOOUGHHH!

And then he charged.

I didn't even have time to turn around before something far away caused the ground to shake.

Your Dreams Taste Like Candy

The Gray Man stopped in place.

"Oh, fuck," I whispered. "Listen to me *very* carefully."

The Gray Man looked at me in soulless attention. I prayed that he understood my words.

"You need to be very, very, *very* quiet," I continued in the softest tone I could muster, "And I'll get you all the chicken bones you like. How's that sound?"

The rumbling had stopped, thank God. Now I had to keep it that way.

The Gray Man stared emptily back at me.

And then he screamed.

Why did it sound like a dying woman's last shriek? That made everything so much creepier than it had to be.

And the ground shook.

It didn't stop shaking.

The Gray Man understood. He turned and ran at an inhuman speed. When he caught up to me, he didn't attack.

He was too afraid.

As the shaking continued, not a single house light turned on, and not a single window opened.

Which meant that *everyone* understood the danger.

So I knew that no one would let me inside, no matter how much I screamed and begged. The first tears fell then, and I wondered if I could kill myself with a nine-iron.

It would hurt less than being found outside after dark.

A flash of inspiration came over me, and I acted without thinking.

CRACK

The nine-iron hit the Gray Man squarely in the kneecap with a sickening burst as I shattered his bones.

AAAAAAAOOOOOUGHHHAAAAGGGHHH! He screamed as he fell to the floor. The ground shook more violently still as he disrupted the night with his wails.

Then a roar ripped the sky apart. It was loud enough to reverberate from anywhere and everywhere all at once.

But I knew it was radiating from the cul-de-sac at the end of Petunia Lane.

Your Dreams Taste Like Candy

I knew that its source would be here in a matter of seconds.

And I knew that the Gray Man couldn't run anymore. He would lie helplessly on the asphalt as his screams drew *it*.

Which meant that I would have just enough time to sprint home, close the curtains, and spend the night ignoring the knocking that would come from every window and every door.

It's not the sounds that got to me most.

Sure, I hated hearing the Gray Man scream in pain that I had caused. And I hated it even more when the screams abruptly stopped.

I could hear the crunching of bones from two blocks away.

No, what gets to me the most is that we *knew* this could happen, and we didn't prevent it.

This is all the new girl's fault. She had every opportunity to follow the rules.

And breaking the rules has consequences. I don't like it, but there are many, many things I live with that I don't like.

Tomorrow night, she'll suffer the punishment she brought upon herself.

And when she runs through the streets, screaming and knocking at every house, my neighbors will know to ignore her.

No matter what sounds they hear, no one will open the door.

No matter how much she begs before she dies, every child will stay quiet.

Because we know better than to violate the Home Owners' Association rules.

THE MAGIC OF CHRISTMAS

December 24th, 2018

Dear Ralphie-

You asked me today whether Christmas magic is real. Does Santa really care so much about one little boy's heart?

Or is eight years old just too late to still believe?

Here's what's real.

Your heart is *everything* to me and your mom. I know that it's hard to imagine a time before the two of us had you in our lives, and it's hard for us as well. Because we were fundamentally *different* people before you arrived.

You changed us.

And the only reason that change was possible is because we believed in you *before* you were born. Were you real at the time? The answer is both no (from a certain point of view), and yes (from our hearts' perspective). You affected our plans, our dreams, and our*selves* before light ever twinkled from your curious blue eyes.

We believed in you.

So you became real.

Imagine the scaffolding on the side of our house. It's there because we believe in a vision of a bigger, better home for us. We can plan for that house, we can treat it like it's *already* real, because we believe in our dreams.

It's more than we can afford, but we have faith that we'll work hard enough to pay the debt one day. *You* were too much to afford before we had you. But I took your mother in my arms and turned my pockets inside out. They were empty, but I said, "Janine, these are magic pockets. Right now they contain only dreams, which is the best thing in the world, because dreams can become anything in the morning light."

So here's the truth:

You don't need to believe in Christmas magic as long as *it* believes in *you.*

Merry Christmas, Ralphie.

-Mom, Dad, and Santa

Elm Grove Police Department

Evidence Item No. 122420181913

Incident Type: Accidental deaths (2)

Coroner's Conclusion: Mike Stanton (36 years old) died of exsanguination at approximately 20:00 on 24 December. It is estimated that the process took 60-90 minutes before unconsciousness forced his body into a state of relaxation that allowed the majority of blood loss to occur. Prior to this unconsciousness, Mr. Stanton was fighting to maintain an upright position that held in his blood. The Elm Grove Coroner's Office (EGCO) believes that the physical orientation caused excruciating pain, but that he was able to maintain it for so long out of a profound (yet ultimately unsuccessful) desire to survive.

Janine Stanton (32 years old), wife of Mike, was pinned under collapsed scaffolding for 60 minutes before rescuers extracted her. The choice to remove her ultimately proved unwise, as the collapsed scaffolding had been acting as a tourniquet to her crushed and pinned left femoral artery. The unfortunate decision to extract her so hastily directly led to her death, which could have been avoided with proper planning.

Your Dreams Taste Like Candy

Notes: Ralphie Stanton (8 years old) received a letter from his father [Evidence Item No. 122420181913] that he apparently believed to have been written by Santa Claus. He proceeded to climb the scaffolding outside of his Elm Grove home, which is currently under construction, with the goal of making what he called a "Santa trap."

In an attempt to establish realism, Mike Stanton climbed on top of his house at approximately 18:00 while dressed in traditional Santa Claus attire. He subsequently caught his boot in a rope trap that had been left by Ralphie, then fell off the roof. The rope pulled taut and swung him into a jagged metal edge of the scaffolding, causing deep lacerations to his abdomen. He then hung upside-down from the rope (still tied around his ankle), approximately twelve feet above the ground. When he lifted his shoulders above the cut, he was able to reduce the level of blood loss. However, Mr. Stanton frequently had to relax his position due to complete physical exhaustion. During those moments, he would experience severe bleeding.

Ralphie Stanton quickly appeared after the fall, but believed that Mike Stanton was actually Santa Claus. When the elder Stanton begged for help, Ralphie argued that Santa was simply attempting to escape his clever trap. The boy proceeded to say that he would not offer assistance until Mike procured several specific gifts from the "magic pockets" described in the above note [Evidence Item No. 122420181913]. When Mike was unable to do so, Ralphie explained that he would leave the man hanging from the roof and "making fake blood" until he surrendered the requested material goods.

Ralphie filmed the "capture" on his mobile phone. The footage revealed that Mike Stanton had begged for his life, shouting, "Santa isn't fucking real!" and "How can you be so stupid, eight-year-olds are smart enough to know that Santa is a goddamn lie for idiots!"

Approximately 60 minutes after the initial fall, Janine Stanton returned home from Christmas shopping to find her son recording her husband's slow death. She immediately attempted to climb the scaffolding in an effort to release Mike, but the "Santa trap" had severely compromised the frame's structural integrity. Her additional weight collapsed the scaffolding, crushing Janine's left leg and trapping her.

Janine's phone landed near Ralphie during the fall. The boy picked up the device and refused to return it. "Santa will make your leg all better with Christmas magic," he explained on the recording. "We just have to pass his test, and everything will be fixed for Christmas!"

The level of joy apparent in Ralphie's voice made it clear that he truly believed his parents were in no real danger.

Janine and Ralphie watched as Mike slowly lost the will to live. The child chose not to react as his parents begged, threatened, and screamed at him in fruitless attempts to persuade him to call emergency services.

Elm Grove Police and Fire eventually arrived in response to neighbors' noise complaints, and Mike was declared Dead On Arrival. Immediately before the ill-advised extraction of Janine, she was able to speak with her son.

"I don't understand how you could possibly believe that fucking note. We didn't plan for you at all, Ralphie. You were an accident that happened after I drank too much at a Christmas party, and I've hated the holiday ever since. You'll learn to hate it too, since it'll remind you of the day you became an orphan."

VAMPIRES SUCK AT BLOWJOBS

"THEY'RE UNDER YOUR BED, YOU KNOW," I EXPLAINED TO MY son as he pulled the covers up to his eyes.

"You're – you're joking, Dad," Brett responded in a voice that was anything but confident.

"Oh, no," I answered in an Oscar-worthy performance of parental gravity. "The vampires *definitely* live in all the dark corners of our homes. Fortunately, I've spread a coating of garlic all around the house for protection. Family keeps each other safe." I winked at him, ruffled his hair, and kissed his forehead.

His terrified eyes followed me out of the room until I clicked off the light.

Fine. I admit it. I enjoy fucking with my son. But at seven years old, Brett is almost done being a little kid. His mom died three years ago, nineteen days after our thirteenth anniversary.

That's when I stopped waiting for the future. Time is a limited commodity with no warranty. For better or for worse, I'm determined to make my experiences with my son the most powerful they can be.

I'll deal with the outcome of those decisions later.

If you think being a single dad puts the "blue balls" into "my dating life," you'd be entirely correct. I was so lucky to find Charmaine; she had a daughter of her own and understood the drill well. We would talk in hushed tones when I brought her home, and she'd slink quietly to my bedroom after I went ahead to determine that the coast was clear.

And she was a championship-level dick sucker.

Watching her was like witnessing Gustavo Dudamel draw symphonic fire from the Los Angeles Philharmonic. She used both hands, nimble lips, a *little* teeth, loved swallowing, and truly, *truly* understood the importance of periodic eye contact.

That's how I knew she was dying.

Or at least it seemed like it. First she gagged, then she choked, and finally she turned purple. I had to deal with three EMTs while my full erection was on display for all the world to see.

I went to the hospital long enough to watch her get intubated, then headed back home to take care of Brett.

He was wide awake and waiting for me.

"Hey, Bud," I offered delicately as I sat down on the bed next to him. "I'd like to explain why I left in the middle of the night."

Brett gave me a knowing look. "You were being chased by the vampire, Daddy." He flashed a big, gap-toothed smile. "But I helped to protect you."

I was bewildered. "What on earth are you talking about, Brett?"

He looked both serious and excited. "Dad, I've noticed a lady vampire that got past your garlic. She would follow you into your room at night, but she always hid in the shadows! I knew I had to protect you!"

I felt my stomach slide through my torso and settle onto my balls like a deflated balloon.

"So I was sneaky, Daddy. I heard her talking in the dark. The problem was that that vampire wasn't hurt by your garlic. I heard her say that she was allergic to peanuts!"

That's when the first wave of nausea hit.

Charmaine was deathly allergic to peanuts. She had told me that just before making a "But I'm not allergic to *penis*" joke that Brett must have secretly overheard.

"So I took the little armor that you use for protection," he continued, his triumphant smile growing, "and I rubbed it in the peanut oil we keep in the kitchen."

This genuinely confused me.

Then I understood.

My world spun.

Your Dreams Taste Like Candy

"Family keeps each other safe, Daddy!"

Brett had found my condoms while snooping around my room a few weeks ago. Rather than getting angry, I explained (truthfully) that they were little pieces of armor that I used for protection.

Charmaine's peanut allergy was *bad*. The small amount of oil that would have been transferred to the condom upon opening it would have been sufficient to trigger a significant reaction once it…

I remembered why I'd had the condom on before the blowjob.

I sprinted past Brett, snatched up my phone, called Avera Sacred Heart (the best hospital in Yankton, South Dakota), and demanded the doctor watching over Charmaine.

The seconds crawled, but I finally got a voice. Before he could form a sentence, I screamed into the phone.

"Check her rectum!"

WHERE NO ONE CAN HEAR THE SCREAMS

HE OPENED HIS EYES, SLOWLY GAINING AWARENESS OF THE ROOM. Me? I'd been rock-hard for a while, of course.

The man grasped at the space behind his chair. I chuckled. Not much he could do with both hands pinned behind his back. Still, he rattled the cuffs, almost like he was checking them.

"Good morning," I said with a smile.

He opened his eyes wider. Took everything in.

I loved watching the dawning moments of realization.

What did he see? A room devoid of all hominess. Water stains were the only decorations on the concrete walls. Inside the room was a table full of equipment, and me.

Nothing else.

But oh so many possibilities existed when those things combined.

He looked around with more effort now. The table was within his view but just beyond his handcuffed grasp, and he stared transfixed at the hammer nearest to him.

"No need to focus on just one tool," I offered in a nearly friendly voice. "There's a lot more to work with."

I let my eyes drift slowly, lovingly across the table. There were pliers for teeth. Scissors for skin. An acetylene torch for cauterizing wounds. Those were the basics.

But there's so much that can be done with a little imagination.

The array was beautiful. A scalpel, twine, glue, surgical thread, three sledgehammers, tweezers, rags, lighter fluid, gauze, two large vices, a

186

catheter, rope, one power drill, thirty-seven drill bits, and a hacksaw to be used in a thousand different places.

Soak it in for a minute. Your imagination can do far worse than my descriptions.

He certainly did. His eyes were as wide as fucking saucers.

I took a deep, deep breath: the thrill of anticipation. Incomparable.

After letting the moment linger, I breathed out and pulled something from my pocket.

"And this, my friend, is my favorite." He looked like he was going to puke.

That would happen later, of course. All in due time.

"This is a Pear of Anguish." I held out the device for him to see. It was shaped like a pear, but was entirely metallic. I gently placed my fingertips on the knob and started to unscrew it. The bulb spread open and splayed its parts outward, expanding slightly with each screw, until it was nearly ten inches wide from end to end. "Do you know where in your body I put the Pear of Anguish before slowly opening it?" I asked gleefully.

He shook his head. It wasn't to say "no."

He was pleading me not to do this.

Fuck, I was hard.

I just nodded. "Anywhere I want to," I explained simply. "Anywhere," I added with a sensual whisper.

His breaths were coming in shallow gasps at this point.

"But the piéce de résistance!" I shouted suddenly. "Is this," I offered in a more calming voice. Here I pulled an IV on a wheeled stand. The bag was filled with blood. "Type A positive, of course. I like to be accommodating. We wouldn't want you dying in the first week!"

He didn't buy my fake comfort, and I didn't blame him.

The man appeared to be dizzy. In all fairness, I had requested quite an assortment of drugs to be in his system.

His lips twitched, and he gasped like a fish as he struggled to find words. At first, they were only whispers. "Why, why, why?" he finally articulated. "Why did you do it?"

I looked at him and smiled almost sympathetically. I sighed. "They always want to know why. Honestly, it tempts me to use a gag." I cocked my head to the side. "I never would, though. The screaming is such a beautiful song."

Your Dreams Taste Like Candy

He shook his head, trying to shake it all away. This part was important. The torture begins long before the pieces start coming off. It begins in the head, not on it.

"Next you'll want to know what happens, and how you can get out of it," I explained with slight exasperation. "The answers are 'a lot,' and 'you can't.'"

"No," he retorted. "Why. Tell me why you did it."

I turned my head to the other side. "Why did I bring you here? That must be obvious. I want to torture a stranger for a few weeks. It's a... hobby of mine, and I have a lot of disposable income. We're a long way from anything, and no one would hear your screams even if sound could leave this vault. Which it can't." I squatted so that I was at eye-level with him. "It's going to be a very long ride. Get ready."

Here he shook his head again. "No. No. No. Not right." He looked directly at me, his eyes nearly pleading. "Tell me this isn't who you are."

I sighed. "This is who I am, down to my core." I folded my fingers together. "There's no doubt."

He shook his head once more. "You're wrong," he explained bafflingly. "Not a stranger."

His hand whipped from around the chair with lightning speed, and he used the momentum to snatch the hammer from the end of the table. I barely had time to gasp before it connected with my skull.

I opened my eyes, slowly gaining awareness of the room.

My head throbbed in steady agony; each beat of my pulse threatened to tear the soft skin of my temples away from the bone underneath. I reached up to caress my wound, and found that my hands were bound behind me.

The man was standing above, hands at his sides with fists clenched, brow furrowed in deep thought. "Not a stranger at all," he said as though our conversation had continued uninterrupted. "You must remember Bobby," he went on with his voice now at a whisper. "I do. One thousand, nine hundred and thirteen sleepless nights until they found the ground beef that had once been my brother. Mom slit her wrists when they showed her the pieces. Dad had died of a heart attack after the first year. I had only one thing left to live for.

Your Dreams Taste Like Candy

"And now I've found it," he said, dropping to his haunches. "A lot of inheritance money can buy a lot of answers. You cannot possibly be surprised to find that the man who kidnaps your victims lacks a certain moral fiber. It wasn't hard to purchase the truth about what you did to him. Another million convinced him to make it appear as though I was your next victim. To make it seem like I was drugged. To use handcuffs that can easily be unlocked." He took a deep breath and let it out slowly. "And he knows that there's no need to fear vengeance from you."

Realization was solidifying itself in my mind. I began to cry. Both my face and my pant leg were soaked in less than a minute.

"I'm sorry," I choked. "Please don't do this. You're good and I'm not. Don't be like me." Pathetic, I know. I simply didn't give a shit about dignity at the moment.

He was unmoved. "The first thing you're going to do is to write your confession, so all your friends and family can know what you truly are."

My eyes flew wide open. "No. No! I'm a CFO, well-respected – please! Even if you kill me, please leave my reputation intact! It's all I have left!"

It only took one swing of the hammer to break my tibia. Remember that scene from Misery?

Worse than that.

I broke quickly.

"And when I'm done with the confession?" I asked, lips trembling. "Will you be the better man and let me go?"

He just stared above my head in silence for so long that I thought he would never answer. When he finally spoke, it was barely audible.

"Bobby was the better man," he explained.

I knew then.

I looked up at the IV of blood and started to shake.

"Yes," he explained calmly without looking at me. "I know that you're A positive as well. I know that this building is too remote to hear any screams engineered within."

He finally looked down and made eye contact with me.

"It's going to be a very, *very* long ride." He breathed deeply, his chest puffing outward before collapsing, eyes blazing like the flame from an acetylene torch.

"Get ready."

HUMAN BEINGS
AND OTHER MONSTROSITIES

-1-

TO BE PERFECTLY FRANK, I HATED TALKING TO GREG.

My particular line of work was pleasant enough to exempt me from much face-to-face time with my immediate supervisor.

Unfortunately, of course, some contact is inevitable.

"So," Greg sighed, easing his girth into the seat behind him. "Why are we having this meeting?"

I dropped my slender frame into the chair opposite. "Um. You called me in to have a meeting, Greg."

He blinked, then sighed in disappointment. "You picked up a previously undocumented cryptid last week, which was sent to Cheyenne Mountain. Why was there an undocumented subject in your area?"

I tried not to be condescending. "Because, well, if we had known where it was, then... it wouldn't have been previously undocumented. All wild subjects have to be undocumented before we can discover them."

He looked at me with a mixture of confusion and disgust. "I realize that finding these subjects can be frightening, Lisa. But that's no excuse to let it affect your work." He sniffed. "And if you can't deal with the rigors of this job, I'll find someone who can. Everyone else in your position is at least 5' 8" and 160 pounds."

My blood began to boil, but I learned long ago not to show any emotion in front of Greg. I forced a smile. "I can assure you that I wasn't afraid. If you'll read the reviews from the extraction team, and the medical report of the missing boy who I found, everyone gave me glowing reviews."

Greg slowly took off his glasses before leaning forward in his chair. "Lisa, I feel that you're often a challenge to my authority."

I had learned to keep my mouth shut in these moments, but I'm sure my face was crimson.

Greg sighed. "The subject that you picked up last week, all 867.72 kilograms of it, has been residing in Cheyenne Mountain's Environmental Niche Replication Program. It's several hundred acres of Colorado wilderness that's cleverly blockaded from any civilian entry."

I nodded. "Thank you for explaining that, Greg... but I was the lead consultant in designing this particular E. N. R. P."

Greg scowled. "We've just got new orders from Washington," he explained gruffly. Here he tossed a stack of papers across the desk at me. "DoiBou needs to clear out this E. N. R. P. of all undocumented subjects."

I stared at him in confusion. "Clear... out? Where will they go?"

Greg shrugged. "Last week's subject has chromatically desirable optic receptors – I think that's the phrase they used."

My jaw dropped. "People like his eye color?"

He stared back in contemplation. "When ground into a powder, it's apparently almost three percent less expensive than the leading black food coloring."

I nearly leapt out of my chair. "You're going to kill him and take out his eyes? Why?"

Greg sighed deeply. "The federal government's official position is that it doesn't exist."

"What?" I spat. "Of course he exists."

Greg shook his head. "The official position is that there's no concrete evidence one way or the other, so there cannot be a policy that recognizes the existence of the subjects contained within the E. N. R. P. at Cheyenne Mountain. Therefore, DoiBou has been instructed to terminate all subjects therein."

I closed my eyes and pulled several of my hairs out.

"If your emotional condition prevents you from being able to complete your task, Lisa, there are stronger people who are capable."

Your Dreams Taste Like Candy

I controlled my breathing. It wasn't easy. "I'm absolutely fine, Greg. But you see that the order to *dispose* of something inherently *implies* that it exists."

He blinked several times. "The official position is that they do not exist."

I sighed. "Yes, I just – look, never mind! If they don't exist, why not simply release him back into the wild? Why are they going to kill him?"

Greg gazed at me stoically. "They're not going to kill him," he said matter-of-factly. "You are."

I stared back, slack-jawed.

"Well, that wraps things up, Lisa," he shot in a chipper voice.

I stood up to walk away, shell-shocked.

"You know, they really screwed up the name of our department," he explained (mostly to himself) as I walked out the door. I turned back to see him brooding and grave. "They call it the Department of the Interior, but it only covers the outside stuff."

I was airlifted to Cheyenne Mountain in a daze. By the time we had landed, though, my resolve had returned.

Though Greg had come with us in the helicopter, I knew that he was outranked once we were on the ground.

"I'm not killing that cryptid," I explained to a mustachioed man at the gate. I could tell that he was in charge, because everyone around him seemed to be afraid of him.

He looked down at me. "Okay," he responded simply.

I sputtered. "Yes – well – so that's it?"

"Sure," he explained. "The only reason you were requested is because they wanted the subject to be euthanized humanely." He turned away from me to stare at the cobalt Colorado sky.

I felt betrayed by how beautiful the firmament was in this moment. I wondered if the same immortal hand in distant deeps and skies had truly wrought both the hunter and the prey.

"It will be a lot easier without that concern," the man continued, his hands clasped behind his back. "A 7 millimeter Winchester ballistic silvertip to the thigh should cause death via hemorrhaging within twenty-four hours.

Your Dreams Taste Like Candy

It is far less risky that the tranquilizer they had suggested you use before termination. Frankly, there's no telling how vicious that wild beast could get while my men are putting themselves at risk."

"24 hours to die? That will be torture! You don't have to do that, he's not dangerous!" I nearly shrieked.

He glanced back. "Don't worry, he won't be a threat if everyone remains in the Jeep. Frankly, I'm glad to hear that you'll be staying out of harm's way. I don't think you realize what you'd be getting into with this monster. You'd better stay with Greg, where it's safe."

My world spun. I grabbed my head in my hands and walked away from the group.

I focused on the crisp alpine air. I took in the fifty-mile view of wilderness, an expanse that was all at once both vast beyond comprehension yet exempt from the passage of time.

I thought about why I took this job in the first place.

Then I returned to the people in charge. "I – I'll do it," I responded meekly. "Give me the tranquilizer gun and the rifle." I blinked away a rogue tear that I was determined not to let them see. "But I'll need a bag of red gummy bears to do things right."

I bounced back and forth as the Jeep drove ever farther into the wilderness of the Cheyenne Mountain E. N. R. P. The rifle slid from side to side in my lap.

"Did George love Lennie?" Mrs. Neese asked as she walked the rows of my seventh-grade class. "Hmm? He shot Lennie in the head. Most people would declare themselves unable do that to a person they loved." She stopped pacing, and for reasons I'll never understand, chose to look directly at me. "But I have to ask 'most people' a very specific question. If choosing not to kill someone is a result of your own discomfort, doesn't that mean you love yourself more than you love anyone else?"

Here she leaned in towards me and seemed to tune everyone else out. "If your definition of love isn't COMPLETELY sacrificing your own comfort, then how would you define it?"

Your Dreams Taste Like Candy

My hands were too numb to tremble as I filled the bolt-action rifle with its deadly contents. I loaded the chamber with a decisive *snap*, then returned it to my lap.

I joined DoiBou because I love the unknown parts of the world. Fear is power, but only to a certain few, and extracting fear is nothing different from extracting human potential.

But sometimes the task of being human requires us to build impossible hope from nothing more than broken pieces.

I am being forced to kill something that I love because I love it.

That much of my humanity, at least, remains intact.

I turned away from the rest of the people in the Jeep so that I didn't have to hide my tears.

The vehicle plunged onward, unabated, into the hidden forest with the futile goal of finding something more monstrous than what was already riding therein.

-2-

I thought about turning the rifle on everyone else in the Jeep. Given the advantage of surprise, I'm pretty sure I could have taken the three of them out pretty quickly.

After that?

The only realistic option seemed to be running headlong into the forest, living like the cryptids we worked so hard to hide, never to be seen again by the world's deadliest animal.

I stared down at the gun in my lap. It bounced harmlessly from side to side, looking docile and tame. I had nineteen bullets to do the job, and thirteen tranquilizer darts, because the true hunter is more concerned with killing than it is with humanity.

And *I* was too much of a coward to shoot these assholes.

Too much of a coward *not* to kill an innocent creature.

The Jeep came to a sudden stop, slamming my face against the headrest in front of me. No one acknowledged my grunt of pain.

Your Dreams Taste Like Candy

"Now *that* is one big pile of shit," the mustachioed man quipped. He turned his head around to face me. "You're up, McMurry. I'm told that you DoiBou folks love this shit. So go do your thing," he finished, flicking his head toward a watermelon-sized pile of fecal matter on the ground.

It was only when they slammed the car door behind me that I realized I would be alone.

"Wait – how to I get back?" I called out.

"It's a two-mile southwest hike back to the edge of the E. N. R. P.," the man shouted as the Jeep spun around. "We'll have Greg waiting for you."

If he said anything else, it was lost in the rumble of the receding engine.

I was alone.

It was an improvement, to be honest. And I didn't even mind hiking the two miles back. But I knew Greg would be *pissed* at having to wait for me, and every minute that ticked by would be another strike against me.

I pocketed the tranquilizer gun, shouldered the rifle, and plunged into the forest to kill an innocent monster.

Chamberlain had a speech memorized from Shakespeare and gave it proudly, the old man listening but not looking, and Chamberlain remembered it still: 'What a piece of work is man... in action how like an angel!' And the old man, grinning, had scratched his head and then said stiffly, 'Well, boy, if he's an angel, he's sure a murderin' angel.'"

I had never understood how anybody could relate to a killer.

I thought about this as I noticed a large swath of broken twigs and branches.

There was *always* a clear line between 'right' and 'wrong' during my childhood.

I reflected on this as I snuck behind a tree and stared into the shadow of a perfectly occluded corner of foliage.

Being a "good girl" was the loftiest goal for me. Honesty would always trump deceit.

I wondered about this while pulling the bag of red gummy bears from my pocket.

Well... you know what they say about well-behaved women.

I threw the gummy bears toward the trunk of a nearby tree. They bounced among its roots and lodged themselves in place.

I waited.

Your Dreams Taste Like Candy

It took several minutes.

And then the shadow moved.

"Ffffffsssssssnuuuuuuuuu?" the voice asked cautiously. A large, brown, furry mass emerged slowly from the leaves. His enormous paw reached toward the ground, flopped about, then snapped shut like a bear trap. The arm then disappeared once again into the shadows, where I saw an ephemeral hint of the snack going into the silhouette of his open mouth.

Crunch.

"Fffffffssssssneeeeeee!" he screamed in excitement.

I reached a trembling hand into my pocket, and closed my fingers on the cool metal of the tranquilizer gun.

The cryptid burst from the shadows. His black, round eyes were blazing with excitement. The row of crooked canines that made up his enormous underbite was coated in a thick sheen of drool that ran down the corner of his mouth and drenched most of his chin.

I pulled the tranquilizer gun out of my pocket and pointed it forward.

All pretenses of hiding now gone, he bent over and presented his brown, furry boulder of an ass to me as he gnawed hungrily at the tree roots.

I aimed.

With an enormous grunt and a deafening crack, a sudden burst of sunlight blinded me. Heart racing, I dove behind the nearest tree. If my gasping breaths didn't give away my position, I was sure that the jackhammer in my heart would do so posthaste.

But when I peeked my head around the corner, I realized that I would remain unnoticed.

The cryptid had been unable to reach the gummy bears lodged in the tree roots, so he had decided to move them aside. He had grabbed them in his hand, and pulled.

And had tossed the whole damn tree aside.

The sudden absence of a leafy canopy is what had caused the burst of sunlight, and the cryptid didn't spare me a glance. He didn't seem to have *any* grasp of how strong he was, and was apparently as unfazed as if he'd just removed a troublesome leaf. He was sitting on his great rear end, knees straight and legs directly out in front of him, munching noisily with his mouth wide open. A piece of candy flew out of his face and landed in his belly fur, causing him to bend his head down and closely examine his navel.

Your Dreams Taste Like Candy

"FFffflluuuu?" he asked in genuine confusion, causing the ground to rumble slightly. He found the hairy bear, held it in front of his face with joy, then called out in triumph. "Ffffllleeeeee!" he explained happily before popping the furry candy into his mouth.

He chewed very loudly.

I didn't know why the world had gotten blurry until I wiped the tear from my face.

And that's when I made up my mind.

"Hey!" I screamed at him, waving the gummy bears high above my head. "You hungry for more mass-produced obesity tablets?"

He snapped his head toward my direction, mesmerized by the candy.

It never dawned on him to look at my gun. He clearly had no idea what it was.

I pocketed the tranquilizer.

Then the cryptid arose, all seven feet of him, and stalked toward me, eyes fixated on the prize in my hands.

"Okay," I breathed nervously, "let's throw caution to the wind and get you out of here. You can be discreet, right?"

He walked into a young pine tree, instantly reducing it to splinters.

"Great," I responded, continuing to walk steadily away from him. "Just... great. Now I designed this E. N. R. P., so I know all its weaknesses. This preserve is designed to be a barrier from the *forest*, so that's the area that gets the most monitoring. We'll walk back toward the main compound and sneak you out near there. Nobody will expect such a bold move. The closer we are to danger, the further we'll be from harm."

He continued to advance on me, staring only at the candy in my hand.

"And of course, you can't understand a damn word I'm saying. I am free to tell you whatever I want right now. I can confess that I think Joe Biden is sexy. Doesn't matter. The only important thing is that you follow me on a two-mile jaunt through these woods."

I took a deep breath, then turned toward the southwest and started running headlong into the forest.

"So what they say, in case you're wondering," I offered as I continued to run from the wilderness monster now chasing me through the woods, "is that we rarely make history."

Your Dreams Taste Like Candy

The whipping of the branches against my face, chest, and legs was enough to mute the voice in my head.

I'm glad for that. I was sick of hearing "So you know this is crazy, right?" on a continual mental loop.

The frustrated cryptid chased behind me in a kind of lumbering power walk. Though I didn't turn around to look, I knew that a wide swath of splintered trees and terrified squirrels surely lay in his wake.

"Ffffffffsssssssnuuuuuu!" he shouted every time I dared to believe that he might be quieting down.

Yep. This was batshit crazy.

I knew this E. N. R. P. well enough (and had spent sufficient time outdoors) to realize that we were getting close to the main compound. But even I was caught off-guard when I stumbled into a clearing and found a building just fifty feet ahead.

My heart stopped. If we were caught, the cryptid would be killed, and I would rot away in some God-forsaken cell beneath Cheyenne Mountain.

I turned around and faced the lumbering creature. "Stop right there and SHUT UP!" I screamed out of pure impulse. Yes, I know it was a stupid thing to do.

But heaven help me, it worked.

He came to a sudden stop, then stared at me, mouth agape.

"Um... good boy! Here you go!" I whispered, pulling a red gummy bear from the bag in my pocket and tossing it into the sky.

He opened his mouth greedily, but to no avail. The gummy bear bounced off of his forehead and fell to the ground. He quickly dove into the dirt and slurped it up, chewing in loud smacking noises.

I turned back around in an attempt to find a way past the compound.

And that's when my blood froze mid-beat.

Greg was standing idly by himself, staring aimlessly at the sky above.

Waiting for me, just like they said he would be.

Shit.

My mind began to race, with only my heartbeat going faster. A plan formulated in my head, seemingly of its own accord. I would have to tranquilize the cryptid (not my first choice, but by far the least of all evils), then hunker down in the bushes. I could spend the time wondering what the "SM" engraved on the gun might mean. I'd move out to get Greg's attention just as the sun was setting, which looked to be about two hours away. We'd write up the report, and I'd sneak out to evacuate my fluffy friend back to the wilderness. The lack of a body would be problematic, but it was a big fucking E. N. R. P., and it would be believable enough to say I'd simply lost him in the woods. What with the fact that I'd been abandoned by everyone (with hardly any equipment, I might add), it could be an easy enough sell.

Swallowing my nausea would be the biggest challenge in offering the "don't blame me, I'm just a girl" argument.

But I'd done it plenty of times before.

The cryptid was now sniffing furiously around the forest floor, sounding like the world's biggest bloodhound as he desperately tried to draw a scent through the tiny slits that made up his nose.

Quietly, I withdrew the tranquilizer gun from my pocket. And as I did so, the edge of the gummy bear packet peeked out as well.

"FFFFFSSSSSSSNEEEEEE!!!" the crypid shouted. The sound echoed off of the building.

Then he sprinted toward me.

It was loud. Especially when he accidentally kicked a tree from the ground in his excitement.

I groaned and turned around.

Yeah. Greg had noticed.

He had started running toward me as well. I stood frozen in the middle as two large beasts ran into a collision course.

"Give me the damn rifle, Lisa!" he screamed. "I told them they shouldn't have trusted you with it!"

Time teetered on edge as I immediately understood what was about to happen.

I had maybe three seconds until both of them smashed into me. The rifle wasn't going to do me any favors, so I spun around and flung it into the bushes behind my back. Then I pulled the tranquilizer pistol out and pointed it at my new friend before turning to block Greg. Hopefully, I could subdue the cryptid quickly enough to convince my boss that killing him was unnecessary.

I held out my hand and yelled at Greg to stop.

He did not stop.

Instead, he reached for the tranquilizer gun as the two of us smacked into each other.

Hard.

Pain. Stars in my eyes. The taste of copper. One hand *shoving* my face into the ground, the other trying to rip my fingers off, heaving, grunting, instinctively trying to clutch the tranquilizer pistol as it was angrily pulled from my grip.

I yelled, tried to shake him off of me, failed, and made one last desperate grab as the gun began to slide away from me.

He slammed my hand against the ground.

FFFFFFFT "Ow!"

Greg rolled off of me, clutching his head.

Gasping for breath, my heart threatening to break my ribs, I got to my knees and looked across at Greg.

He was sitting upright, a vacant look clouding his face. A large angry dart, filled with enough sedatives to kill Ozzy Osbourne, was sticking out of my boss's temple.

For a moment, the world stopped spinning. The intense *wrongness* of the situation crystalized in that instant, burning my memory with the indelible sight of his suffering.

"No no no NO NO NO *NO!*" I screamed, lunging at him. I reached my hand forward, feeling my fingers wrap around the dart in mid-leap.

I pulled.

There was resistance as the needle popped out of his skin, but it emerged intact. I collided with Greg's chest, and we fell to the ground.

For half a second, I didn't move.

I dreaded the sight of what lay before me. I didn't want to look.

I knew I had to look.

I slowly pressed on the ground, lifting myself up so that I could gaze down at Greg's injury.

He was immobile. The only sign of life in my boss was the blood that poured steadily from his temple.

I looked down, shaking, to see that his blood was all over my hands.

-4-

No, I didn't actually want to kill Greg. Active hatred is difficult for me to harvest; no one can make immoral decisions unless there's *something* good within them that they have chosen to overlook. Besides, creating hatred means splitting your soul, you see, and hiding part of it.

Honestly, I just wanted Greg to go away.

But not like this. I don't even know if I was screaming as I shook his frame, begging him to wake up, convinced that his entire life had been snuffed out by a stupid fight.

I checked his mouth for respiration.

He moaned.

I *know* I screamed that time. I had fallen flat on my ass as he was sitting up. But when I had finally quieted myself and focused on my injured boss, I didn't understand what I was seeing.

He was smiling.

It was a vacant, creepy sort of expression that hinted his mind was even more absent than usual. He glared at me and parted his lips even wider. His teeth were rimmed with blood.

A chill ran up my spine, and then back down again. The lengthening shadows and crisp coolness of the air did nothing to stave off the impending shivers. "Greg?" I asked softly. "Greg, are you okay?"

His empty stare locked on me as drool began to slide down the corner of his mouth.

I understood all at once. I had pulled the tranquilizer dart out of his head almost immediately, but enough must have seeped into his temple to produce…

Greg's head fell bizarrely to the side, though his eyes remained fixed on me.

…well, it produced *this*.

What options did I have? I couldn't leave him to die, but my superiors were going to be *very* curious about the sudden onset of apparent brain damage.

And there was, of course, the issue of the seven-foot beast that had followed me out of the forest.

This whole situation was going to be quite awkward.

"Ffffffffssssnisshhh?" came the rumbling voice from behind me.

Your Dreams Taste Like Candy

I was nearly bowled over as the cryptid brushed clumsily past. To my horror, he reached out for Greg.

Before I could do anything, he had laid a great, hairy paw upon Greg's head.

And carefully lifted his skull from its crooked position.

"Ffffffffsssssssneeeeeee!" he breathed happily.

My heart stopped as I saw him reaching for Greg's jaw. Regardless of his intentions, he could rip Greg in half without realizing it.

But my fears were put to rest when I saw that the cryptid was putting red gummy bears inside Greg's drooling mouth.

"Wait," I started, suppressing a laugh, "I don't think he can chew right-"

I stopped when the cryptid grabbed Greg's jaw and began mashing his teeth together, gently causing him to chew up the gummy bear. My hairy friend did not seem at all bothered by the resultant stream of drool that cascaded down upon his arm.

When the cryptid was satisfied with Greg's mastication, he tilted the man's head back. Greg gulped involuntarily, then dropped his jaw once more as the cryptid released it.

Greg smiled.

"FFFFFFSNNUNUNUNU!" the cryptid shouted. Then he scooped the man up in his great arms and buried his face into Greg's chest, wrapping him tight as could be while twisting back and forth. Greg's limbs danced freely, but he offered no resistance.

Greg had become a doll.

Then the cryptid jumped up and down with excitement. He shook the trees and caused the ground to tremble.

"WHOA there, boy! I think we need to get everyone out of here before someone starts asking me some *very* awkward questions!"

I had taken two steps away before I turned back toward the bushes.

"I do *not* want to leave this here," I said mostly to myself as I plucked the rifle from the branches. "There's more than enough incriminating evidence lying around as it is."

It was hard to get the cryptid moving at first, what with his new toy and all. But my gummy bears eventually won him over when he realized that

Your Dreams Taste Like Candy

Greg wouldn't eat pine cones, and we were once again racing through the forest as the sun truly began to set.

I came to a halt as I recognized the hidden edge of the E. N. R. P. An occluded barrier ran cleverly underneath the foliage. It emitted pheromones, subsonic and supersonic pulses, and random magnetic fields that were designed to keep out the wildlife.

There was also a fence hidden underneath the leaves as a final stopgap to anyone who didn't get the message.

To clarify, the fence was for humans. Only humans needed that many hints to understand.

But the far western corner of the barrier stopped just before it met the wall of the compound. That gap allowed Interior Department employees more complete access to the grounds, and security concerns were offset by the hidden cameras stationed at regular intervals around the wall.

I *really* hoped that I remembered the exact location of every camera.

I could feel my own pulse in my ears as I very slowly and very carefully snuck my way along the edge of the wall. The cryptid, for the most part, seemed to pick up on my body language.

Not for the first time, I wondered just how much of our behavior animals truly understood, and how intelligent it would prove them to be if they had been faking ignorance since the break of civilization.

Inch by inch, we picked our way along the edge of the wall. The cryptid followed my lead, dragging Greg's limp form across the grass. Past the hidden border.

Out into the wild.

It didn't seem that we had been picked up by the camera, because no MP or Interior guys were waiting to meet us.

I breathed easy.

The cryptid continued to take several steps after I had stopped. He continued walking until he was twenty feet ahead of me.

But at twenty feet, one inch, he stopped. Turning around slowly, he looked at me in alarmed confusion. Greg still dangled placidly from his arms, and he seemed greatly content in his place.

"You go on now," I commanded. I didn't realize how hard things were going to be until I heard the hitch in my own breath. "And you take Greg with you. They would just subject him to a lifetime of medical experiments here. Besides," I continued as the first involuntary tear began to fall, "I can tell that you love him, and I think he needs that in his life."

Greg continued to smile emptily.

I don't have any *proof* that the poor cryptid understood even the slightest amount of what I was communicating.

But I knew.

And he knew it, too.

"Fsnu," he explained meekly.

I shook my head adamantly. "You need to get out of here now. That's it. Vamoose." I gulped. "Goodbye."

His enormous black eyes began to glisten. The teeth of his underbite trembled, and his lower lip started vibrating quickly.

I finally lost it when he took a solitary step in my direction.

"STOP IT!" I screamed at him. "You need to get the fuck away from here! Now! They could still be coming for us! I just set you free! Go! Don't wait!"

He slackened his arms, holding them wide like he wanted to give me a hug. In that moment, his raw innocence was set on display with all the blatancy of a splayed corpse at the deli counter.

I saw red. "*That* is the kind of stupid innocence that will get you killed!" I shrieked at him.

He remained in place, clearly confused.

Then he took another step in my direction.

It was too much. I picked up a rock from the ground and hurled it at him. He immediately stopped when the rock careened into his soft, fuzzy stomach.

But it was his spirit that I'd hurt, not his belly. He stopped dead in his tracks.

"Fsnip?"

My rage boiled over. I flung another stone at his right shoulder, then a different at his left. *Thump, thump.*

When he continued to stare at me in hurt confusion, I took aim at his forehead and fired. As it sailed through the air, some distant part of me wanted the rock to miss, because I couldn't bear the thought of watching him suffer.

That distant part was disappointed.

CRACK

Your Dreams Taste Like Candy

The missile to his forehead halted his advance, rooting him firmly to the spot. The cryptid's own tears were flowing freely now. A look of the most profound betrayal was carved into his enormous, innocent face.

"RUN AWAY!" I screamed before wiping my eyes on the sleeves of my shirt. Then, quietly to myself, "far away from here."

He let me be still for a moment.

Then the cryptid extended his paw in my direction.

He was offering me the last of his red gummy bears.

I understood in that moment just how powerful his innocence was, and how difficult it would be to break it. Even if he escaped today, there had been too much of a ruckus to keep him hidden from the government, which would be searching for him. He would never again be safe in the wild.

And life in captivity would be hell for a creature that did not understand distrust.

I nodded to myself with confidence, but every twinge caused me pain that was both physical and metaphysical.

Numbly, I lifted the rifle and loaded it. The bolt snapped into place with a grim finality.

"I'm sorry" was all I could muster.

I raised the rifle, aimed, and pulled the trigger.

The bullet ripped past the cryptid's right ear, spraying blood into the air as it tore the edge of his tender flesh.

"FFFFSSSSSSHHEEEEEEEE!" he screamed, dropping Greg and curling into a fetal position. He rocked back and forth as blood ran across soft paws that pressed hard against his damaged ear.

I loaded the gun again. My fingers worked by feel, as my vision had become blurry. After snapping the bolt into place, I wiped my eyes and looked down at the cryptid.

Tears were tumbling down his face like tiny waterfalls. His mouth was open, and his breaths came in agonized, ragged sobs of "WAH-WAH-WAHHH!" The pointy teeth, which had once appeared so large and imposing, suddenly seemed very small.

He trembled as he looked up at me once more. The cryptid instinctively raised his left arm in a protective stance as he flinched – but the right one reached out toward me.

He was offering the final gummy bear as a truce.

Your Dreams Taste Like Candy

"You're not GETTING it!" I screamed. I raised the rifle and aimed it at his head. "Do you want another bullet?!"

"AARRRRP!" he yelled back, dropping his last gummy bear as he used both arms to brace himself.

I aimed near his head and fired again. The bullet came within inches of his other ear.

This time he took the hint.

The cryptid sprang to his feet and began to run away from me.

Then he stopped.

And turned around.

He sprinted back to where he had just lay, scooped up Greg, tucked him under his arm, and once again ran away in complete terror.

He never looked back.

"Learn to be afraid of us," I blubbered to myself before sitting down on the grass and dropping the gun. The sun was starting its final descent now. Its orange and gold light illuminated the lush, green landscape in a warm glow. I remembered the root beer float.

It was wrong, all wrong.

I dropped my head into my hands and let the tears flow unabated. "Be afraid of us. It's the only way to live." A heaving sob racked my body.

"You need to leave us alone, all alone."

-5-

I walked, zombie-like, toward the compound's doors. Every tear had been wrung from my face like water from a well-twisted sponge. Barely aware of the rifle in my hand, I trudged on with the vague notion that things couldn't get worse.

That's when the Jeep came screeching toward my direction, spraying dirt and gravel as it slid to a halt. The mustachioed man was staring at me, eyes blazing with emotion.

"Get in."

Your Dreams Taste Like Candy

After surrendering the rifle, I was marched deep into the compound. A small group of men escorted me through three different security doors before depositing me into an opulent office. They shut me inside by myself, and I collapsed into a chair.

Do criminals from Cheyenne Mountain get sent to normal federal prison? I doubted it. The bowels of this particular military installation went quite deep, and I'm sure it contained secrets that everyone was better off not knowing.

I don't think I'd ever felt more alone.

I was distantly wondering whether the tears might make a reappearance after all when the mustachioed man walked through the door and rested in the chair opposite me.

"Stay seated," he commanded crisply. "Just watch." Here he snatched up a remote control and switched on a monitor that had been hidden in the wall. An image sprang to life that caused my stomach to melt deep into my colon.

That's how I found out I *didn't* know where every exterior camera had been hidden.

The footage clearly showed the cryptid wandering idly forward, Greg dangling loosely at his side. My form couldn't be seen. But I could tell from the angle that I must have been just out of sight. My eyes began to burn again as I saw the cryptid turn around, then take a tentative step toward me. While no audio was available, I could clearly recall every word that I hurled his way.

Every insult that I could muster.

Every tear that I shed.

I didn't want to watch, but I couldn't turn away when I saw the first bullet hit his ear. The second one seemed so *angry* as it caused a wave of dirt to explode by his head. The image then showed him getting up to run away before turning back to pick up Greg. The two disappeared off screen, and the footage cut out.

What was there left for me to do? I'd disobeyed orders, shot my boss, helped the cryptid escape, and allowed Greg to be lost to the forest. I sincerely doubted that I'd end up amongst a zany crew of misunderstood prisoners a la "Orange is the New Black." No, I figured I was much more likely to find myself on the business end of an alien probing stick for a fuckup of this magnitude.

The man cleared his throat. "I don't know if we've been properly introduced. I'm Captain Wrede, special liaison for inter-departmental cooperation. What I just saw on that monitor was appalling."

I tried to think of something courageous to say – but for the life of me, not a single word came to mind.

"That must have been *very* frightening for a woman," he continued.

The nausea, anger, sadness, and fear all cancelled each other out to make a neutral neural soup.

I listened.

"The fact that this cryptid was able to overpower, abscond with, and undoubtedly kill your immediate superior indicates that it is *far* more dangerous than our intelligence had previously indicated. Its resistance to .375 H & H bullets indicates that it is far *stronger* than previously believed. Your attempts to save your boss, then stand your ground after driving the beast away, indicate that you are of much tougher mettle than we had previously understood.

I did not know what was happening, so I remained very silent.

"So several of us looked over the various reports on your performance that had been filed throughout the years. When we actually sat down to read them, they painted a much different picture of you than the one we had gotten from Greg." Here he nodded confidently to himself. We passed a very long, very quiet moment together.

It was quite tense.

"Well," he quipped, not just breaking the silence but absolutely shattering it, "You'll have noticed that there is a sudden vacancy in the head office of DoiBou. I've been in talks with Secretary Bernhardt's people, and they think you're the right man for the job."

My head spun. With so many questions that I wanted answered, it seemed impossible to get everything out at once.

So I chose one at random. "You've already talked to the Interior Secretary's office in the incredibly short time since I shot – I mean, since all this happened?"

Captain Wrede eyed me suspiciously. "Certainly you must realize how quickly things happen when there's - *motivation* to enact change."

Your Dreams Taste Like Candy

The hair on my neck stood up, and nearly every other question died in my throat.

I had a feeling that the next words I said would be very important.

I took a deep breath. "So," I led with the most authoritative voice I could muster, "You'll understand that I need an increase in DoiBou's budget for tracking rogue cryptids."

Within an hour, I had redecorated Greg's office and thrown out all of his porn. It took three bottles of hand sanitizer.

I plan to keep a close eye on all local cryptid reports. My plan is to shoot every one of them on sight.

There doesn't seem to be the budget for any more bullets, so tracking devices will have to be a worthwhile substitute.

That's just the first part of my plan for the future of DoiBou. And while I like my office here in the Hayes/Fillmore Wing of the Cheyenne Mountain Satellite Compound, I fully intend to spend most of my workday outdoors.

Before leaving that night, Captain Wrede came by my new office. He looked impressed.

"Good to see you, Captain," I announced sharply, bringing his attention back to me.

"I'm ready to begin."

BROTHER, COULD YOU SPARE A DIME AND SOME WEAPONS?

-1-

MINIMUM WAGE ISN'T ENOUGH TO PROVIDE A LIVING.
Hell, it's not enough to provide *survival*.
Let's look at the math.

My wife and I each bring in $400 a week before taxes. After taxes, Kendra and I have $608.70 to sustain our existence. $300 is set aside for rent (it's what we can afford while staying in a safe-ish Charlottesville, Virginia neighborhood). $74 for groceries is used *very* quickly by three people; Ellie is eight years old and growing like a weed. That's one dollar per person for each daily meal, with $11 left over for toiletries. I work six miles from home, and Kendra clocks in eight miles away. That's 140 miles of gas between Monday and Friday, or $25. Utilities are another $25. $36 is set aside to pay for the remaining balance (and maintenance) on Kendra's shitty 1999 Toyota Corolla, $50 is needed for the monthly repairs on my 1997 Ford F150, $40 goes toward our credit card debt, and $50 covers interest on said credit card debt.

That leaves me with eight dollars and seventy cents to bring joy to my family.

Did I mention how little money we set aside for toilet paper?

Ellie didn't say a word when I gave her one of my worn-out t-shirts for her first day of third grade. She had outgrown her old clothes, and we had spent that week's $8.70 splurging on Pepsi and microwave fish sticks.

210

Your Dreams Taste Like Candy

No, my daughter didn't say a word, but there was shame in her eyes. I cried that night. Kendra held me while I sobbed.

She didn't say a word, either.

When Ellie was diagnosed with type 1 diabetes last week, I checked my life insurance policy out of sheer despair.

It turns out I'm not worth that much.

"Even with all the government assistance, Ellie's insulin will cost us $400 per month," Kendra explained calmly. We were sitting at the kitchen table, both staring fixedly away from one another. We were too far apart for physical contact. "That's $100 per week."

"We'll just get further behind if we stop the credit card payments," I offered dryly. "We're feeding Ellie too much pasta and ramen as it is, and the shitty food probably triggered the diabetes in the first place." A single tear ran down my face. I didn't wipe it away. "We can't cut back on car payments and gas, because we need them to get to work."

"We could let them shut off the electricity."

"That wouldn't be enough."

"And the water, gas, and phones."

"Still wouldn't be enough."

"How much is the off-brand shampoo?"

"I haven't bought shampoo in six months, I just run bar soap through my hair."

"I wish your mom were alive."

"I wish my dad weren't a bastard."

"We could move."

"No safe neighborhood rents apartments for $600 per month."

"Maybe Jim will let you sleep on his couch. Ellie and I could stay in the Corolla."

I stood up without a word and walked three blocks to the bar.

Your Dreams Taste Like Candy

Going to the bar is a different experience for me than you might expect. My first step is to grab the bottle of Kirkland Signature moonshine that I keep hidden under the passenger seat. The $7.99 I spent in 2017 has been responsible for all of my debauchery since then. I stole six healthy gulps that night before staggering down the street in search of freedom from myself.

John at the bar is a friend of mine, so he lets me walk in completely shit-faced and drink water at no charge.

It's the best I can get within my financial constraints.

"The thing is, John," I slurred, "even Willy fucking Loman at least *believed* that he could provide for his family in death. I don't even get that! I have no choice in the matter. It's like grabbing a live wire. No matter how much your balls get fried, you just can't let go!"

I get oddly philosophical while drunk. It's the only apparent use of my degree in English literature.

"So the question, friend," came the silky voice of the man sitting next to me, "Is what you would do if you *had* a choice?"

I slowly turned to face him as John quietly slinked away to the back room.

"I'd choose my family's well-being, shithead. The only reason I *can't* make that choice right now is because I'm a fucking loser whose only professional ability is to dig myself deeper with every week that brings me closer to death."

"Living is the method of dying," he responded darkly, "And only the dead are free. Should we call those richer, who could do with less?" I could *hear* his smile without looking at it. "What are you willing to sell for your daughter's life?"

I imagined living without Ellie.

But I could not imagine a *reason* to continue living if she were gone.

And in that moment, it really didn't matter that this man was about to lie to me.

I nodded slowly. "Whatever you're buying."

We turned toward each other. The smile playing about his lips brought no mirth to his ice-blue eyes. "I won't offer a specific dollar amount. Instead, my employer can promise a lifetime of insulin." He raised a provocative eyebrow.

Your Dreams Taste Like Candy

I downed the last of my water, raising it high above my head as I slurped the final drops before pounding the glass down on the table. I made unsteady, inebriated eye contact with the man.

"You want to know the cost," he guessed correctly. "It's straightforward: all of your inhibitions."

My own guffaw surprised even me. "Okay, friend, you've got yourself a deal. If all I've got to lose is *me*, then there just isn't that much at stake."

He nodded, then slid me a tumbler of whiskey that I hadn't noticed him drinking. "You might be hesitant, but when you wake up-"

I snatched it from his hand and drowned the bitter concoction in a single gulp.

And then, thank God, my day finally ended.

I awoke naked next to a strange woman.

Two strange women, actually. And another guy.

Everyone was naked.

And we were outside. It was late morning.

The fuck?

I tried to think, but it was like forcing Jell-O into place with a bowling ball.

I pressed my hands into the soft mud and forced myself into a sitting position. The spins did not leave my head even after I held my skull in place.

A note fluttered from my chest and landed gently on my crotch. I picked it up and struggled to read through the blurriness.

Slowly, the letters stopped dancing on the page. Moans emanated from my companions as I began to understand what I was reading.

"Where the fuck am I?" The man asked from behind me.

I ignored him as full comprehension set in.

"Life is for the strong, to be lived by the strong, and, if needs be, taken by the strong," read the note. My English degree was setting off internal alarm bells, but I could not quite remember why.

I kept reading.

"You'll find this game worth playing, Rainsford."

Your Dreams Taste Like Candy

My stomach dropped, but it would not do me the courtesy of stopping once it hit the floor.

Upon fully awakening, one of the women screamed. In response, the second woman screamed, and then the man screamed at them both.

"Where the *fuck* are we and who the *fuck* are you?" the first woman wailed.

I didn't have the energy to turn around and face them. My mouth was so dry that it took all of my willpower to force any words at all.

"I don't know who put us here, but I think I know why," I explained flatly. I finally turned to look at them as the woman stopped screaming. We all stared at each other in a moment of petrified silence.

"We're about to be hunted."

-2-

In all probability, I would have sat for hours in that daze if the first woman hadn't broken the silence.

"What the hell is that message?" she asked in a panicked voice.

She stood up and walked toward a nearby tree. Normally, I would have been consumed by the image of a curvy, naked thirty-something blonde woman, but my eye wasn't even slightly drawn in that moment.

She stopped in front of a wooden sign. I bolted to my feet and ran after her.

The sign was carefully painted. Icy comprehension whispered clearly in my ear: *someone has a very specific plan for us.*

The other man and woman stopped behind me as I took in the painted message:

It's dangerous to go alone! Take this.

Beneath it was a pile of clothes.

In a dreamlike state, we pulled garments from the pile and held them close.

214

Your Dreams Taste Like Candy

My set was a perfect fit.

Within a minute, I was wearing a t-shirt, briefs, basketball shorts, tube socks, and running shoes.

A chill shot through my spine as I realized that someone had almost certainly measured me while I was unconscious.

I snapped back to reality when the blonde woman screamed.

That's when it became apparent just how large the other man was. I happen to know that I'm exactly 75.3 inches tall; standing at least 6' 6", the man dwarfed me.

The blonde woman didn't stand a chance against him.

He ripped the shirt off of her and tossed her into the mud with casual effort. Then he squeezed uncomfortably into the stolen shirt, which was at least three sizes too small for him.

It was completely covered in a military camouflage pattern. He grabbed a too-tight pair of pants from the ground and quickly forced himself into those.

They had the same pattern. And despite the clearly uncomfortable squeeze around his biceps, the effect was striking.

Suddenly, I wished that I had taken the camouflage outfit.

I suspected that it would be practical very soon.

The blonde woman, still prone on the ground, gasped in a quiet sob. "Fuck you. You had no right to take that from me."

In response, the man snatched a pile of clothes from in front of him and threw them at the woman. "Stop your bitching and be grateful. I left you plenty."

She grabbed the outfit and scrambled into it, tears streaming down her face. She stood up, and it became very clear that the clothes were not meant for her. They cascaded ridiculously across her limbs, and her arms were too short to protrude from the ends. The pant cuffs ended in several rolls of excess fabric that sat on top of her oversized boots.

Most noticeable, however, was the fluorescent pink and blinding yellow striped pattern that covered both the shirt and pants.

"They chose sizes that were tailored to the four of us," the second woman whispered, finally breaking her silence.

I turned to face her for the first time. She was young, maybe twenty, and tiny. Her straight, shoulder-length brown hair contrasted with her pale, mousey face. The girl wore a tank top, running shorts, and shoes that were far too big for her.

"But some clothes are good for hiding, and some are best for..." she crinkled her nose in discomfort. "For being found."

The man strode over to her in three quick steps. "Is there a fucking problem with the way that I handled things?"

Mousey girl looked like she was caught between fainting and puking. "I – I'm sorry, please, I'm sorry." She backed up against a tree.

The man glanced down at her shoes, and then at his own feet. "If you're such a lady genius, then tell me why we only have three pairs of shoes for four people."

The first tears streamed down her face. "I don't know," she mumbled, "I'm so sorry, I don't know."

"Well," the man responded in a dangerous whisper, "Are you going to give them to me, or am I going to take them from you?"

I finally found my voice. "What the hell, man? Everything is fucked right now. We're going to need – friends – to get through whatever this is. Let's – let's be cool, okay? Don't take her shoes."

He turned toward me and gave a look of pure disgust. "If she needs them so bad, then maybe you'll give up yours?"

I froze. He waited for me to move.

I didn't.

"Then it's settled," he responded calmly.

He left mousey girl standing barefoot in the mud, crying softly.

I wanted to comfort her. Really, I did.

But I just couldn't.

We were already in survival mode.

For the first time, I tried to absorb my surroundings.

We'd been placed in a forest, probably still in Virginia. It was late morning. Tall oak trees dominated the rolling landscape, which was covered by patchy grass and damp mud. There were no birds singing.

My eyes wandered to the place where our clothes had lain. It was a small, wooden platform, about the size of a crate.

There was a message on it.

We had overlooked that fact in our scramble to grab the clothing.

I stepped closer. Like the one on the wooden sign, this message had been planned well before our arrival:

Your Dreams Taste Like Candy

Master using it and you can have this.

Without thinking, I dove for the wooden platform and lifted the top above my head.

A nine-millimeter pistol sat at the bottom of a dark cavity. I reached for it greedily.

My world spun. Down was no different from up. *Angrily*, pain shot through the top of my head. I reached. Found the ground. Steadied. Head fucking *hurt*. Tried to understand.

The man was holding the pistol contemplatively.

I understood.

"Why the *fuck* did you throw me on the ground?" I spat angrily. "My head hurts like hell." I touched my fingers to my temple. It was wet and sticky.

"I needed this," he mumbled without looking at me.

My blood boiled.

"We all want to get home. We should share it," I sputtered.

"No," he responded dismissively as he checked the clip and loaded the chamber.

The two women sobbed on either side of me. The pain in my head suddenly swirled into a vortex of nausea. I puked.

"Okay, folks, this is how it's gonna be," the man announced authoritatively. "We're neck-deep in Shit Creek, so everybody's going to paddle together or we're all gonna drown. This guy says we're being hunted, and that is unacceptable. Our location is known by our enemy, so we need to move, and it has to happen now. Will there be dissent?"

The crying continued from both sides, but neither one of the women spoke. It took all of my concentration to balance as I stood on shaking feet.

"So it begins," he announced matter-of-factly. "Move now, or get left behind."

He turned and approached the blonde woman. "That outfit was made to stand out. We just can't have it." He aimed the pistol at her knee.

He fired.

Blonde woman's left leg exploded in a mess of blood, and she screamed so loudly that I had to clamp my hands over my ears.

"What the FUCK?" I shouted.

Your Dreams Taste Like Candy

"Whoever's hunting us will deal with her as we vacate this area," the man yelled over her cries. "We need to split their focus as we exit a known location. I took no pleasure in it, but it had to be done."

He walked away from the screaming woman and approached me. I staggered back in fear.

The man stopped between mousey girl and me. He looked at each of us in turn. "Living is only possible for those willing to *survive*." He nodded. "I'm going to take this weapon and leave immediately. Our chances are maximized if the three of us work together, but the choice is yours. Follow me, or stay here and die."

-3-

The man turned and walked away. The sense of *breaking* overwhelmed me in that moment; the most equipped member of our group was departing, mousey girl stood rooted to the ground, and the most needy person was likely to die where she lay.

"Wait!" I screamed.

The man turned to me, but he continued walking backwards.

"Let me at least make a tourniquet for her!"

"The whole point of leaving her here is to buy us time, and every second counts," he explained firmly as he paced away. "If we hesitate, her sacrifice is worthless. Besides," he went on, nodding toward her, "a tourniquet would just prolong the inevitable. Be kind and let it happen quickly." He stopped walking. For a moment, he seemed genuinely sad. "My guess is that you're out here because you've got something worth living for." He sighed. "I advise you not to throw it all away for what you can't change." He turned and trotted into the trees.

The blonde woman was coated from neck to boot in blood, but her crying had diminished greatly. "Please," she whimpered.

Your Dreams Taste Like Candy

"Please," Ellie begged, wiping her tears on my ragged jacket, "just – just tell me that I'll be okay. Diabetes won't change me, will it?"

I had never felt like such a failure as a father. I wondered what her life would have been like if she'd been born to anyone besides me.

"I'll tell you what I can promise, honey," I responded, resting my hand on the back of her head and pulling it closer to my chest. "There are going to be some really hard times ahead for all of us. I promise that in those moments, I'll do whatever it takes to make your life as good as I can possibly make it, no matter how difficult that may be."

I felt empty as I turned away from the blonde woman and looked toward the mousey one. "We'd better move," I explained softly.

Then I broke into a jog.

A few seconds later, I heard her padding after me.

I had thought it would be impossible to leave a dying woman behind. But the impossible becomes remarkably plausible when we're forced to evaluate our true potential.

I caught up to the man. He took large, quick strides, and he didn't turn to face me when I moved in behind him.

"Terrible situations can't be made un-terrible," he quipped gruffly. "Anyone who wants to live had better embrace that reality."

I was out of breath from running, and I didn't have time to catch it as I weaved in and out of the foliage. He stayed two steps ahead of me as we moved.

"There are advantages in working together," he went on. "So let's cut the bullshit, man. You and I are each other's best allies. Be honest with yourself: what do you think would have happened if you had let me go and tried your luck with just her by your side?" He jerked his thumb over his shoulder.

Fifty yards away, mousey girl struggled to pick her way around the bushes and trees. She wasn't able to move very quickly in bare feet, and she kept slipping in the damp mud. I felt terrible for her.

But I didn't slow down.

"The highest elevation point in the vicinity is that hill," the man explained, pointing just ahead. "I'll get a better idea of where we should go from the top of it."

Your Dreams Taste Like Candy

He didn't wait for a response from me, and I offered him none.

Within two minutes, we had fulfilled the man's goal. I instinctively waited sixty feet away while he headed for a stump at the center of the hilltop's clearing. "Varsani Peak," he called out as he read yet another wooden sign. "627.62 feet." He scrambled up onto the thick, wide stump so he could get a better vantage point.

While he was observing the surrounding landscape, mousey girl came tottering up to me. She slipped and grabbed my arm for support, so I helped lift her upright. Her wide eyes betrayed pure terror, and I was struck by just how young and vulnerable she seemed in that moment.

She snapped her head around and saw that the man was looking away from us. Then she turned quickly back and pulled out a Desert Eagle .50 caliber pistol.

That was the straw that broke the camel's back. It was just a squirt, but I actually shit my pants.

"You were running too quickly to see that this had been left for us," she whispered rapidly. "This note was next to it," she hissed as she shoved a piece of paper into my hands.

It was very clear that she trusted me with the note, but not with the gun. I chose to ignore that for the moment.

I looked down and read as fast as my panicked mind would allow. The words sank in immediately, and I suddenly understood how the game had fundamentally changed in an instant.

"You know that's a *much* more powerful gun than the nine mil he's carrying?" I hissed.

She nodded solemnly, then tucked the Desert Eagle into the waistband of her shorts behind her back.

We looked up just in time to see the man take one last glance at the valley below him. Then he turned around and peered inquisitively down on us both. Without waiting for a cue, I marched up toward him.

"I can see a river not too far away," he explained cautiously. "We'll follow that. It's our best bet."

I reached his stump well ahead of mousey girl. Before she could arrive, I cut him off.

"We've got a problem," I blurted out.

He jumped down from the stump and quickly approached me before she could intercept us.

Your Dreams Taste Like Candy

"She found something that you missed. There was a much better pistol laid out for us, and she has it. She's hiding it in her waistband right now, and she's going to kill you if you don't take it from her first."

-4-

Mousey girl couldn't keep a secret. The man realized this immediately. She turned paper-white and nearly fell to her knees.

I knew I had made the right decision.

I took several deliberate steps backward as he grabbed her delicate shoulders and spun her around with a near-effortless flick of his hands. She twirled, he caught her, and then she was still.

The girl offered no resistance as the towering man plucked the Desert Eagle from her waistband and shoved her violently away. She careened into the ground with a *splorch*, her fingers and knees sinking deep into the loose mud.

"This isn't what I wanted, little girl," he lectured condescendingly as he checked the magazine and chamber. With a sharp *click*, the man loaded a round. "This is the decision you made. I'm not responsible for it."

She sprang to her feet and sprinted, wheezing and gasping in desperation. In attempting to circle around a tree for cover, she lost her footing. Bare feet haphazardly slipping in the mud, she tried and failed to find purchase with the ground.

I jogged backwards, but did not turn away from the scene in front of me.

The man breathed deeply, aimed, and pulled the trigger.

At first, the only things I felt were vertigo and an aggressive ringing in my ears. That was followed by a noxious wave of smoke. When I realized that the sudden darkness was only due to my squinting, I opened a tentative eye.

The man was sprawled on the ground in a bloody mess. Mousey girl leaned heavily against a nearby oak, shaking but unhurt.

I ran toward the man.

Your Dreams Taste Like Candy

Both arms were completely gone below the elbows. What remained of his stumps was nothing more than a vile spaghetti of skin flaps, bone shards, and blood. He had been aiming with his right eye, so that particular organ was utterly obliterated in the explosion. Enough skin had been stripped from the right side of his face that pure white bone was visible beneath the deepest shreds.

He coughed. A well of blood and teeth flowed softly from his mouth. He gasped for air.

I don't understand why I did it, but I knelt down by his side.

"Oh God," he whispered. "There's no one left to take care of my daughter." His voice was so quiet that I feared moving; the slightest adjustment might be enough to drown out his voice. "I only took that fucking deal because I was promised a lifetime of insulin." He rolled his remaining eye toward me. "Her mother's dead, and she has no family left. Where will she go?"

I poured all my effort into remaining still, convinced that my tiny movements were making too much noise.

I couldn't hear him anymore, though.

He was dead.

Suddenly repulsed, I jerked backwards.

And slipped in the mud.

My face landed directly in his exposed intestines.

The innards were hot and steamy. Layer after layer cascaded around my face, spreading wide to envelop my head and pull me deeper inward.

I slammed my palms downward and shot my head into the fresh air, then immediately wiped the chunky goop away from my face.

After several aggressive smears, I stopped cold.

I knew that smell.

I looked at my right hand.

It was *covered* in shit.

I slowly peered down at the man's shredded abdomen.

Yep. His large intestine was splayed wide open. One *very* long worm of feces stretched prominently across the center of his gut, with my handprint embedded deeply in the grime.

The warm, textured geyser slid sleekly up my esophagus and erupted violently from my mouth. One branch of the spunk snaked its way through my nasal cavity, suffocating me as twin rivulets of puke squirted powerfully from my nostrils.

When the upheaval was finally over, I collapsed on the ground in sheer exhaustion. It compared eerily to the fatigue that I experienced immediately after coitus, but this time it felt as though I had been fucked from inside of my own body.

Disgusted, I searched for a place to cleanse myself. I had to settle on a nearby pool of pitch-black water.

I did not enjoy the irony of washing in a mud puddle to make myself *cleaner*.

After I scrubbed everything that I could manage, I approached mousey girl. She was still trembling against the same tree. Blanched, exhausted, and terrified, she didn't seem to care about how dirty I was.

"I'm sorry that approach scared you, but he needed to believe that you were completely terrified. For what it's worth, he reacted just as I'd hoped."

I pulled the note out and read it once more.

Give this away

With cocky aplomb

Beware of the trigger-

This "gun's" just a bomb!

Waves of doubt crashed over me with the weight of retrospect.

There had been no way to know if the note was a lie. I had simply assumed that the man would force himself on mousey girl, that she would be petrified, and that he would try to shoot her.

I could have been wrong about any of those things.

I could have misinterpreted the note.

The entire setup could have been an elaborate lie.

I did the best I knew how to do in the moment, painfully aware that other people would live and die by my inadequate efforts.

I wanted mousey girl to speak. I needed her gratitude, her wrath, her explanation of what my actions had meant to her – anything.

She looked past me, nodded, then turned away.

In silence, we went on.

I almost suggested looking for the one nine-mil or trying to salvage his size thirteen boots. But a glace at the stewy pasta that had formerly been a human being confirmed undoubtedly that all equipment had been annihilated, and that whatever pieces remained were very, very gross.

We had walked for no more than two minutes when we encountered the next wooden sign.

Mousey girl read it and screamed.

-5-

And while she screamed, I found myself completely unable to move.

The wooden sign was heavily worn. It had clearly been there for quite some time, bearing a simple, unchanging message:

The hunt is over. You are as safe as you choose to be.

I walked numbly past the sign, expecting a significant change as I passed through the invisible barrier that the message represented.

I was surprised to find everything the same on the other side.

"And that, my friends, is *choice*," came a voice from nearby.

I was so covered in foulness that there was no way to discern if I shit or pissed myself.

In all honesty, I probably did both. But I was beyond caring at that point.

"Would you choose to have a seat?"

I found the source of the voice standing not twenty feet away. His smile brought no mirth to his ice-blue eyes.

Part of me yearned to strangle the man, while another part wanted to hug him in relief.

Instead, I placidly did as he asked.

Your Dreams Taste Like Candy

A rustic picnic bench sat next to an ancient wooden table. Mousey girl and I walked to it and sat down in a daze. He stood authoritatively on the other side.

"You want to know how the hunt can be over when you never met the hunters," he stated matter-of-factly. It was a declaration, not a question – and he was entirely correct. "Yet part of you already knows that you *did* meet the hunters, and they were quite successful against their quarry."

Sudden understanding overwhelmed me. My stomach, already weak, betrayed me once more. I turned and vomited chunky bile onto the forest floor.

"I am duly impressed," he added. "It's very rare that *two* hunters survive the half-mile walk."

Mousey girl was dizzyingly stoic. "Will we get our promised payment?" she asked coolly.

"Remind me of our agreed-upon terms," he responded formally.

"You promised a lifetime of insulin for my daughter, and you'd better fucking deliver." I tried to sound threatening, but my scratchy, wavering voice reeked of desperation.

"And *your* price," he asked mousey girl in a businesslike tone.

"My girlfriend was just diagnosed with ovarian cancer," she answered meekly. "She was brought to the U. S. illegally as an infant, and her mom's employers fired her when they found out about the medical request. She can't afford new insurance or the surgery and chemo that will improve her odds." Her voice finally cracked. "The treatment plan is there, we just-" She sobbed once and fell silent.

"Do you believe that my employer will live up to his end of the bargain?" he asked silkily.

Rage bubbled in my gut. "He *has* to." My sentence fell flat.

I felt acutely aware that he was standing while we were sitting.

He let the silence linger.

"He will," the man continued. "It's really not that much money in the grand scheme of things."

He seemed content.

"Wait," I shot back, panic rising once more. "Wait. The man – he said he had a daughter. She – she needs insulin. Will you save her?"

Your Dreams Taste Like Candy

"No," he responded simply. "Her father chose not to overcome his own inhibitions and see what was in front of him. The deal was not completed."

"Tell me who she is," I sputtered. "Let me share *my* daughter's insulin, let me help her!" My breaths came in ragged, heavy gasps.

"No," he answered in the same tone. "Look at what is in front of you. Understand what is real. That girl's medical condition is exactly the same as it was before you came across the knowledge of her. Thousands of people are dealing with the same exact issues. You chose to be led into action by an exchange of knowledge – but were never moved by the permanence of truth. You're perfectly aware of suffering around you, but simply don't care if you have no direct experience. If you could ignore the girl's illness before it affected you, there is no reason to expect a change simply because you've allowed your emotions to think on behalf of your brain. This weakness is why you are the one accepting deals that are arranged by those who choose to be powerful."

My brain seemed to float. I tried to grasp any of the million spinning thoughts that twinkled in my head. I latched onto the only concept I was able to articulate:

"Why?"

He made no attempt to smile this time. "Dying is the method of living," he responded darkly, "And only some are free."

He turned to walk away.

"Stop," mousey girl ordered. He remained still, but did not face us. "How do we know that you'll deliver what you've promised?"

"You're entirely at the mercy of trusting us," he answered simply. "Stop pretending that you were unaware of this fact. Every person relies on the goodwill of every other person, every single day of his or her life. Would you cross a street or eat a meal if that weren't the case?"

Neither of us had a response to that.

"Just explain how we can get home," I finally requested.

He pointed to his right as he resumed walking away. "Interstate 64 runs parallel to the path you've been following. It's 300 feet past that copse of trees. I left your phones and clothes by an Adopt-A-Highway sign. You can't miss it."

And with that, he disappeared from sight.

Your Dreams Taste Like Candy

The sound of traffic materialized almost immediately after we started walking in his indicated direction. A few minutes later, we emerged on the side of the road.

We looked left, right, and left again before spotting the man's promised sign. "Highway adopted by Crozet High School – celebrating 106 years," it announced to the world.

Only the two of us seemed to care about the treasure on the ground below.

Uber had never seemed so magical.

"Wait," I nearly screamed as the car stopped in front of her apartment. "What's your name?"

She smiled sadly. "Isn't it easier if we choose not to know?"

She was right, of course. Names are only given to define perspective. The hunt is lost the moment we cede control.

And the hunt can only ever be won by those who lack the weakness of empathy.

Unless, of course, everyone chooses to get along.

THE NICE MAN INVITED ME INTO THE CREEPY HOUSE

EVERYONE KNEW THAT MR. SILLIS WAS GUILTY.

Everyone also knew that Mr. Sillis was rich. That's why he lived in a giant house on the end of Hill Street. It's the reason six of the most expensive defense attorneys in the state were by his side at the funeral.

It is, in fact, the reason that no one went to jail after they laid his wife and young son in the ground.

He said he wasn't guilty.

But everyone knew how dangerous he really was.

And no one questioned why he never shed a tear.

"Don't go trick-or-treating at the Sillis house on the end of Hill Street," every parent in town would say to their children. The kids would roll their eyes, because they'd heard the same warning dozens of times.

So when little Suzy Walker, four feet tall, walked up the Sillis driveway on Halloween night, she was all alone. She smiled innocently as her little black cape bounced along behind her, head bobbing slightly as she worked her way up the steep path.

Mr. Sillis looked surprised when he opened the door. "Hello there, little girl. I, um, wasn't expecting any trick-or-treaters." He looked around her. "Are you all alone?"

"Yep!" she squeaked with an innocent smile.

Your Dreams Taste Like Candy

Mr. Sillis looked up and down his driveway again, and began to smile himself. "Why don't you come inside? I might have some candy in my kitchen." He stepped aside, and little Suzy Walker trotted right in.

He quietly closed the door behind her.

When he looked back, she was staring at him expectantly. "I'm pretty hungry, you know."

He nodded, rubbing his hands together. "I... can understand that hunger. Please... follow me."

She didn't move. "It's been a while since I've eaten, you know. One meal can sustain me for *quite* some time. So I like to be... *selective* in my choices." Her feet remained in place, but her hand reached up and locked the door. A smile grew on her face, and fangs grew from her gums. "And screams taste like candy. But I bet you already knew that."

No one who looked like little Suzy Walker was ever seen again. But she wasn't missed.

That's because no one by that name lived in that town. Anyone, except for the reclusive Mr. Sillis, would have known that.

Mr. Sillis was never seen alive again.

He wasn't missed, either.

But that was for different reasons altogether.

THE FITFUL SLUMBER OF AZATHOTH

-1-

THE LIGHTS WENT OUT, AND THAT WAS A REALLY BAD FUCKING SIGN.

There was no noise with the darkness, and that was a really *strange* fucking sign.

I heard urgent footsteps making their way down the hall. Without knowing exactly what the shit was happening, I decided to sit on my bunk with my hands on my lap.

There was enough moonlight peeking through the high windows to illuminate the area directly in front of my cell. I watched it as the footsteps slowed, then halted right in front of me.

C. O. Hensley was staring directly at me. I could barely make out the silhouette of his face, but the shotgun in his hands was extremely clear.

C. O.s didn't use weapons unless shit was about to hit the proverbial fan.

That meant bad things for people in my situation.

Then the cell door began to open.

Fuck.

I had nothing with which to defend myself. Not that it would matter against a shotgun if I did.

The hairs on the back of my neck felt like they were on fire. I turned my face away, because the thought of my mom staring down at hamburger meat in the morgue was too much to bear.

230

Your Dreams Taste Like Candy

My dad was an asshole, and you'd have all the evidence you'd ever need if you met the motherfucker.

He was fighting with my mom, again, when the cops showed up. Again.

"Fighting with" isn't really the right term. That implies some sort of equality.

I was afraid to move out of the house at age twenty-two, because I was afraid of what my dad might do to my mom.

Turns out, so were the neighbors.

The cops only knocked once before letting themselves in. I was afraid to step away from the chair where mom sat long enough to answer the door.

There was shouting.

Then the cops were involved in the shouting.

They tried to move my dad away. He was an asshole about it as usual, and ended up in cuffs.

They tried to move my mom away. She was scared. She didn't get out of the chair.

There was more shouting.

One of the cops pulled a taser and aimed it at mom. I didn't think. I snatched it out of his hands, threw in across the room, and asked him what the fuck he was doing. He just stood there, slack-jawed, and said nothing for a while.

They found a crack pipe near dad's wallet. Possession of paraphernalia, along with a few priors, meant that he'd be going away for some time.

They found an eighth of an ounce of weed in my bedroom. I lived in the same house where my dad's pipe was discovered. Things might have been different if I were richer, or if I had a different dad, or if my skin were lighter. Ultimately, the conclusion was possession of a Schedule I controlled substance, possession of paraphernalia, and assaulting a police officer for the taser incident.

There were two things that I didn't have to worry about after that.

One was my dad hurting my mom.

The other was two to five years' worth of rent.

"I'm unarmed, C. O. Hensley, and I'm in full compliance with your instructions." My heart was jittering like a popcorn maker, but it made little difference. If he wanted to shoot me, he would. Afterward, they'd compare the word of a live officer to that of a dead convict.

Your Dreams Taste Like Candy

Hensley didn't need to worry.

I didn't even know what was happening.

I closed my eyes.

"Stand up, Inmate 1913." He didn't sound like his usual, overbearing-jackass self.

He sounded… scared.

My voice was shaking. "I'm standing as requested, C. O." I got to my feet with my hands raised.

"Open your fucking eyes, Inmate," he spat at me.

I did as instructed. His face was still inscrutable in the shadow.

"Heads up." He pumped the shotgun with a cold *clack-clack*. I froze for a fraction of a second before my tight end's reflexes kicked in.

The shotgun sailed across the cell, and I snatched it out of the air.

This made no fucking sense at all.

Then C. O. Hensley *turned his back on me.*

"You'd better get out of that cell if you want to survive the night." And with that, he started walking away.

All of my survival instincts were at war with each other. Be seen with a gun? Suicide. Ignore a C. O.'s orders? Not unless I wanted time added. Stay in this cell?

That's when the prison shook. Somehow, I knew that whatever was moving it had taken hold from above, and was moving the ceiling.

The whole fucking ceiling.

The prison is the size of a city block.

That's when I ran into the hall.

-2-

I prepared myself for anything. Had the world gone to shit? Would I see a gunfight? The aftermath of a gunfight? Monsters *eating* the aftermath of a gunfight?

Your Dreams Taste Like Candy

Scenario after horrible scenario slipped through my haunted imagination as I raced across the metal balcony and down onto the main floor.

I had never fired a weapon in anger. The shotgun seemed impossibly heavy in this moment, as though it would be more a burden than a savior.

The hair from my scalp to my toes stood on end as I followed where I thought Hensley went. It was dark every step of the way, but I knew it well enough.

Fuck, I thought as I barked my shin and face-planted on the dark floor. Okay, I didn't know it perfectly.

I froze as I looked blindly above me. Why did it echo like that when I fell? What was different?

I snatched the shotgun from the ground and crept carefully toward the chow hall. That would be the only place big enough for a gathering of people, so I hoped we'd find someone there.

I pondered for only a second about what such a gathering would entail before pushing the thought from my mind. I didn't want to think in this moment. Nothing made sense, and thinking might drive me crazy.

I slowly pushed open the door to the chow hall. Its large bay windows would be more than enough to bathe the room in moonlight. I held my breath and peeked my head inside.

Nothing.

No living people. No dead people. No sign of a fight. No sign of human habitation.

No Hensley.

With nothing but silence, my imagination was beginning to take over. That's a bad thing.

The scariest monster imaginable is the one that we can't see, because fear can only exist in the unknown. I crept forward with this thought tap-dancing across my brain, creating new mental scars with each step. I walked deep into the room, growing bolder and louder as I went, *willing* something to find me. *Anything* was better than not knowing. "Hey," I breathed in a loud whisper. "Hey," louder this time. "Hey! Heeee-"

That's when a hand slapped over my mouth, another grabbed the shotgun, and an arm pulled me backward.

Your Dreams Taste Like Candy

Everyone knew something was going to happen in the yard that day.

There were even bets on how things would turn out.

San Ignacio was a small enough prison that only a couple of gangs ran the show. Duke led the only white prison gang, and Reg ran the black one.

Do you have any idea how territorial human beings can get over the smallest stretch of land? If not, look into trench warfare during World War I.

It started with some benches in the yard.

See, a bunch of new inmates were coming in all at once. The thing is, this new crop happened to be mostly black. Reg knew this. Duke knew this. Reg knew Duke knew this.

And when Duke saw Reg talking to the whole fucking new class in the yard on their first day, both of them knew that things would change.

One way or another.

And every C. O. knew it, too.

So when twenty inmates from each gang started mulling around the benches that USED to belong to the white gang, the C. O.s were ready. Ten of them marched right between the two factions in a move that surprised everyone watching. Did they want to get killed?

I'd managed to stay out of this shit for the most part. I'd had to grease a few palms in ways that I'm not proud of, but Reg had mostly given up on trying to recruit me.

But I sure as shit was going to watch what happened. How could every C. O. be willing to risk pissing off both gangs?

By not pissing off both gangs, it turns out.

C. O. Chulley was in charge that day. He was 300 pounds of mean, and proud of it. The parade of C. O.s marched behind him, separated the factions, then turned to confront Reg and his guys.

Defeated, Reg backed off.

The white gang kept the benches.

And Duke gave Chulley a knowing look as he walked past.

I understood why Reg was pissed after that. Hell, we all were. Duke's guys were visibly arrogant for weeks.

But it was still Reg's own damn fault when he melted three plastic forks into a shank and jumped Chulley in the hall. That was fucking stupid.

When the C. O.s were done with him, Reg couldn't walk anymore. He's going to serve out the rest of his sentence in a prison hospital.

It turns out that some stories just don't have any heroes.

Your Dreams Taste Like Candy

"*Shhhh, shut the fuck up!*" the voice hissed into my ear. "Do you want them to hear you?" I was forced into a crouch and led to the end of the chow hall. I didn't resist; I wanted *answers*, and was going to follow them wherever they might be found. I was pulled to a group of lunch tables that were barricaded around one corner of the room.

The moonlight was just strong enough to make one thing clear about the dozen or so people hiding behind them: they were afraid.

The arm forced me into their midst, bent me into a crouch, and thrust the shotgun back into my chest. "Here," Hensley said forcefully. "We don't need them taking any more of us."

I clenched the gun and looked around at the bizarre sight in front of me.

Inmates and guards intermingled, and each was armed with the weapons that were supposed to be locked up tight in the armory. Everyone looked tense, but there was something completely *off* about their faces.

I realized that they weren't afraid of each other. Of all the differences between prison and the outside, the greatest for me is what people mean to one another. On the outside, they're other people. In here, they're the *opposition*. Every person you see wants what you have because they don't have enough of their own. No one is your friend. Not really. A friend is something you can only have when you're both free.

I looked at the faces, eyes wide in the moonlight, and felt vertigo rush through my head. Chulley was there, knuckles white as he clutched his weapon. Duke was next to him, eyes wide and unblinking. Hensley crouched next to me, nearly nuzzling up to my shoulder.

He looked at me intently, and placed his finger against his lips.

I read once that people tend to doze off under extreme fear.

That's the only explanation I can give for being jerked suddenly awake.

The group was trying desperately to remain silent as they shuffled around in the darkness. They were failing as several people slammed against the tables and floor.

Your Dreams Taste Like Candy

My head swam as I clutched the shotgun tightly and I tried to figure out just what in the blue fuck was happening. Several people were poking their heads just above the benches in panic. I snuck up behind them, heart racing, then looked over the edge in an attempt to understand.

I didn't understand. It looked like thick creeping vines were reaching out of the blackness, coiling, writhing, stretching outward toward us as they grew at an impossible rate. Could we even shoot such a thing? There had to be at least eight tendrils. Were more hidden?

I was nearly knocked off my feet by Duke's flailing arms. He was being pinned down by Chulley and two other guards. The group fought harshly in the moonlight. Despite the struggle, all of them forced themselves to stay as quiet as possible.

I moved toward the wall and pressed myself against it as far as I could go. Next to me, Hensley sat motionless.

Chulley and his friends quickly overpowered Duke, who broke the silence with his yelling. "NO! Not me. Fuck off. Fuck you!" He started to shriek.

No one else joined either side of the struggle. We just sat and watched.

Duke managed to make eye contact with me once he could no longer move. "Help me, man! Please!" He grunted, then tried, and failed, to kick. "Come *on*, man! Do you really think they'll spare you next?"

My blood froze in place at that moment as I looked around. No one wanted to make eye contact with me.

I still didn't move as they pulled Duke out from the safety of the benches and into the darkness beyond. I wondered if everyone else would be as silent if *when* my time came.

I didn't really wonder, though. I knew.

And I knew I had to watch what happened to Duke.

The three of them thrust Duke forward. He collapsed onto the ground as his captors scurried back toward the safety of the benches. At first I thought that nothing would happen.

I was wrong, of course.

The tendrils found Duke and quickly bound themselves to him. He began to scream before one of them stuffed itself deep into his throat, and his voice was instantly cut off. He silently bobbed back and forth as the tentacles pulled him to the ground. Slowly, they slithered back with their prize into darkness, until there was neither sight nor sound left of Duke.

Your Dreams Taste Like Candy

The last I saw of him was the look of his bloodshot eyes reflecting the moonlight.

Everyone held their collective breath for a moment. This, I realized, was a game of sacrifice. They must have decided while I was sleeping that their only option was to appease whatever was before us. So much for not being afraid of each other.

That thought was stuck in my head as I saw a stray tendril re-emerge from the darkness. That plan was on my mind as the second one crawled forth and made its way toward us.

That knowledge was guiding me as I weighed my options.

Don't judge me. I'd do it again in a second.

Chulley was the slowest of the group returning to the benches. I raised the shotgun, took aim at his right kneecap, and fired.

I don't think anyone realized how silent things had been until the blast rent the darkness.

Chulley screamed as I pumped the gun and fired at his other knee. But that scream was drowned out by a deep, guttural roar as the tendrils descended upon him, binding his arms and broken legs before squeaking with him back into the unknown.

But no tentacles invaded his mouth. They let him scream this time.

And again, it seemed that no one would interfere with the sacrifice. Good. I looked wildly around the room and saw no more tentacles; my plan had worked.

That's when Hensley leapt over the benches and charged forward.

I didn't think about my reaction this time. I was running before I knew it, with both the gun and the benches dangerously left behind.

In another life, I had been a tight end. Clearly, Hensley couldn't say the same about himself. I overtook and tackled him almost instantly.

We rolled on the ground before I forced us to a stop, pinning his arms to his sides. The room seemed to shimmer in a fevered dream. I couldn't see any of the rogue tentacles around me, but I couldn't see much of anything at all. In the darkness, though, I could hear them. *Chitter chitter chitter chitter*

I bent down over Hensley and whispered harshly into his ear. "*I just saved your ass, and Chulley just saved all of us. You're fucking welcome. Please don't do anything stupid.*"

Your Dreams Taste Like Candy

Chitter chitter CHITTER CHITTER

"Things are about to go bad, Hensley," I hissed as I pulled him to his feet. The walls began to vibrate.
"Very fucking bad," I continued. *"Run."*

-3-

He stared up from the ground, looking at me inscrutably. I wanted to smack the shit out of him. "What the *fuck* are you doing, C. O.? *Move!*"

He stared back for another interminable second before climbing to his feet and turning away from me.

Back toward the tentacled abyss.

I grabbed his shoulder and pulled back. "Get behind the tables!" I screamed as quietly as I could.

He turned back toward me and grabbed my shoulders, giving me a stare that was somewhere halfway between fear and hope. "They'll get past the tables soon enough. I think we can slip through the door to E Block while it's eating Chulley."

So *many* things about that didn't make sense.

"C. O., that doesn't make any-"

I got lightheaded with the punch that he landed on the back of my skull. In the eerie calm that came with the bizarre, tingly distance that ensued, I followed him without question. He pulled me forward, toward the tentacles.

Then right through the door towards E Block.

That section of the prison was separate from the rest. Awareness slowly filtered back in as I found myself running alongside Hensley in the dark. Like the rest of the prison, there was only silence, emptiness, and obscurity. I had no idea where we were going as Hensley led me forward.

I finally realized that I should not follow so willingly. That it was time to question this man's motives.

That's when he opened a door and stuffed me into a small room.

238

Your Dreams Taste Like Candy

He followed me inside and quietly closed the door behind us. I was about to tackle him, to strangle him, to demand to know what was going on.

That's when I looked down and realized that I still had the shotgun. The shotgun that he had given me.

"If you're going to shoot me," he interjected as though reading my mind, "I'd prefer you do it now and get things over with." He flipped on a flashlight that he found from seemingly nowhere, casting an unsettling series of shadows across his visage. "I clearly don't have the balls to do it myself. But if you're *not* going to oblige, you can stop moving so slowly and *help me the fuck out.*"

I stared at him, slack-jawed. That's when he pulled out the book.

I looked wildly around and tried to get my bearings. We were in a guards' office, right in the middle of E Block.

The crazy person's ward.

Well, the crazy/extremely dangerous/dangerous-because-they're-crazy ward.

There was a *slam* as Hensley threw the book on the table. The very strange book, that looked like it was covered in skin. I looked at him in revulsion. "What the fuck do you think you're doing with that, C. O.?"

He stared at me darkly.

"Don't act like I don't know what that's supposed to be. I did more than just play football when I was at Cal. You think that just because I'm a prison kid, I've never heard of the *Necronomicon?*"

He acted like he didn't hear me.

"We need to find Digor Lish," he explained gravely before turning to walk out of the room.

It was dark, but I'm sure I turned whiter than bird shit. I ran forward, and slammed the door in front of him.

I hadn't been in attendance that day. But based on the number of times the story was repeated, I might as well have.

They didn't know his name at the time, but detectives from six different states had been seeking Digor Lish for two years when they finally descended on the house at the end of the road.

Your Dreams Taste Like Candy

S. W. A. T. had surrounded the residence, and aerial surveillance had been monitoring it for a day before they went in. Thirty armed men were called up to capture this prize.

The bomb squad had found nothing unusual, so Alfa Team moved right on in the front door. The plan was to meet Bravo at the back, but they never made it that far.

Just past the hallway, obscured from any outside windows, was the living room. In the middle sat Digor Lish.

The path to reach him was strewn with human viscera on all sides. The different body parts were indistinguishable in the blended mess. Six months later, forensics would determine that thirty-seven different people had donated pieces of their corpses to that unholy swamp.

Digor Lish did not acknowledge the presence of anyone as they marched in and gagged. He simply continued chewing on what appeared to be angel hair pasta. It dangled down over his heaving bosoms, jiggling as he chewed. Digor Lish did not have a stich of clothing on his 350-pound frame, which highlighted just how much blood was coating his alabaster skin.

It wasn't pasta, of course. It was a bundle of nerves that led down into the spine of the corpse on the ground. The body was face-up, with the nerves snaking through a gaping cavity in the man's torso.

Face-up was a misnomer, to be honest. The man was missing every part of his face from his forehead down to his chin. Instead, a bloody casserole was punctuated only by shiny, white teeth where a mouth had once been.

Digor Lish refused multiple commands to surrender. Instead, he stared hungrily into the men who had come to arrest him as he continued to chew.

That's when the corpse revealed that it was, in fact, not a corpse. The man reached a feeble hand up to his own temple, pointing to it with a thumb in the air. The horrified police realized that he was begging them for a death that he'd heretofore been denied, and wanted nothing more than his own brains splattered against the wall.

The police never admitted which one of them mercifully obliged.

And that's how E Block came to house Digor Lish.

Three nine-fingered guards had asked for a transfer since his arrival.

Hensley looked at me, sizing me up.

"I don't know why you need my help right now, *Hensley*, but it's about time to start talking," I spat at him.

He nodded. "Okay."

I was caught off-guard.

"We can sit and chat, I can tell you everything. Conversely, we could not waste what little time is left with an explanation you wouldn't believe anyway. The choice is yours."

As if on cue, the roof shook again, and this time it sounded like it was tearing away. The walls trembled, and dust tumbled down in the dark.

The image of the terrified guards and prisoners flashed through my mind. "The rest of them-"

"Are probably dead by now, because they're pussies. They lived longer than anyone else because they were pussies, it's true. But that just made *it* want to play with them more. Are you a pussy, Inmate?"

He always was an asshole.

My mind was officially frazzled.

And that's how I found myself following Hensley through the dark.

We had to go through an extra security door just to gain access to the control panel that would allow entry past the other security door so that we could stand in front of his cell. With each barrier, I grew a progressively stronger feeling that I'd have been safer with the tentacles.

When Hensley finally opened the triple-padlocked door, it groaned in protest. I had a feeling that it didn't get opened much.

There was a light coming from inside. I peeked around the edge of the door and saw that it was coming from a small fire on the floor.

At the back of the room stood Digor Lish. Most of his body was clad in a black robe. Enough of his face was showing, however, to reveal that he'd been unable to remove the mask forcibly placed upon him by the guards.

It was the same mask worn by Hannibal Lector.

That mask, combined with his dark hood, created a chilling effect from the obese man.

Hensley exuded terror, but held his ground. He gripped his own shotgun, finger on the trigger.

Digor Lish didn't acknowledge our presence. Instead, he growled. That growl developed into words, and those words became a chant.

My blood turned to ice. For the life of me, I could not understand why I didn't just wait to die with the rest of them behind the tables.

"Ia Ia!" Lish yelled to the ceiling. "Cthulhu Fhtagn!"

Your Dreams Taste Like Candy

-4-

For the briefest, stupidest moment, I actually believed that nothing would happen. Maybe it would all be okay.

It was not all okay.

The ensuing sound was so loud that I actually *felt* it rip the sky. I dropped to my knees and let the gun fall to the floor, wrapping my arms around my head in a fruitless attempt to block out the noise.

When it ended, I wondered if I had gone deaf. The ringing in my ears disproved that soon enough.

My mind was foggy as Hensley pulled me to me feet. He was shouting something, and his voice tuned in and out of my head.

"...look up, Inmate...listen..." I was only able to pick a few words out of the ringing, but I heard enough to face skyward.

When we were in elementary school, Mrs. Dunwich taught a unit on impressionist art. She showed the class a picture of Van Gogh's Starry Night and nearly teared up. When the class asked her why, she said because it was the way that God must see the world. Our feeble attempts to build mighty structures were nothing compared to the magnitude of the heavens, which to God were nothing more than a single brushstroke. The greatest mystery the universe offers is not life but size, and this one painting shows just how small we truly are.

I was a speck of sand as I watched the shadow lean over the now-roofless prison. The shadow occupied the space of an expansive storm cloud, but moved as a living being. It was darker than the night sky around it. But the outline was more than enough, more than too much. The creature's wingspan reached from end to end of the building, spreading out of sight. Writhing tentacles the size of tree trunks dangled from its face, which was punctuated only by two glowing, red eyes.

"I said *don't* look up, Inmate! Are you fucking stupid?" Hensley screamed as he grabbed my shoulders and forced my face down. Digor Lish was yelling his chant at the now-open sky, seemingly unaware of our presence. The fire at his feet, though small, was burning brighter, as though *angry*.

I didn't know how badly I was trembling until I tripped over my own words. "What... shit what was – the fuck?"

It sounded clearer in my head.

"Don't ask, Inmate," Hensley growled as he shoved a flask between my lips. I drank half a gulp and sputtered. "And don't spit that out!" Here he took a swig of his own before shoving the flask into his coat pocket, then tucking the *Necronomicon* under his arm. "That's Kentucky grain alcohol." Here he pumped his shotgun and looked over at Digor Lish. "We'll wish we had more before long."

I was panting. I had *so many* questions.

But they would have to wait.

A sick, slick, licking sound emerged from our left, drowning out even the horrible chants of Digor Lish.

Though something told me that the emergence of the sound was connected to his words.

Despite everything, the being that emerged to our left was clearly the most immediate threat. It stood eight feet tall, with rigid, segmented sides like a bug's thorax. Dozens of stalks emerged from its top, swaying gently like sea grass in a warm current. On the edge of each stalk was a snapping mouth, opening, closing, lazily waving a thick, black tongue. It slid forward on a bed of writhing, slimy tentacles that reached out and pulled forward. They were seconds away from wrapping around our feet.

I had no time to react. Hensley slammed the *Necronomicon* into my hands. "*Read*, college boy!" He screamed.

I thought for just a second, then decided not to think at all.

I squatted so that the book would be visible in the firelight. Looking down at the page Hensley had left open for me, I struggled to understand was I was reading. "Uh, Hensley, I don't even know what to... this isn't English. How-"

"Time is a factor, Inmate," he spat back.

Would you ever consider screaming profanity into a quiet library? I felt that same sensation of *wrongness* as I spoke the impossible letter arrangements on the page before me.

Your Dreams Taste Like Candy

I heard a *slorch* as the thing in front of us paused with one tentacle about to wrap around Hensley's heel. Slack-jawed, I looked up at the creature.

That's when I saw the other tentacle. It had slipped quietly around my back, and was just about to brush up against my neck. It had me completely entwined.

It was temporarily frozen. But as soon as I stopped speaking, the tip of the tentacle gave a little jiggle. It was just so *eager* to tickle my throat.

I looked down and resumed reading, faster now. I didn't stop as I listened to Hensley's staccato footsteps move past the tentacle and approach the creature.

The sound of the shotgun blast shook the hallway. The frozen tentacle ripped past my head, brushing my cheek, leaving a thick coat of globby slime to drip past my collar and trickle down my back.

Two more shotgun blasts were overrun by the sound of the creature's inhuman screaming. It sounded like Hensley was torturing a vacuum cleaner with a bag of angry pigs.

One final shotgun roar ended the screaming for good. And, in the relative silence that followed, the vile chanting of Digor Lish again came to dominate the room.

I placed the *Necronomicon* gently on the floor (I think it gave my fingers a gentle squeeze as I laid it to rest), then picked up the shotgun I had dropped earlier and aimed it at Lish's head.

Hensley grabbed the barrel of the gun and pointed it forcefully downwards. "You stupid fucking faggot, don't you think I'd have killed him already if that were possible?" His words sounded angry, but when he looked at me, white knuckles still on the barrel, his face showed nothing but raw fear. "*He* is the channel between the worlds right now. Imagine a hundred linked train cars going over a fork in the track. If you try to *change* from the left track to the right one halfway through, the whole train is fucked, and everyone dies." He looked over at Digor Lish, who still seemed unaware of our presence as he wailed, hands high in the air. "Wherever we're going, it's together. All of us."

At that moment, we heard a groan come down from above. We both reflexively looked upward.

Descending from the inky sky was, impossibly, a man being lowered on a rope. Though bound hand and foot, he was otherwise naked. The man was audibly sobbing as he slowly approached solid ground.

Hensley went white. "Oh, God," he whispered. "It's the warden. Lish is going to feed him to *it*." Here Hensley actually started to cry, and that scared me more than anything yet.

"Once it's eaten," Hensley croaked, "we'll all be pulled to the other side." He looked at me with woeful eyes. "I hope you still have shells in that shotgun, Inmate. You'd better put the barrel in your fucking mouth."

-5-

Hands shaking, eyes and nose flowing, Hensley put the barrel of his own gun under his chin.

He pulled the trigger. It made a soft *click*.

He wailed, pulled another shell from his pocket, and quickly loaded the shotgun.

To be clear, he was a fucking asshole. There were plenty of times when I would have volunteered to bequeath him a firehouse enema and laugh as it happened.

But that didn't stop me from grabbing his gun, and pulling it firmly away from him.

Hensley collapsed on the ground, inconsolable. I dropped his shotgun to the floor, holding my own weapon in my right hand, and the *Necronomicon* in my left. I looked up at the impossible sight in the sky.

The naked warden now dangled fifteen feet above the floor. The way that he sobbed so *unabashedly* was even stranger than the incessant chanting floating from Digor Lish. Imagine that you came home from school one day as a young child to find your parents collapsed on the floor, wailing and sobbing. Imagine they just didn't *care* that you saw them in such a state.

Picture just how badly your own worldview would be turned on its head.

Your Dreams Taste Like Candy

The warden had always been the general of the invading army, King Shit of Turd Mountain, and things happened when and because he said they did.

Now, as he descended toward the earth, even the drool that slid from his lips seemed beyond his control.

San Ignacio State Penitentiary was a shithole. About that, no argument could be made. But stand in one place long enough, and it becomes your shithome.

My corner of the yard was in the warm sun each morning, and evolved into a cool patch of shade every afternoon. I would go, sit, and close my eyes. For a brief few moments, I would be free.

It's funny. I never thought about how free I wasn't until they put me in jail. The species likes its bars, because the confines make it safe.

The scariest thing about prison is that the bars are no longer invisible.

I was sitting in my corner with my eyes closed, being free, when the nastiest of the prison gangs decided that my peace wasn't worth their time.

"Why dontcha stand up and say hi?" I could hear the nasty smile in its voice.

I opened my eyes and rose nervously.

C. O. Chulley was speaking. C. O. Hensley and another guard were standing beside him, chuckling uncontrollably.

The reason for their giggles was more than obvious. Chulley didn't even bother to hide the joint in his mouth.

"Tell me, Inmate," Chulley said slowly, "have you got some nachos you're hiding from us?"

C. O. Hensley burst a loud guffaw at this.

"No, my mistake," C. O. Chulley continued, grinning maniacally, "you're all about the fried chicken, aren't you?"

My face and neck burned as C. O. Hensley doubled over in laughter. I saw red.

The change in their behavior was difficult to describe, but it was immediate. They didn't slouch, and were trying so hard to subdue their laughter. C. O. Chulley plucked the joint from his mouth and pinched it out between his fingers. It hissed.

They were looking over my shoulder at the man approaching in quick, crisp steps. His fitted suit contrasted sharply with the uniform that the rotund C. O. Chulley was wearing.

"Hello warden," C. O. Chulley offered when the man stopped next to us.

246

Your Dreams Taste Like Candy

"Chulley, I need to know that you're not wasting my time and money," the warden said darkly, looking C. O. Hensley up and down. "You said that coming to the yard would be worth that aforementioned time. Show me."

"Yessir," he said sharply. "I wanted to show you what we were doing to address the contraband issue." Here he lifted the now-dormant joint. "Inmate 1913 was hiding something under the fence. It's why he's always scurrying into that corner. He's using it as a drop spot for our problem contraband," he finished gravely.

I was dumbfounded. A million different retorts spun through my head. I looked for one that would get me in less trouble than remaining silent, but found none.

The warden looked at me like I was an errant raccoon shit in his foie gras pate. "Why haven't you removed him yet?" he asked, his voice dripping with disgust. "We cannot hope to rehabilitate the rest while the worst offenders spoil their efforts."

Most of my mind was boiling with inarticulate rage. The rest of it was weighing just how many years I'd be willing to add to my sentence for a single right cross into Chulley's fat jaw. My head was still spinning when Chulley and Hensley each grabbed one of my upper arms and started forcing me off the yard.

"And Chulley," the warden snapped suddenly. Chulley stopped and turned to face the man, dragging me forcefully with him.

The warden looked at us each thoroughly in turn. He seemed bothered by something inarticulate. Finally he nodded once to himself. "Be sure that you're looking out for my nephew. I can rely on you for that, right?"

"Yes, Warden Hensley. Of course, sir."

The warden nodded once more and turned around. He and his crisp business suit marched quickly off the yard and out of sight.

The warden shook in his bonds, thinning gray hair flopping uncontrollably as he cried. His tiny old-man penis jiggled pathetically. I turned away in disgust.

"I'm sorry," Hensley cried from the floor. "I'm so sorry."

"We have to cut him free when he gets to the ground," I responded urgently.

"You *can't*, you stupid fucktard," Hensley gurgled through his sobs. "What do you think is pulling him in?"

I looked up at the rope that suspended him. It disappeared into the pitch black sky above. Yet something about the way he descended made it apparent that a force was pulling him to Digor Lish, and that the desire of gravity was just a coincidental afterthought.

"He's connected to Lish," Hensley continued in a shaky voice. "We can't touch him, or we'll be part of it, too. All we can do is watch."

A low, grumbling roar emanated from above, causing the walls and floor to tremble. It sounded triumphant.

I shook my head slowly. "We can't interfere directly with Lish, or we fuck everything around us. Yet if we do nothing, then whatever is watching over us right now gets to eat your uncle and we'll get pulled over to the other side."

Another powerful roar from above. It was getting restless. Hensley cradled his knees in his arms, rocking slowly back and forth.

"But if I *touch* the warden, I'm bound to his fate. Am I right?"

Hensley confirmed this with his silence.

"You know what I learned that day on the yard, Hensley? The one with the marijuana?"

He looked at me with something that almost might be called regret.

"It was a lesson that stuck with me." Here I pumped the shotgun once. It made a satisfying *cha-chink*. "There's no peace in this place. All you can do is find your home in the chaos."

I aimed the gun high above Digor Lish. The warden met my eyes and screamed. "No! *No!* This isn't how I wanted things to end, there are so many people I love-"

I blasted him once, and his head exploded like a dropped watermelon. His arms and legs continued to twitch without purpose. That part, at least, was normal.

The tear was not.

The point in space where his head had ripped apart was *also* shredded, as though someone had torn a piece right out of a page.

Hensley looked up. Digor Lish looked up.

And the creature from above wailed in fury.

The tear continued to spread, inching out in all directions like cracking ice. The scope of the tear ignored the magnitude of perspective, reaching across my field of vision at a constant rate regardless of background size.

The tear reached Digor Lish first. It extinguished his fire with a hiss, then caught him by the ankle. The 350-pound, cloaked, masked monstrosity let out a single gasp, and was sucked into the white oblivion.

Your Dreams Taste Like Candy

I looked down at Hensley, who met my gaze with an eerie calm. The tear was reaching out for him.

We both knew that running would do no good.

He never turned his eyes away from me in the last moments. He simply said "Elsewhere."

And then he was gone.

The tears came for me next, of course. There was no one else to take. I imagined, for a moment, that I would heroically fight them off until the final moment, defying the will of the Greater World with a resistance that would be overcome only by death.

But that didn't happen. It came for me, and I simply stood, waiting until the tendrils held my arms and plunged me into the white nothing.

I didn't remember falling, or landing, or waking up. I remember just *being here*. I don't know when it started.

It's 2019.

Not 2015 like it was when all of this happened.

You know that feeling when a person is standing too close behind you, making the hairs on your neck prickle?

I get that feeling all around me. I know when specific people are near or far, because I *feel* them long before I can see or hear their presence.

That's how I know that Hensley exists somewhere in this place, though I have no idea exactly where.

I am certain that Digor Lish is alive, and he's somewhere much closer.

But worst of all is that *thing*. It's not just nearby. It's part of *here*, the way a reader holding a book has a whole universe in the palm of his hand.

For the moment, it's slumbering.

But it's so, so angry.

And this time, I have no idea what to do when it wakes up.

FORTY-EIGHT YEARS AGO, I COMMITED THE ONLY UNSOLVED HIJACKING IN U. S. AVIATION HISTORY. THIS IS MY FINAL CONFESSION.

BY GUEST AUTHOR DAN "D. B." COOPER

-1-

I FLEW TWELVE TOURS OF DUTY IN KOREA, AND ANOTHER THREE in Vietnam, but the most terrifying moment of my life was when my wife told me that she had lung cancer.

I don't remember much of the day itself. I do know that it was raining hard. A pine tree collapsed in our front yard, and that arbitrary act finally triggered my tears. My wife hugged me and rocked us back and forth as I stared at the fallen pine and *knew* that everything was pointless, it was all a waste – that every happy moment would be lost forever when its final witness died.

I was a zombie for three days. Then I got the phone call that made everything worse.

A bit of background: my post-military life had led me to a job with the Reno Police Department. It had seemed a perfect choice at the time: my combat training had suited me for the task, the alpine environment soothed my then-undiagnosed PTSD, and it had great benefits.

Or so I thought, until the phone call revealed that my wife's treatment wouldn't be covered.

Your Dreams Taste Like Candy

I was so shocked that I simply said "thank you" to Timothy from Human Resources and hung up.

A few additional phone calls revealed that my military service was extensive enough to leave me with a 7.53-inch scar on my right thigh and the aforementioned PTSD, but not quite good enough for comprehensive spousal health insurance.

Dazed, I spent the rest of the afternoon on the phone. I finally got an anonymous voice from an anonymous hospital to break the news:

It would cost upwards of $150,000 to provide my wife with the very best treatment options. It would require a lot of out-of-state travel and likely months of missed work, which is what drove the price tag so high.

That was five times the value of our house.

My wife was going to die.

It's impossible to explain what breaking a spirit really means to someone who has never experienced that particular damnation. I'd seen two buddies of mine come home from Da Nang with missing arms, and two more from Cambodia (yeah, that's a different secret altogether) who had each lost a leg above the knee. To a man, they gave dreamlike descriptions of how odd it felt to be missing parts of *themselves*. It seemed that their brains simply wouldn't accept that their flesh was slowly rotting in a fetid swamp.

I think it was a survival mechanism.

That's the only way I can explain what I did after I looked down at my shell of a gently sobbing wife and truly understood that she would soon be at room temperature.

Dreamlike, I found myself sneaking into the Reno P. D. late at night.

It was shockingly easy.

I waved at Debbie on the way in, then used my clearance to access the Human Resources offices at the back of the building. No one was there at 2:00 a. m. to stop me. I turned on the overhead lights, since that seemed less suspicious than bumbling around with a flashlight.

The file cabinets were locked. But I'd done a hell of a lot more than tear past locks while I was in Korea, and I quickly had them open.

I didn't know what I was looking for until I found it.

My health insurance file was relatively thin. Like I said, no one had encouraged me to seek help for the PTSD, and the scar on my leg only left me with the slightest limp. No need for the insurance company to waste money on that expensive doctor, right?

At least, that's what the author of the note paper-clipped to my file believed. It had been attached to my wife's medical paperwork.

Can legally be denied at Stage 4 for predicted terminal prognosis. Stall for 4-6 weeks AT ALL COSTS to increase likelihood of metastasization.

Tears seemed inadequate.

I quietly closed the folder and slipped it back into the drawer filled with dozens of identical files.

I paused.

My heart was already racing; being caught here could cost me my job, or even my freedom. I'd found what I'd needed, and could walk away right now.

But I plunged my hand back into the drawer and opened another file. Where I found another note.

Patient's insulin is projected to cost over $3,000 annually by fiscal year 1976. Given his age of ten, lifetime financial obligations would be greatly irresponsible for us to burden. Substituting an NaCl-laced placebo for a single prescription will address the issue permanently.

I felt like I was floating above my own body. I pulled out another file.

Donor X has paid $50,000 to advance his standing on the liver transplant list. This patient has consequently had his designation downgraded to "moderate priority" to explain the change in rankings.

I couldn't read anymore. I had to act.

But no court would accept this stolen evidence; attempting to smuggle the files out would do nothing other than getting my wife killed faster.

This is where I learned to redefine fear. Even in combat, my fear had been relegated to a specific time and place. They could be escaped physically, even if not mentally. But in this moment, when I realized that the most important part of my existence was in the hands of a man with neither face nor heart, my blood ran cold in a way that never truly warmed again.

I wanted to yell, then scream, then take my service weapon and fire at everything that moved. I saw red. I hated. I *hated.*

Instead, I put everything neatly back where I'd found it, waved to Debbie on the way out, and drove straight back home.

Your Dreams Taste Like Candy

That's when my wife told me that she had reached out to her former employer. She'd worked for Northwest Orient Airlines for ten years, and had hoped the cancer treatment might be covered under a worker's compensation agreement. I was confused for a second.

Only a second.

Then I remembered why she quit. There had been too many days when she came home coughing uncontrollably. She's been Northwest Orient's on-site liaison for major purchases, meaning that most of her time was spent at plane manufacturing sites. She said that the fumes from the welding floor were getting to her, causing prolonged dizziness, making it hard to breathe.

Once, she had coughed up blood.

Lung cancer.

I realized then just how tiny a cog she was in someone else's valuable machine.

But this tiny cog was the only reason my world kept turning.

We sat in our living room's little window seat that night, rocking slowly back and forth without saying a damn word. Her hair, always resistant to any attempts at taming, gently raked a few loose strands across my chin as I held her close. She smelled like jasmine and flour.

When she finally broke the silence, her voice was barely audible. "Promise you won't get mad when it hurts and I snap at you? I don't want that to be your last memory of us."

I kissed one knuckle on each finger before whispering, "I promise," into her ear.

It was shockingly easy.

Because the beginning of the story is the best place for a naïve fool to be. Most significant journeys would remain untaken if the traveler knew just how badly the most painful part would hurt.

But I was only thinking of one thing as I watched a plane take off from Reno-Tahoe in the distance.

Things look a *hell* of a lot easier when you've got nothing to lose.

Your Dreams Taste Like Candy

2

"I can always turn back" was the mantra that got me past my own inertia.

Was I really going to hijack a plane? No, I told myself – I was just *setting up* for it, not actually doing something wrong. I could always turn back before I became a criminal.

Which made sense. I had been a law-abiding citizen for my entire life. I'd nearly died for my country.

Then I remembered the note attached to my wife's medical file. The people controlling her fate wanted me to become a widower.

That's what I had gotten for following the rules all my life.

And suddenly, I didn't feel so bad about destroying the system that was trying to kill my wife.

I thought about how shockingly easy it had been to break into files that were supposedly top secret.

The reality is that I had been conditioned to believe in un-crossable boundaries. We all have.

Those limits are real simply *because* we believe in them.

But the thought of losing my wife in my early 40s – of spending the next half-century alone – peeled back the visage of a world that had been created through belief and obedience.

In its stead was a plan.

The pieces fell into place almost of their own accord, and the idea presented itself to me fully formed. I looked for a reason to believe that it wouldn't work. But each possibility generated the same result:

If I don't, she will die.

So I kissed my wife goodbye three days before Thanksgiving. She cried then – not in an angry or combative way, but with tears that were too exhausted to fight. "Please," she whispered.

"Trust me," I responded.

We looked at each other for several minutes, but didn't say another word.

That was our entire conversation.

It was all that needed to be said, and neither of us could bear any more talking.

Your Dreams Taste Like Candy

I extracted $200 in cash, leaving my credit card and driver license at home. I gave a fake name to the motels along the way, changing it each time I had to use one.

"Dan Cooper," I responded to the man selling tickets at Portland International Airport.

It was the first and last time I ever said the name.

For reasons I don't fully understand, people came to use the alias "D. B. Cooper" when talking about me. The name stuck.

I tried to smile as I handed over cash for the ticket, but my entire face was numb. I paid $20 (flights were much cheaper then, and required no photo ID), he handed me 87 cents in change, and I walked away like someone else was controlling my body.

Waiting to board was the worst. I almost turned back when I saw a little girl of about six wearing a blue dress and combing a Barbie doll's hair. I considered what I was about to do to her family, and I nearly vomited.

Road flares, a voice in my mind interrupted. *You're only using road flares that look like a bomb. No one's getting hurt.*

I almost laughed at the internal voice. *I* was going to lose everything if they called my bluff. My wife would die alone while I withered in a forgotten federal prison cell, waiting decades to be released back into a life that I no longer wanted.

No, someone was definitely going to get hurt.

Sometimes, that's a good thing.

My heart nearly jackhammered out of my chest as a stewardess stared curiously at my briefcase while I boarded. I tried to smile.

I failed.

But I walked confidently past her and headed for the rear of the plane. Like I said, flying was different in the 1970s. No one checked any of my bags.

The first signs of a combat flashback were stirring as I sat in the back row where I could watch everyone. As soon as I did, the stewardess made a beeline for me.

For the moment, I forced the flashback away. I had to.

This was it.

"Excuse me, miss," I called, waving slightly.

She flashed that fake airline smile and asked me how she could be of assistance.

Your Dreams Taste Like Candy

"Bourbon, please," I responded. I felt exhausted already.

"Of course," she answered with saccharine sweetness. "Coca-cola?"

I nodded, and she turned away.

I didn't think I could do it.

She returned with my beverages and a grin. After handing them over, she sat right near me in one of those folding seats used only by airline crew.

I wanted to cry. This was too much. I had to give up.

Every tool I needed was in my briefcase, but I just wasn't strong enough to use them. Part of me always knew that I would be too weak. As the plane took off, I closed my eyes and did everything I could to hold in the tears.

"Going home?" came a voice from behind me.

I wiped my eyes and turned around in surprise. "Pardon?"

It was the same stewardess who had brought me the bourbon. "Are you heading home for Thanksgiving? It's always crazy for us the day before." Her smile seemed real this time. "I've been in the air for nineteen hours straight. All *I* want to do is get back to my family and then take a nice, long rest."

The first tear finally escaped, but I wiped it away before she could see it.

Finally, I smiled too. It was genuine.

I pulled the pre-written note from inside my briefcase and handed it to her. "Me, too."

She took the note politely. My adrenaline spiked.

Then she dropped it, unread, into her purse.

I frowned.

"Um. Excuse me, Miss?"

She seemed irritated now, but the saccharine smile was back in place as she turned to look at me. I waved her closer and leaned forward.

"I really think you should read that message." I pulled up my briefcase, but kept it closed for the moment. "I have a bomb."

And just like that, there was no turning back.

Your Dreams Taste Like Candy

3

If you ever want to witness a person receiving the shock of their life, try showing them a bomb during a plane flight.

I watched the stewardess's face change so fundamentally that I knew she'd never bounce back the same way.

It only took one glimpse to have this effect, and that's all I offered her. My copper wire and road flare deception looked real enough, and the shock of the situation drove it firmly home for the poor woman.

I closed the briefcase before she could take in every detail.

She didn't see how much of the case I was concealing, or how much I had hidden below the flares. And if all went according to plan, no one ever would.

Her face had gone paper white. And for the rest of her life, I hope she was remembered for just how cool she remained during an impossible situation.

"What do you want from us?" she asked in a stark, businesslike tone.

I tried to swallow, but my throat was too dry. "Two hundred thousand dollars in unmarked, non-sequential bills. Four parachutes will be waiting for us in Seattle. When we arrive, the plane gets enough fuel to fly to Mexico City."

She nodded, then got up to leave.

"Oh, one more thing," I added quietly.

She froze.

"Another bourbon, please. I'm parched."

She quickly (but not nervously) turned around and headed for the cockpit.

That's when I discovered that waiting patiently is the most nerve-racking thing a person can do in a stressful situation.

Everyone around me was peaceful. Most were families. Nearly all of them were certainly traveling for Thanksgiving the next day. They were either talking quietly or napping. Each person was pleasant and relaxed.

The paranoia started bouncing around in my head then. How could I be the only one who understood that the entire plane had been taken hostage? I felt so fucking alone, because they were in one world while I was in another at the back of the plane, and it was getting way too hot when no one else noticed, hot just like in Saigon during the summer when the plane we were flying came in too low for the landing but we realized too late and all I could do was be grateful that I was in the back of the cabin with the ground coming up too fast in the heat-

I gasped quietly as the overhead speaker crackled to life. I quickly wiped the tears away as the captain spoke.

"Ladies and gentlemen, please be advised that our plans to land in Seattle have been changed."

I forced myself to be calm. The only way that I could deal with the flashbacks was to force them deeper inside, and I had gotten quite good at it. I did not understand at the time just how profoundly I was damaging myself.

"Due to a minor technical difficulty, our arrival time will be delayed for a few minutes. We apologize, and thank you for choosing Northwest Orient." The captain signed off without another word.

The crowd murmured quietly. I saw the girl in the blue dress lay her head down on her mother's lap. Mom gently brushed her untamable frizz, and I found myself thinking of jasmine and flour.

I was causing this. *I* was the reason that these families had now become negotiable hostages. My head spun, and I suddenly wanted out.

No.

I was not the reason for this horror. This was squarely the responsibility of a few soulless men who saw my wife as a financial transaction instead of a human being.

'Well,' I thought as I pulled a pair of sunglasses from deep inside the briefcase, 'a hell of a transaction is what they're about to get.'

The stewardess (I later found out that her name was Florence) came back and sat down next to me. She informed me that everything had been relayed to the appropriate people, and that preparations were being made.

I nodded, then handed her a five-dollar bill. She looked at it like I was offering a particularly large beetle. "What's that?" she cringed.

I gazed at her in confusion. "I got two drinks."

That's when I realized that I wasn't a customer to her. Not anymore. I was a monster, and monsters don't play by the rules of normal people. Why wouldn't I just steal my drinks, given how horrible a person I clearly was?

She took the bill incredulously, and even tried to give me change.

Florence thought I wanted every penny I could steal.

I finished the bourbon in a single gulp.

Your Dreams Taste Like Candy

The next hour was a painful wait. Florence was the consummate professional, keeping me abreast of the situation as she moved back and forth between the pilot and me. A nervous energy buzzed through the passengers.

I watched the landscape below as we circled around Seattle. The sun sets pretty early that time of year, and it wasn't long before twinkling city lights were the only challenges to the Pacific Northwest darkness.

"We're ready," Florence announced as she shattered my thoughts. The flashbacks had been dormant for the moment, but I had learned to accept that they were around every corner and always would be.

I took a deep breath. "Good. Let's land this plane."

It was surreal watching everyone bow to my wishes. All of the window shades were pulled down to hide what was going on inside. We pulled to a far-off, brightly-lit section of the airport so that I *could* see what was happening outside.

The passengers' murmurs were shifting toward panic.

"Why is that truck refueling us?"

"Can we get off?"

"I want to go home!"

I closed my eyes, but the images I found there were worse, so I opened them and focused my attention outside.

My heart stopped. The truck had quit refueling.

Florence sat down next to me. I forced my breathing under control.

"There's a problem getting the fuel in. Northwest Orient has requested permission to try a different truck."

Perhaps they were calling my bluff. If so, there was no card I had left to play.

"That's fine," I offered in a voice far too calm for how I felt.

When the second truck had the same issue, I had basically given up. They were clearly testing my limits. They wanted to see if I was real. Sure, it put a few dozen airline passengers at risk. But would the man sitting atop a huge corporation love $200,000 more than a human being?

"Please," my wife had said. "Trust me," I offered back.

Yes, these people would certainly roll the dice with a handful of lives when enough money was on the table.

I wondered if they would let me out of prison long enough to say goodbye to my wife before she died.

Your Dreams Taste Like Candy

I knew, of course, that they wouldn't.

When Florence sat down next to me once more, I was mentally preparing to surrender.

"A Northwest Orient representative has just delivered the money and parachutes," she explained calmly. "It's all on board awaiting your inspection. We would like to know if the passengers are free to go home."

My controlled exterior masked an internal storm. What was real? When the passengers left the plane, nearly all of my bargaining chips would go out with them.

I checked the money and parachutes. They were genuine. There was nothing left to do except *decide*.

I looked down the aisle at the girl in the blue dress. She had her arms wrapped around her mother, but she was staring at me.

The look on her face was one of pure horror.

I nodded. "Let them go."

Florence signaled in the direction of the cockpit, and the passengers came to life. Only she and I remained still.

"I'm letting you go, too," I explained softly.

Florence looked gravely back at me. "I understand that, Mr. Cooper. But you're not letting everyone go, and some of my friends are staying behind as your hostages."

I nodded curtly, but said nothing.

"So could you explain something to me?" She drew a deep breath. "Why are you keeping five people on the plane, despite requesting only four parachutes?"

Calmly, I took out a cigarette, lit it, and blew a soft stream of smoke into the air above my head.

"Do me a favor, Florence. Just make sure that everyone does *exactly* what I say."

-4-

"You can have anything you want, Mr. Cooper," the co-pilot explained.

I probably would have laughed if I were capable of movement. But the numbness of shock held all facial expressions to inaction.

If I could have had anything I wanted, I certainly would not have been sitting with four strangers in the cabin of a nearly-empty plane at 7:13 p.m. on Thanksgiving Eve with a "bomb" in one bag and $200,000 in another.

I quietly took a long drag from my cigarette, let it out slowly, and stared at the space between pilot and co-pilot. With my dark glasses on, they couldn't tell where I was looking at any given time.

"I need to get to Mexico City," I deadpanned. "But there are conditions."

Here's where I need to backtrack a bit. As I mentioned earlier, my wife had spent ten years working for Northwest Orient in their manufacturing division.

It was no coincidence that I had chosen that airline to hijack. My wife had first shown symptoms of lung cancer after breathing in so many chemicals in their plant that she had to retire early. They had denied her worker's compensation claim in order to save money.

As I stared at the bag of cash that Northwest Orient had surrendered to me, I reflected on just how poor a choice they had made in this particular money-saving endeavor.

You see, lung cancer isn't the only thing that my wife had brought home.

As a supervisor on the plant floor, she had intimate knowledge of and access to airplane design. If she'd been born half a century later, the world would have encouraged that woman to study engineering. Despite my bigger paycheck, she was smarter than me by far.

Throughout our marriage, I would smile and nod as she described her workday, then mindlessly help her store the excess paperwork that she sometimes brought home.

Your Dreams Taste Like Candy

The first time I had really paid it any mind, however, was just before this excursion. And the paperwork I found contained a *lot* of information about the 727 aircraft.

There was even a placard with instructions for opening the airplane's stairs.

"And what are your conditions?" the pilot asked wearily.

I swiveled my head just enough to let him know I had heard him. "I need you to fly at the slowest possible speed necessary to keep us in the air. Keep the wing flaps low, and don't pressurize the cabin."

The flight engineer (in the 1970s, that was one of the cockpit employees) looked at me like I had two heads. He stared at the parachutes, then back at me, and simply said, "No. Not in the rain and the dark. Not here. Not now."

I snuffed out my cigarette. "Is there going to be an issue with my requests?"

The captain cleared his throat. "If we follow all of those... *particular* instructions, it will severely restrict our flight efficiency. It's unlikely we'll be able to go more than a thousand miles without needing a fuel stop."

"Then we'll take a fuel stop," I responded simply. "Where would you need us to land?"

The pilot and co-pilot leered at one another. I don't think that either of them truly believed that this conversation was actually happening. Surely, they would awaken from a fevered dream soon enough, and the world would be restored to its proper state just in time for breakfast.

"Um," the co-pilot offered, "I think it would be pushing things to reach McCarron in Las Vegas, so..."

"If it is necessary to make multiple refueling stops, then that is what we'll do. What airport is on the way to McCarron?"

"Reno-Tahoe is the farthest that I would be comfortable travelling under those conditions," the pilot quietly responded.

"If that's what you feel is best for the aircraft, then I will accept it," I explained calmly. "Now let's get moving. This flight's been delayed long enough."

Your Dreams Taste Like Candy

And with that, the cockpit crew got up to fly the plane back toward Reno.

The heart of any con, you see, is getting the target to believe that it was his idea all along.

A flight attendant waited in the cabin with me while the cockpit crew closed themselves in. Her name was Tina, and she was clearly terrified to be left alone with me. I wanted to comfort her, but I knew that it would be impossible because of how I looked, and I hated *hated* the fact that I wanted to do the right thing but she saw me as violent, yet I know she was even a little intrigued, and I wanted to ensure her that the streets of Da Nang were *safe* because we were here doing the right thing when a gunshot came out of *where?* and the woman's head exploded like a watermelon

The plane left the ground with a jolt and I was gasping for air.

"I said are you *okay*, Mr. Cooper?" Tina asked from three seats away.

How bad must I have looked if she was actually concerned for my wellbeing? I nodded quickly, tried and failed to force a smile, then reached for another cigarette. "Thank you for your concern, Tina. You've done everything I asked, and you've done it well. I sincerely apologize for any difficulty I've caused you." I blew a stream of smoke through my nose. "Now that we're up in the air, please join the cockpit crew. I'm going to need you to remain there throughout the flight."

She looked at me with – what was it – concern? Then she nodded and headed wordlessly into the cockpit.

I was alone.

I took the opportunity to finish my cigarette, because I knew damn well that it might be my last.

We fear death greatly enough to build faiths around its escape. But the overwhelming majority of what makes life worth living is just the damn everyday pleasures that we disregard in fleeting moments. The cumulative impact of those diminutive joys is great enough to drive ninety-nine percent of our waking hours; it defines us more than do our own names.

So I relaxed, for five minutes, until the cigarette went out on its own schedule.

Then I got to work.

I reached deep into the briefcase. It was large and spacious, and it held all I needed. I pulled out the placard and set it aside. Then I removed the tightly packed duffel bag and unfolded it. I quickly shuffled the money into my own duffel from the easily recognizable knapsack Northwest Orient had used (let me tell you, $200,000 is a *lot* of cash). It was a tight squeeze, but I fit everything in.

Well, almost everything. I set three of the money packets aside.

Then I pulled the change of clothes from my briefcase. I took off my tie and threw it onto a seat, then quickly stripped down, glancing warily at the cockpit door the entire time. Once I was naked, I threw on the new set of clothes and crammed the old ones into the briefcase. I couldn't fold them neatly, because I was shaking too much, so they barely fit.

After that, I grabbed my knife from inside the briefcase, pulled open one of the parachutes, and cut out a long stretch of cord.

I turned back to the three loose packets of money, pulled out a single twenty-dollar bill, and slipped it into my pocket. I had left my credit card at home and spent nearly all of my cash driving to Portland. I realized that I'd want access to money without opening my ransom stash in the middle of a god-forsaken gas station.

They probably wouldn't notice a single missing bill.

But since three packets of money would hopefully turn up in the forest a few days from the hijacking, detectives would almost certainly stitch together the exact story that I wanted them to assume.

I stuffed the three packets into the briefcase with the clothes, knife, and "bomb," but I didn't latch it closed. I wanted it to burst open on impact and scatter its contents.

Then I used the pilfered cord to bind the briefcase tightly around two of the intact parachutes.

It was go-time.

Carefully following the instructions on the placard, I opened the rear door of the plane.

The placard was instantly sucked from my hand and into the frozen night. The wind was forced out of my lungs as I grasped a nearby chair while the outside world opened with a vortex and a roar.

"Mr. Cooper!" the intercom cackled. "What are you doing? Do you need assistance?"

"I'm fine!" I screamed over the howling wind, though I have no idea if they heard me.

I plodded steadily to where I had left the parachute/briefcase bundle, shakily picked it up (it was a heavy load), then walked slowly back to where the open door was sucking air into its maw with violent ferocity. I struggled to balance as I teetered on the edge of the exposed stairway.

The roar was *deafening*, as though the night itself was screaming in protest.

I had to get this just right. The plane's sensors would be able to tell if a weight pushed up from the exposed stairs; from the cockpit's perspective, it needed to seem like an adult male had leapt from the edge.

I aimed, heaved, and prayed.

The parachutes and briefcase sailed through the air and slammed down hard on the bottom step. The cord was useless, and the entire bundle burst open.

Then it disappeared in an instant.

That's when I lost my balance and pitched forward. For a second I was floating, and the fragility of every damn thing in the world was just so crisp and clear in that moment that I wanted to cry.

I caught hold of the handrail and squeezed tight enough to peel the skin off my hand. For an instant, I hung at the screaming edge of oblivion, knowing that I had been mere inches away from falling hopelessly into the faraway night.

-5-

I clutched the handrail as the whirlwind of rain and wind spiraled around me, clawing at my grip and trying desperately to pull me into the night sky. I could *feel* the world telling me just how little my own life mattered to the engineers of a much greater plan.

But I fought against the sensation in the same way that I had battled uphill with every new development since my wife's diagnosis. I forced myself upright. I pulled my leg up a single step - then another, and another after that.

I was back in the plane.

"Mr. Cooper!" the intercom screamed. "Mr. Cooper, the aft door is open! Do you need assistance?"

Your Dreams Taste Like Candy

Everything now hinged on whether the crew would follow the final instructions I had given them before they'd entered the cockpit:

"Under no circumstances shall you open the cabin door before landing to refuel. You will be tempted to do so. Please remember that I can initiate the bomb just by dropping the briefcase. No emergency is worth destroying the plane. Do not test me."

They continued to shout, and I continued to ignore them. The only real protection I had at this point was their fear of me. And despite my bomb being imaginary, that fear proved to be a weapon that was very real in its own right.

I walked away from the door and stepped past the two remaining parachutes. Those were, of course, unnecessary; requesting four chutes had implanted the idea that I would take hostages, and that was all I needed.

The only property of mine left in the plane was $194,000 in the duffel bag that I had brought from work.

For a moment, I froze in contemplation of this fact.

I had actually *done it*.

Well, not quite yet. I was, after all, still on the plane.

But the thought of succeeding actually started to feel *real*. I might not, after all, grow old entirely alone.

I snatched up the duffel and stepped away from the parachutes, certain that someone else would be happy to dispose of them on my behalf.

Then I climbed across the seats and headed toward the 727's crew rest compartment. When I got there, I waited, and I prayed.

It took two hours for us to arrive in Reno. They were, without a doubt, the longest two hours of my life. I wanted nothing more than for the wait to end.

Then the plane descended. Adrenaline kicked my pulse into overdrive. I wondered if it was possible for my heart to crack my ribs from the inside.

Suddenly, I didn't want the wait to end.

But it turns out that Time just didn't care about my priorities.

I stood up and grabbed the bag as the plane taxied to a stop. The whiteness in my knuckles spread across my hand as I prepared myself for what was going to happen next.

"Mr. Cooper, are you there? The FBI has requested to board the plane. If this will cause you to detonate the bomb, you need to let us know now. Please respond, Mr. Cooper!"

For a moment, there was silence.

Your Dreams Taste Like Candy

Then there was none for a long time.

The door in the front of the plane burst open to screams of "FBI!" Footsteps ran through the center aisle as I heard the cockpit door hit the cabin wall, followed by yelling from inside. Like dominoes, noise tore across row after row as it drew toward me. I took a deep breath and shouted.

"Crew rest compartment's clear!" I called as I jumped forward.

The nearest FBI man whipped around and aimed an assault rifle at me. Then he looked down at the clothes I had changed into.

The clothes that I had brought from work.

"Reno PD, what the *fuck* are you doing in this aircraft? You're on *fucking* ground support right now!" He yelled at another FBI agent near him. "Reca, get this shithead off my plane and *make someone's head roll for this!*"

The man obeyed without question, shoving me violently down the aisle toward the exit.

I stepped out into cool night air and saw one of the greatest sights of my life.

Hundreds of people were gathered in the rain. Lights shone on FBI and Reno PD running around in a frenzy, but there must have been half a dozen different agencies present.

I scrambled down the stairs, bag in hand, and moved to get lost in the crowd.

"Whoa there, pal," the FBI man said as he grabbed my arm. "Just *who* the fuck are you, now?"

My breath stopped. I tried to take in air, but my lungs refused to cooperate.

"Christiansen! Rackstraw! We've got someone!"

Two men in FBI gear ran toward me as the agent clutching my arm started barking information into his walkie-talkie.

Finally, I found my voice. "Get my captain! He'll explain everything! This is Reno PD jurisdiction! Please!"

The man shook my arm forcefully. Fortunately, the duffel was in my other hand. "What the fuck are you saying, man?"

"He told me to get in the plane! You're interfering with direct orders from my captain!"

Your Dreams Taste Like Candy

He looked at me like I was something foul he had scraped off his shoe. Then he stared hard at my uniform, and yelled fresh information into his walkie-talkie.

Obviously, the captain of the Reno Police Department was at the scene. When he arrived and identified me, the FBI quickly lost interest and left me to my boss.

He was not so dismissive.

"You were *in* the goddamn plane?" he asked desperately. "I just lied to the FBI to save both our asses. Are you trying to get us fired?"

I stared at the ground. The best way to handle an angry person is to let them talk uninterrupted, and I did that now.

But it was a busy night, and he didn't have much time for me.

"I don't know what to say," I offered when he was done. "I haven't been the same since my wife's diagnosis. My head's not on right."

He softened just a little. "Look, this is *not* the time to lose control of yourself. Just – just leave. There's been a hijacking, and we don't have time for fucking around. Go on home to your wife."

There was more disappointment than compassion in his voice.

I nodded, turned, and walked away without another word.

As I was leaving, the captain looked down at the bag I was carrying. I had been careful to select one that prominently displayed "Reno Police" across the side.

"Wait!" he screamed. "What are you carrying?"

I pretended I hadn't heard him, and quickly slipped into the rushing crowd of people. I darted out of sight as fast as I could manage without drawing undue attention, and I never looked back.

The uniform enabled me to walk calmly past the police barricade. Andy was guarding it, and I waved at him as I carried the ransom money away from the airport and toward the rental car I had left in the parking lot three days earlier.

I couldn't relax during the entire drive home. I needed to see my wife before letting my guard down and believing that the night was *actually* over. And when I parked in front of our house, the warm light glowing in the kitchen told me implicitly that everything was going to work out.

I smiled. I was home.

I went quietly through the front door, set the money down, and headed for the most-needed hug of my life.

Your Dreams Taste Like Candy

When I didn't find my wife in the kitchen, I headed to our bedroom and flicked on the lights.

She was lying on the floor, eyes glassy with a trickle of blood leaking from her mouth. The *wrongness* of the sight prevented me from understanding what I was seeing at first.

Then I screamed.

I grabbed my wife and shook her limp body. Her head lolled sickeningly back and forth, but she gave no signs of life.

In a blurred panic, I picked her up and ran for the front door.

I made sure to grab the duffel bag of money on the way out.

The rainy, harried drive to the hospital was the most dangerous thing I did that night. But I'm certain we arrived faster than an ambulance could have.

They admitted her right away, and I was ushered into a sterile gray waiting room filled with magazines and the crying families of dead people.

I couldn't just *wait*. So I ran for the reception desk.

"You need to give her the best doctors! Chemotherapy! Radiation! EVERYTHING! Please, I have money, all the money you could-"

"Sir!" the woman behind the desk said politely but firmly. "Money isn't the solution to this problem." She sighed. "I promise you that our doctors and nurses are doing everything they can. Please, have a seat and wait for what's next."

And then there was nothing left to do but sit.

Part of me was numbly shocked that everyone else went about their business like this was just an ordinary day, and not the most horrible thing in my life. I wondered how many people at any given moment are experiencing the worst pain they've ever felt, and how much it would mean for an unaffected world to act like it cared just a little bit.

The beginning of a story, you see, is the best place for a naïve fool to be. Nearly all significant journeys would remain untaken if the traveler knew just how badly the most painful part would hurt.

That's when I looked up and saw a vaguely familiar face. I needed to break the loneliness before the last vestiges of sanity finally slipped through my fingers, so I nearly ran to her.

Then I recognized who it was.

Tina, the terrified stewardess from the plane, was leaving one of the rooms. Since I hadn't physically hurt her, she must have checked into the hospital as a direct result of the terror that I had caused. The look on her face made it clear that she had been crying.

A flashback was coming up fast. If she recognized me during an episode, the FBI would have me in handcuffs before I recovered.

I sprinted out of the hospital, leaving my wife to an unknown fate.

After twelve hours had passed, I couldn't wait any longer. I went back to the hospital on Thanksgiving morning and headed to my wife's room.

She had not regained consciousness. The doctor was with her; he looked grim.

The exact details of the conversation were wiped from my memory in a deluge of anger and pain. I know that I begged the doctor, that I promised him money, and that it had no effect. The cancer had just gone too far. What had been done could not be undone.

He left me alone in the room so that I could have some time with her. I knelt down and interlocked her fingers with mine. I told her that I was sorry, that I had tried, that I needed her forgiveness for failing. I begged her to wake up just once to tell me goodbye. I had to let her know how hard I'd fought. I *had* to. I couldn't let her go while she believed that I'd been doing something pointless. I wouldn't accept the notion that she had been alone when the world turned itself off to her.

Yet cancer didn't care what I wouldn't accept.

The most wanted man in America, and ostensibly the most dangerous, cried helplessly as an arbitrary arrangement of cells ruined his life forever.

She never woke up again. My wife died that night after being alone for three days. I won't ever know what her final conscious moments were like.

But if she loved me as much as I had loved her, it would have been agonizing to die without the person who made her world go round.

I left the hospital that night, grabbed the money, and never returned to Reno. I called my captain and told him that I couldn't go back to a life that would never be as good as it once had been. He said he understood, and we never spoke again.

Your Dreams Taste Like Candy

The entire country was looking for me, so I found a forgotten corner of the Southwestern U. S. and stayed out of sight. I bought a tiny abode in the desert for dirt cheap and didn't touch the ransom cash for years. I lived off of prior savings, because the serial numbers of the stolen money had been sent to every bank that used American currency.

After three years, I decided it was time to head over to the local rundown medical clinic.

"Hi. I'd like to pay for everyone's bill, please."

That had, after all, been the original intent for the money.

After treating the day's 26th patient, the head of the clinic pulled me aside.

"I can't help but wonder about this cash," he said warily.

"Well," I responded coolly, "It's good to maintain a sense of wonder."

That was the end of our conversation.

I grew old.

The most terrifying part about losing my wife was the fear of spending the next half-century alone. That fear proved valid. It wasn't the type of gut-punch horror that sends the pulse racing, though. Instead, it was an almost-numb sensation that I experienced while moments passed by that *should* have been shared with someone. No moment can ever truly be replicated, and once gone it's dead forever. Those moments are quantified and finite, and mine were forever diminished versions of what they could have been.

I had no one to comfort me when I was diagnosed with advanced esophageal cancer last month.

And I have no heir to accept my money. That part isn't so bad; I spent all but the last $1,913, and I've left enough clues in this text for anyone to find it.

It's nothing to get very excited about, though. You can't take it with you when you go.

In the end, all I really wanted was to grow old amidst the lingering scent of jasmine and flour, but I guess the world decided that was just too much to ask.

Your Dreams Taste Like Candy

So I stand at the edge of the faraway night, wondering if there are answers to be found in a faith-filled leap, but mostly certain there is only darkness.

HOW I DIED

THERE'S A GHOST THAT HAUNTS MY ROOM, AND HE'S THE BEST part of my home.

I don't think my Daddy wanted a daughter. Or at least, he didn't want one after his wife couldn't be my Mommy. All he ever said about her is that we can't stop death, and then got really quiet.

He never wanted to talk about her after that.

I always wondered how much control he had over his own life. If you can't stop death from happening, why would you stop life from happening? Because that's the choice he made.

He never took me places. Friends weren't allowed inside our home. To be honest, he never seemed really happy being my Daddy.

There might have been more to that story. But like I said, my room is haunted, which prevents me from seeing all of the things that happen inside my house.

I was very scared the first time that the ghost came for me. I felt like I was falling asleep, but then I was falling. I fell faster and faster, and I wanted to wake up, but something was pulling me far away. I couldn't breathe, and everything was really dark.

Then it was warm and peaceful. I met the ghost, but I couldn't see him. It didn't make any sense, but all of my senses were gone. I knew that he was in front of me, but my body was missing, and there was light. I felt the light instead of seeing it, and that made it real.

"I've come to take you away," he said. The ghost didn't use words, but I knew what he meant just the same. "Why are you taking me from my bed?" I thought, and he understood. "It's only for a short time," he explained. "I will be in your place, in your bed, and your father won't be able to tell that it's me instead of you. When it's over, you can go back home." "But where will I go until then?" I thought, and the ghost quickly answered back. "You will stay here, where it's warm and safe. I will fetch you when tonight is over."

I wanted to ask more, but he was gone.

I was warm and safe.

And when I returned to my own bed that night, I still felt warm and safe.

It would have made sense to be afraid when I fell through the darkness and into another world. It would have made sense to doubt the ghost who pulled me from my room and took my place at night. Yet I wasn't afraid. I could feel goodness in the ghost.

But I felt sadness, too.

It got stronger as time went on. The ghost would be in front of me for just a second when I came into his world. Each time, he got colder. Each time, he spoke less.

I wanted to make him feel better, but I didn't know how. I wondered, then, if this was the part of growing up that no one talks about. Maybe everyone can see pain in the people around them, but just don't understand what to ask about why it's there, even where the suffering person only needs to *share* a story that nobody knows how to talk about.

I wanted to tell my Daddy stories about the ghost that came into my room at night. But whenever I tried, he got very red and quiet. Sometimes, he would walk away, and I would hear a breaking sound. Later, I would find fresh fist-sized holes in the walls.

Every so often, the other world would swallow me up while I was talking to Daddy, and the ghost would take me in the middle of the day. It would still be daytime when I returned, but my Daddy always avoided me until the next morning.

I don't think he wanted to hear my stories. I never understood why; all I wanted was someone to share them with.

And it's not even important to believe the story a friend tells you. Most of the time, the friend just wants to know they're valuable enough to be heard.

Your Dreams Taste Like Candy

Even though I was very young, I still understood that a man should value his daughter.

I didn't know how to solve the problem, so I learned to stop talking about it. No one wanted to hear what I had to say.

So the problem spoke for itself.

It just got bigger and bigger because no one was listening. And suddenly, everything changed.

I counted nineteen punches in the wall that night, and thirteen seconds later, my door was rattling on its hinges. I didn't understand *why* I had to be afraid, but I knew *that* I did. Sometimes, there is no "why" when people are scared.

I put my faith in the door's lock.

My faith was broken.

I was falling. The ghost passed by me on the way down, and I could feel the fear wrapping around him like swirls of pure white cream in black coffee.

I was rising. But I immediately started falling again, and nothing made sense, and everyone was spinning around each other.

Then I was in the ghost's home. I was warm. I was safe.

I was pulled out again.

I landed on my bed hard enough to bounce. I gasped for air and sat up. It smelled like pennies. I felt a thick layer of sticky, red liquid pour down my shirt.

My father's silhouette remained still at the other end of the room. I was confused, because he didn't look angry.

"I'm so sorry," he whispered, strange and familiar all at once. "But I can't stop death. No one can."

I was uncomfortable, and I wanted to cry. But the worst kinds of tears are those shared with people who don't care, so I had learned not to cry around my Daddy.

He took in a deep breath, and I understood that *he* was crying softly in the dark.

"Who died?" I asked quietly.

He froze for several seconds. "You did."

I felt the liquid on my chest, then looked down at my fingertips. An angry shade of red was barely visible in the moonlight streaming through the window.

Your Dreams Taste Like Candy

I panicked. "There's no reason-"

"It doesn't matter if there's a reason," my Daddy continued slowly. "Growing up means letting things go."

I struggled to breathe. "What has to be let go?"

His voice rattled. "I'm so sorry. I tried to stop it. But your Daddy's anger was too much this one time, which means it was too much forever." He extended his trembling fist into the tiny swath of moonlight.

It was covered in red.

I gasped. "Am I going to-"

"I switched you," he responded simply. "You could only go into the other place when someone was willing to stand in for you. So no, you will not die."

My head spun. I wanted to throw up.

"You *were* going to the other place," he continued, "and then death came, and it couldn't be stopped. So it was time to switch again. I'm sorry you went back and forth so many times. But someone had to be in your place, someone had to be in Daddy's place, and the most important thing is that death had to take one of us." He cried loudly now. "I'm so sorry. I don't know why it was my responsibility to care for you, but that's just the way things are."

He wiped his eyes. "I didn't think he was a good Daddy. It couldn't be stopped, and you deserved to be saved from death much more than he did."

I wanted to ask so many questions, but they all got stuck on the way out of my mouth.

"But I couldn't leave you all alone. Not after spending so much time protecting you by switching our bodies when your Daddy came for you at night."

He got very quiet.

"You're the ghost?" I asked in wonder. "And now you're in my Daddy's body?"

He nodded in the moonlight.

"And my Daddy is-"

He nodded again. "He made a decision to bring death into the room, so I made the decision that *he* would be the one to face it."

I began to understand. "But – when can you go back to your home, where it's warm and safe?"

He gave a very long sigh. "Death closes doors that can't be opened again."

I trembled. The shaking wouldn't stop. "But that's your home! Won't your family miss you?"

He sniffed. "Yes."

We were silent for some time.

"I'm sorry," he finally said. "I don't know how to be your dad. There aren't any instructions. I have to start failing at it, or I won't learn anything at all." He finally wept, openly but gently. "I'm sorry that you're stuck with me. I tried to do my best, but sometimes we can only choose the smallest failure."

I sprang out of bed and crossed the room before wrapping him in a hug. I could tell right away that it was a different person, even if the body was the same. I felt something that I never had before.

It was warm and safe.

He gasped between muffled sobs. My tiny shoulder was pressed up against his mouth as I hugged him, so he struggled to speak.

"When you and I would switch, I only took your place for a few minutes at a time. Besides that, I've never been a – well, a *person* before. I don't know how."

"It's okay," I responded quickly. "No one does."

He took three shallow breaths. "When I was in your place... your father broke me a little bit more with each visit. I don't know if I'll ever be fixed."

Guilt overwhelmed me. "Oh." I breathed deeply. "Well, maybe fixing isn't something that happens once. Maybe being fixed just means that you always try to get a little better."

He looked down at me, eyes wide in the weak moonlight. "How can I possibly do that?"

I let go of the hug, took him by the hand, and sat us both down on the edge of my bed.

"Well," I began, "what I've always wanted was someone to listen."

About the Author

P. F. McGrail resides in Los Angeles with no fewer than five demons who live in his head and tell him what to write. This is his second short story collection, following "Fifty Shades of Purple." You can find his free weekly tales at www.reddit.com/ByfelsDisciple.

Made in the USA
Coppell, TX
17 December 2020